ROBERT LLEWELLYN WROTE HIS FIRST NOVEL at the age of twelve. By the time he'd published *The Man on Platform 5* (his first grown-up work of fiction), thirty years had passed. In the intervening period he'd worked as an artist's model, a bespoke shoemaker, a tree surgeon, a screenwriter, a comedian, actor and TV presenter.

He has appeared regularly on British television since 1987 in various guises including under quite absurd amounts of rubber in *Red Dwarf*; covered in grease and dust in *Scrapheap Challenge*; in terrifying machines on *How Do They Do It?* and sitting in a car chatting in *Carpool*.

Robert Llewellyn writes under a rack of solar panels in Gloucestershire, and *News from Gardenia* is his fifth work of fiction.

News From Gardenia

News from Gardenia

Robert Llewellyn

unbound

This edition first published in 2013

Unbound
4–7 Manchester Street   Marylebone   London   W1U 2AE
www.unbound.co.uk

Typeset by Bracketpress
Art direction by Mecob
Cover design by Kid-ethic.com

A CIP record for this book
is available from the British Library

ISBN 978-1-78352-009-1 (trade pb)
ISBN 978-1-908717-12-2 (trade hb)
ISBN 978-1-908717-13-9 (ebook)
ISBN 978-1-908717-11-5 (limited edition)

Printed in England by Clays Ltd, Bungay, Suffolk

For my children Louis and Holly

and maybe one day their children

and then possibly, their great grandchildren,
just so they can have a laugh.

Preface

IT WOULD APPEAR THERE ARE ONLY TWO groups of people who truly ponder the long-term future of the human race. Certainly not politicians, you can't really blame them as their entire universe is mired in short-termism. Not the financial services sector even though they commonly use words such as 'futures' to explain the ultra-short-term thinking they gleefully indulge in. I have discovered only engineers and scientists take a truly long-term view, oh, and the annoyingly clever young philosophy student I met last year.

Most of us think about next week, maybe next month, but rarely further than that. I'm no different; to be more accurate, I wasn't until I started writing this book. It is illuminating to read how people in the past ruminated about the future; we have the unfair advantage of our current experience to know just how wrong they were.

One silvery autumn day in 1978 I lounged on the banks of the River Thames near my parents' home in Oxfordshire and read a book. The book was *News from Nowhere* and the bank of the river was an entirely appropriate place to read it. It's the story of a simple journey along the river Thames set in the 1980s. However, the book was published back in 1890 by a man far better known for his decorative wallpaper: William Morris. It is an unapologetically utopian view of a future that was entirely possible, but as we now know, cruelly unlikely. The book had a profound effect on me, not so much because I wanted to live in the bucolic, egalitarian and gentle society he envisaged, but because it made me look at the world I was about to inherit in a new way. It helped me question the assumptions that parents, school and the establishment assured me were normal and the 'only workable solution'.

So, without apology, I have taken that idea of William Morris' and jumped further into the future. However, through the process of creating the book I have come to understand that *News from Gardenia* is not a utopian novel. As we know, utopian visions are full of pitfalls and cruelty. The list of leaders who tried to impose Utopia on their long-suffering subjects is all too easy to recall. Hitler, Stalin, Mao, Pol Pot, a right old bunch of mass-murdering, fanatical nut bags.

Creating a positive, constantly changing and developing vision of a future world is therefore very dangerous. In fact the first words I wrote when I sat down to write this book was 'dystopia is so much easier'. Evidence for this can be found in the torrent of end-of-days fantasies of *The Terminator*, *Mad Max*, *The Road*, *I am Legend*, *The Book of Eli*, *Oblivion*, *World War Z*, the list is endless. The message is tireless and simple: the human race is stupid and we will destroy ourselves. Or maybe more subtly, all those poor people (zombies) will overrun us and only one white man, with a gun, obviously, will survive and save his daughter.

Excuse me while I yawn.

So all I have tried to do is create a world where eventually, instead of the human race destroying the small planet we inhabit, we get it right. It's not perfect, it's not likely, but it is entirely possible.

News from Gardenia is the first part of a trilogy. *News from the Squares*, also published by Unbound, is the follow-up. Book three, as yet untitled, will appear ... as soon as I can write it.

Robert Llewellyn, July 2013

FEEL CONFIDENT THAT THROUGH THE LONG annals of human history plenty of people have regretted not making a greater effort to understand someone they loved. If they lose that someone and have to live with the regret it is a pain that never leaves them. However, I doubt many regretted it more than I.

'What?'

I never knew what 'what?' meant when I was just standing doing nothing, looking at Beth. Beth was the woman I once loved; I loved her so much I took her completely for granted. In that particular behavioural failure I don't think I stand out. I was just a bloke, she was just Beth; she was always there. I didn't have to think about it, her, the relationship, all that women's magazine stuff. I never thought about it at all. Beth just was. I suppose I saw her as a non-problematic sub-system, reliable, proprietary peer reviewed code in my operating system.

So I was standing there looking at Beth, for, I wish to point out, entirely romantic as opposed to lustful reasons. I hadn't said anything and yet suddenly I was being snapped at. I liked looking at Beth, I loved her and looking at her was one way I indulged in that love. I didn't understand why this particular, essentially inoffensive word 'what?' had been spat at me.

It seems a long time ago now. It is in fact an absurdly long time ago – I was so young, but at the time I genuinely believed I was old and past it. And yet I had seen a mere thirty-three summers pass me by.

I had managed to cram quite a lot of achievement in to those few years, much study, much travel, much incredible luck really.

I am an engineer and self-confessed gadget freak. It's true that back then I had short hair because I was experiencing early-onset male pattern baldness. However, unlike many of my generation I was very slim, almost skinny. I didn't work out or go jogging or follow some quirky neurotic diet. It was just the way I was wired. I was wound so tightly, according to Beth, my body virtually vibrated with energy. I twitched and fiddled away any possible weight gain as I sat in front of my numerous computer screens.

So there I was, standing in the doorway of our newly built home in a quiet cul-de-sac that had once been an orchard on the edge of the village of Kingham in Oxfordshire. Yes, Kingham. Voted 'England's friendliest village' in 2008.

I wasn't aware of this; apparently there was a sign announcing the award on the way into the village but I'd never noticed it. Even if I had been aware of it I wouldn't have paid much attention. My mind, basically, was elsewhere.

I now understand that this attribute was the source of the 'what?' problem.

The 'what?' had been delivered by Beth Harris who was, back then, my wife. We had been together for five years, the entire time spent in this small, tidy and easy-to-manage house. It was nothing spectacular but it was fine, we owned it outright, no mortgage – I'd sold some shares in a company I'd helped set up and I had the cash. The deeds of the house were in both our names, a fact that I was uniquely uninterested in but Beth thought we needed to talk about. Beth always thought we needed to talk about things, but I found that once things were sorted out, like the ownership of the house, I didn't really want to think about them again. I certainly didn't want to talk about them.

I had nothing to say so I listened as best I could. I barely understood a word she was saying.

Beth was thirty-two years old, a history teacher at the nearby Kingham Hill private school. Lovely Beth, she was a woman of

bubbly and bright disposition – I think that's a fair description;
if she'd been murdered that would have been what some lazy
hack would have written about her in the newspapers.

Don't worry, she wasn't murdered, she died in her sleep at the
age of ninety-eight. Lovely Beth. However, when I was standing
in the kitchen doorway, she did not have a bubbly and bright
disposition.

'What do you expect?' she spat. Amazing how you can make
a simple question like that so full of venom and bitter history.

'I don't expect anything. When have I ever expected anything?' I said. I remember my voice going a little squeaky mid
sentence; I found that rather annoying.

'You expect me to be here when you get back, which is very
bloody rarely.'

Beth wasn't looking at me as she spoke, she was looking out at
our small garden, which backed onto an eighteenth-century barn
that had been converted into what Beth had once described as 'a
lovely, spacious home'.

A home in which Beth did not live. A home in which she
desperately, fanatically wanted to live. Beth had even managed
to communicate to me that she hated modern houses; she had,
apparently, always wanted to live in a converted barn.

I knew this, somewhere I knew it, although at the time I was
standing in the doorway I wasn't thinking about it. We had
rowed about it before. There was a time when we could have
afforded to buy the ridiculously expensive barn conversion, but I
didn't like it. The floors were wobbly, not good for tables with
more than three legs, the interior stonewalls were bare and bits
of grit were always falling off. Not good for computers.

There's generally a bit of back-story in any relationship that's
been lived in a few years. Unresolved conflicts build up like fluff
around a cooling fan. Beth and I had been together for five years
and we'd created a comfortably large clot of fluff. The cooling fan
was essentially not functioning. The motherboard – if we're

going to stick with this particular analogy – the motherboard was overheating.

Modern house, old house, private school, state school, religion, science, working overseas, working up the lane.

Essentially none of it was functioning efficiently, although I had no idea this was the case. As far as I was concerned it was all fine.

Beth turned to face me. Her face was red and slightly swollen, and I remember I felt a sudden urge to comfort her but her clenched fists warned me away. I may have been a nerd, an engineer, a gadget fanatic and was generally considered to be a little insensitive, but even I could read this body language.

'You're never here. Even when you are here you're always sat in front of a screen. We never talk.'

'We're talking now,' I said, almost pleadingly.

'Oh shut up Gavin. You know what I mean.'

'I don't.' It was true, I really didn't.

So Beth sighed in a big dramatic way, looked at the floor and took a deep breath. 'It feels like, okay, it feels like I am here all the time, I go to work, I come back, nothing, there's no one here.' She stared at me with nothing but hatred in her slightly red eyes.

I couldn't understand – what was there to be so angry about? That sounded great to me.

'I'm lonely, Gavin. There's no one to talk to.'

Okay, that was news. I was hearing that. I'd heard it before from other people and I found it very hard to understand. Loneliness – I didn't know what that felt like. I have always found my own company very stimulating.

'When you do come home, I'm pleased – I'm such an idiot, I'm pleased because I'll have some company, but you are always up in the top room with your poxy computers doing, doing God knows what.'

I shrugged and smiled. 'Yeah, I do this crazy hobby thing, called working for a living, paying the bills, et cetera.'

I should not have said that, it was childish but she was getting on my pectorals.

'Oh piss off Gavin. All I wanted to do today when I got back from church was go to the farmers' market in Chipping Norton.'

'The farmers' market?'

'I told you about it, I emailed you that it was half term and I could go with you, maybe go to a nice pub for lunch, spend some nice time together.'

'You emailed me?' I questioned. 'Did you put it in the diary?'

That was another mistake.

Beth had trouble remembering to put stuff in our joint Google diary; I was always updating it. It was a shared diary, she had the login details – it wasn't exactly hard. It was the quickest and simplest way of telling her my entire minute-by-minute schedule for the next three months. I don't think she ever used it. Such a good service too, so easy to use, and free. I thought she'd like that. But no.

'That's what I wanted to do,' she shouted. The shouting thing really wasn't necessary; our house was very small. I could have heard her even if she whispered. 'And what are you doing? Flying in your stupid little plane to blasted Basingstoke to go and talk with some other engineers who no doubt have a poor idiot woman at home going equally mad.'

I stood there shaking my head. 'I'm not going to lie to you, Bethington.' This was my affectionate term for her, one she'd never complained about, but even my emotionally unconnected self registered that this was probably not an appropriate time to use it. 'Look, I'm sorry, I'm not trying to cause a row, but I truly have no idea what you are talking about. Nothing you've said makes any sense to me.'

'You bastard,' said Beth. I smiled and shook my head again. I've been called worse, plenty of times.

'What am I supposed to do?' I asked slowly, as if I were talking to a child. 'I'm working on the biggest project I've ever worked on, it's a huge collaborative effort spanning five countries and over one hundred engineers and I'm part of the team that's running the whole thing. Do I text them and say, "Can't make meeting today, got to go to the farmers' market"?'

I made texting thumb movements as I spoke, not just a sporadic mime either, I would say pretty damn accurate double thumb movements because in my mind I was using an Android open source phone with an on-screen keyboard. It was rapidly apparent that Beth wasn't interested or even aware of the subtlety of my mimetic skills.

'Piss off!' was the review of said skills, and Beth stormed out of the kitchen. I sneered after her. I was surprised how easy it was to go off people. I'd gone right off Beth.

I picked up my bag, slung it over my shoulder and left the house. Really, I left. That was it.

2

I HAD JUST OVER A THOUSAND FLYING HOURS under my still-trim belt – I only mention the trimness because so many of my contemporaries had become anything but trim, and the trimness helped me with range, less weight you see.

At least four hundred of those hours were solo flying, and at least fifty of those in my newest acquisition, a Yuneec E430.

Built in Shanghai, obviously, and sold in the UK by a company in Potters Bar, the Yuneec was, as I often described it, 'cutting edge aviation technology'.

It had certainly raised eyebrows when the machine first arrived at the flying club I was a member of. I'm not good at joining clubs, but the flying club membership meant I had access to an airfield and some good technical backup, which is quite useful when it comes to light aircraft.

At a cursory glance the Yuneec E430 looked like any other light aircraft, small and a bit frail looking. It was only when it was running, zipping along the old World War Two runway just before take-off, that other flying club members had informed me they noticed something odd. I had to explain to them, even people who were experienced pilots, that this particular aeroplane was electrically powered.

'What happens when the batteries run out?' This question was generally accompanied by a knowing laugh.

'You have to land very quickly,' was my standard reply. 'In exactly the same way you have to if you run out of fossil fuel in an old-fashioned plane.'

I would often try to get the explanatory sentence in the conversation over the sound of laughter and nudging from this comically old-school audience. The flying club had many members in their late fifties, men with unusual facial hair, stout waistlines and great love and enthusiasm for their old planes.

The simple truth was that my little plane functioned well, it was very quiet and had proved incredibly dependable. Most importantly, and something I know I droned on about in the flying club bar, it was very simple to maintain. I was forever seeing people tinkering with their old fossil engines; they were always going a bit wrong, or misfiring, or packing up mid-flight.

The motor in the Yuneec E430 never went wrong, it didn't matter how high I was flying, nothing needed adjusting, there were no high-altitude fuel mixture problems; it was very simple and straightforward.

As for recharging it, every airfield I landed on had a 70 amp power outlet and I carried a very long extension cord in the snug cargo hold.

The plane was the most expensive thing I'd ever bought and of course Beth viewed it as a total waste of time and money. She hated flying. Every time I went anywhere in the plane she told me she expected never to see me again. How right she was.

She would often save light plane crash stories on her iPad and email me the links. She had only been in the plane once, soon after I bought it. Foolishly, on reflection, I'd not been able to resist showing off just a little by performing a couple of very gentle aerobatic turns. I mean that, really nothing intense – the Yuneec E430 is not built to compete in the Red Bull aerobatic competition. However, these manoeuvres resulted in her screaming non-stop until we landed. I want to reiterate that we landed very gently, very safely; everything was fine. I tried to calm her down. I said to her clearly, 'Calm down, we're okay, there's nothing wrong.'

She climbed out of the plane and stormed off over the fields. I didn't see her again for two days, making matters worse by not ringing anyone to find out where she was (well, I was very busy at the time and I knew she'd be fine once she calmed down).

I found out on her eventual return that she had walked to Chipping Norton, caught the bus to Kingham train station and then caught the train to London to stay with her fearsome mother. I was very relieved I hadn't called her — her mother might have answered her phone. Nightmare.

After I took off that day, the day of the 'What?', I remember glancing at the battery indicator as soon as I was airborne — 93 per cent, plenty for what I was doing. The plane had a range of around a hundred and twenty miles on one charge and I was doing sixty at the most. The weather was reasonable for the time of year, slightly bumpy due to occasional cumulonimbus clouds above me but all in all, tip-top flying conditions.

I had read reports of some fairly hefty solar activity which could affect satellite navigation systems but as I was flying across well-known territory to an airfield I'd been to before I wasn't that bothered about it.

I'd taken off from the flying club at Enstone in Oxfordshire. It was a Second World War airfield perched on a rolling hilltop just to the east of Chipping Norton.

I'd then headed north east to start with, giving me the opportunity to fly deliberately low over Jeremy Clarkson's house. I waved but I don't think anyone saw me. I then banked and headed due south toward Blackbushe airfield in Hampshire. I had a meeting in the nearby town of Basingstoke, in the small rented office of the UK arm of Tempus Engineering. I was freelance but very involved in the day-to-day politics of the company. I had a USB key fob in my top pocket with the entire project on it, encrypted obviously. This was a big renewable energy project with many millions already invested. It was probably the biggest ever renewable energy project, and made the Three Gorges dam look like a community power micro-generation installation.

We were going to build a deep-water multi-gigawatt power-generating installation off the coast of north-west Scotland, using the Gulf Stream. It was going to take ten years to complete but in theory at least, it would produce more energy than five nuclear power stations.

My plan for the day was very simple. The airfield was fourteen miles from the town centre, but that was no problem. Tucked into the small cargo area on the plane was a fold-up electric bicycle I'd helped design. I was going to land, plug in the plane for the return journey, zip through the Hampshire lanes to the meeting, plug the bike in while I was there, zip back to Blackbushe and get back home in time for tea.

Maybe even get back home in time to try and make up with Beth. As I flew I found myself going over the row as I remembered it. I must admit I couldn't remember what started it. I wondered what I could do to make things easier for her. The problem was, in essence, that if I wasn't working I was bored.

I wasn't pinning all the blame on Beth – she wasn't boring, I knew that. It didn't matter whose company I was in, I just didn't find other people that interesting. If other people were connected to projects, to concepts, to something I was working on, then I enjoyed that interaction. But just sitting with a person talking about nothing, anything, I suppose sitting with someone and talking about feelings … I'm not saying it's wrong, bad or stupid, I just don't know how to do it.

So if someone was talking to me about feelings, I'd start to play with something. I suppose I was a bit of a gadget fanatic; I never found gadgets boring, well, not for a while anyway. When I did get bored of them I put them in the big plastic box in my office and ignored them until they became interesting again about ten years later. Gadgets didn't complain or give me dirty looks or storm off to stay with their mothers. I truly considered the possibility that I might be at fault, that when Beth tried to punish me with her absence and I didn't notice, this might be very hurtful to her. Of course what I didn't know then was that if I didn't see Beth for more than about three or four days, then I would start to miss her.

I glanced at my iPad, which I used as an additional sat nav display. I'd even built a little aluminium holder to keep it in place during a flight. The plane came with a very good navigation system but I had logged so much data on Google Maps I liked to be able to check things as I flew over them.

I loved flying the Yuneec; it was so much quieter and smoother than the piston engine planes I'd learned to fly in. I sometimes flipped one side off my communications headphones just so I could listen to the low hiss of the wind flowing over the canopy – that was pretty much the only sound I could hear. Very little vibration from the engine and although not fast – the top speed was around 90 miles an hour – it would cruise along at that speed for ages, no problem.

I scanned the horizon. It was a beautiful clear day and I could see for miles.

My attention was caught by a fairly large cloud formation in my flight path, which seemed to be sitting lower than the small puffs of cloud higher up. I had checked the weather reports before I left and there was no mention of storms, but this did look decidedly storm-like. I could clearly see Didcot power station beneath the cloud – the power station was a very good waypoint due to the height of the chimney.

I knew that Didcot didn't pump that kind of smoke out of the very tall chimney; it had been converted from coal burning to natural gas so that wasn't what had caused it. It wasn't a storm cloud, just an unusual formation, and it was directly in my route. I decided to reduce my altitude and fly beneath it. The plane would happily cruise along at 10,000 feet, but I often flew lower. I knew I wouldn't be disturbing anyone having a snooze in their back garden as the plane made no more noise than a glider.

I do remember distinctly feeling the plane rise a little as I started to fly beneath the cloud. Looking down I could see hard shadows being cast by trees and buildings. Nothing unusual, you might think – it was a sunny day – but the sun was already high in the sky and the cloud was big and dense; it should have cast a shadow. I couldn't see one. It was as if there was no cloud, but when I looked up, there was definitely a major cloud above me. I could see no sign of the sun.

Wisps of cloud whipped past the windscreen. The plane wasn't fast, but the cloud seemed to be slipping past me at a much greater velocity. I checked the sat nav. According to the display I was heading in the right direction, everything seemed in order but I did feel a little uneasy. In all my flying experience I'd never seen anything quite like this cloud.

I glanced out of the side window again expecting to see fields, the main line from London to Reading, motorways, housing estates. I saw only grey mist. I felt the plane jolt a little and I gripped the controls tighter; something unusual was definitely going on. I quickly glanced behind me. The rear window afforded a view of the tail and everything seemed fine.

Fine that is except I was now completely surrounded by thick cloud when I had made deliberate efforts to fly below and avoid it. I could see nothing in any direction. Glancing at the sat nav screen again, I felt slightly reassured. I was at 1,800 meters, cruising at 113 kph in a south-south-easterly direction, just as I should have been. The only potential hazard for miles was the main chimney at Didcot power station, but I'd clearly seen it before I went into the cloud and that was only 300 meters tall; I was well above it.

Another sudden and unexpected movement, more of a violent sway, and boy did I grip those controls tightly. I'd flown through much worse storms than this but I still cursed under my breath. I should have gone around the wretched cloud.

I heard the quiet note of the engine rise and fall, and then saw to my great alarm that the map on the built in sat nav was spinning around. This was not good. I could sense that the plane was flying in one direction – I wasn't spinning out of control, which was what the sat nav was telling me. I glanced down at the iPad. The map had frozen and I could see the little spinning

symbol at the top of the screen – the map app was awaiting more
information.

I peered ahead and thought I saw something in the mist. By now the sat nav was behaving completely irrationally, slowly turning and giving me no indication of speed or altitude.

The cloud appeared to be thinning and I saw a ray of sunlight.

'Thank Christ for that,' I remember saying, but as the phrase was leaving my lips I pulled the controls hard to the right. There in front of me was something I can confidently say I had never seen before. A thin blue line, like a laser beam, but more blue than anything I'd ever seen. Like a crack in the cosmos, or a blue light coming through a partially open door seen from a darkened room.

'Jesus wept,' I remember saying as I wrenched the controls, making the plane bank and dive more violently than I had ever done before. The engine revs reached maximum pitch and I experienced the unmistakable tingling sick feeling of expected impact and instant death.

The world opened up beneath me, suddenly and in incredible detail. Bathed in sunlight, a wide-open landscape of green, like an ocean of deep green. It was trees, so many trees stretching on for ever. In amongst the foliage I could pick out the occasional roof of a house. What I was seeing made no sense. I should have been looking at dense suburban Didcot, or railway yards, or the bloody power station, not some unnamed forest.

I levelled out at what I guessed to be around 500 meters. I could see well ahead; there were no hazardous objects in my path.

I glanced at my iPad and could see immediately it had no signal. The word 'searching . . .' was clearly visible top left, the map was utterly motionless and the blue indicator dot giving my position hadn't moved at all since I last checked.

'Fucking piece of Apple shit,' I spat out. 'I really need you now. Where the bloody hell am I?'

The plane flew true and steady, and that was when I first remember seeing the battery indicator. I thought everything had gone wrong. It was reading 100 per cent. It wasn't 100 per cent when I'd taken off – I seemed to recall it had said 93 per cent. I tapped the indicator panel, knowing it was pointless tapping digital displays, but I didn't know what else to do. When in doubt, tap something. I glanced back at the iPad – the battery indicator at the top of the screen also showed green, fully charged.

My mobile phone was in my top pocket and I pulled it out: full battery, no signal. I shook my head; this was turning into a bit of a nightmare.

I decided the best thing to do was find somewhere safe to land and try and work out what the hell was going on. But with no sat nav and a very unfamiliar landscape slowly unfolding beneath me, it wasn't going to be easy.

I switched on the autopilot and picked up the iPad. I re-booted it, opened the sat nav app and waited while it scoured for satellite signals. I waited longer: nothing.

'Bloody satellites can't all be down. What the hell is going on?'

I pulled down my comms mic and pressed send on the control stick.

'This is Yuneec 554, do you read me?'

It was only then that I realised I'd been listening to the low hiss of communications failure on my headphones ever since I'd come out of the cloud.

'This is Yuneec 554, somewhere in the Didcot area. Do you read me, over.'

Nothing, absolute radio silence. I was partly relieved no one could hear me, as admitting I was 'somewhere in the Didcot area' was a sign of very serious pilot error. I should know exactly where I was at any given time. Everything on the digital indicator told me the comms were working, the plane was working, the batteries were 100 per cent still, but there was no response.

'What in planet fuck is going on?' I said to myself.

I flipped off the autopilot and took the plane in a long slow bank to the left. I was cursing and goggle eyed, heart rate off the spectrum and going like a strimmer motor. What hove into view was too big to be taken in. The thin blue line was there in front of me again. Surely no optical illusion of this size and solidity was possible – this looked physical and real, and yet it just couldn't be. It was a glowing thin blue line stretching from the earth beneath me up into the sky. It had no discernable end point; it was just a straight electric blue line, like someone had Photoshopped it onto a real landscape. I glanced down to my left as I banked, seeing an unusual industrial complex where the blue line came to a halt. Some stainless steel pipe-work and small buildings, like nothing I'd seen before. I knew I was quite near the Culham laboratories but I'd visited the complex a few years previously and seen nothing like this installation on the site.

I flew due south, now only using a compass which was embedded into the cockpit display panel. Ahead of me I could only see forest, but there was no forest of this size near Didcot power station. But then there was no Didcot power station either. I must be somewhere else, but I knew I hadn't been flying long enough to get anywhere else.

The ground below me was so well organised and tidy it almost looked like France, but there is no way I could have got to France – my batteries wouldn't have lasted long enough. Although for some reason, even though I'd now been flying for over an hour, the batteries were still reading 100 per cent.

'What if the storm's shagged up the electronics?' I said to myself. I considered the possibility of a major short in some connection causing the battery-monitoring software to flip to 100 per cent regardless of the actual state of the batteries. I knew I had to land, and fast.

To my right a patch of colour caught my eye; it was yellow, a field, a flat, smooth field. I banked to the right and reduced altitude in order to get a better look. As I approached the field

I could see people on the ground, three people standing around a tractor and trailer. One of them was waving at me – they could see me. For some reason that reassured me. I felt so weird that the fact that someone could see me made me feel like I was still alive.

I scanned the ground. It was yellow because it was a field of oil seed. Not really a suitable landing area – oil seed grew a lot higher than nicely mown grass, but I couldn't see anything resembling a field anywhere else. I hoped that as the plants were still yellow they would be fairly soft, the stems snapping easily, not the stiff harsh plants they became just before harvest.

I could sense the direction of the wind and banked the plane again until I was flying into it. I reduced height again and slowly approached the field. The small group of people I'd passed earlier were clambering into the trailer of their tractor; it looked like I might get a welcoming party.

I slowed the plane as much as I dared before I brought it down. The landing was violent, uncomfortable, but thankfully very brief. The prop scythed its way through the yellow plants, the windshield went momentarily yellow; the oil seed slowed the small machine very quickly. When I finally came to a stop I sat back in my seat and only then became fully aware of just how tense I'd been. I've had a few bumps and scares in my flying career, but nothing remotely like this.

I pulled out my phone. I wanted to call Beth – suddenly I was experiencing emotions, I was actually having feelings. I needed something this bloody dramatic to realise that I did actually need this woman, someone I was connected with. I wanted to tell her I was okay and apologise for being such a numpty at breakfast time.

No signal.

I glanced out of the right-hand window and saw in the distance the tractor making its slow way through the field of bright yellow plants.

3

I UNDID MY SEAT BELT, OPENED THE CANOPY
and clambered out of the plane. The first thing that
struck me was the silence. Not some spooky man-made
laboratory silence, but the complete lack of the rumble. I realised
that it was a sound, or lack of sound I'd only heard once before
when I was in a mountainous region of Norway.

Man-made rumble, even in remote rural areas in the United
Kingdom, was always discernable. I stood still for a moment,
straining my ears as I tried to sense what was different. It wasn't
silent – I could hear copious birdsong all around me – but it was
peaceful in some way I found slightly unsettling. The familiar
rumble I'd heard all my life, the hum of traffic, distant aircraft
and machinery, was absent. There was nothing. It was like
Christmas day or a quiet early Sunday morning in midsummer.

But I knew it was a Friday in mid-May and I was near the
urban areas of Reading, Didcot, half a dozen flight paths heading to and from Heathrow. There was the M4, dozens of busy
A and B roads crisscrossing the area – this, after all, was a major
reason behind my choice of transportation.

By car my journey would have taken two hours on the heavily
congested British road network, instead of twenty minutes by
electric plane.

I glanced at the approaching group of what I took to be farm
workers. The machine they were on was moving, but it too
seemed silent. I could quite easily hear the happy chatter of
the people on board the trailer, but no familiar clattering diesel
tractor engine reached my straining lugs.

As they pulled close I realised at once I'd never seen a machine
like it and let's face it, I was just the sort of techie bloke who

should know all about it. This was well within my field of knowledge and yet the tractor-type machine the people were being conveyed by looked most peculiar. It moved along silently except for the sound of the large almost balloon-like soft rubber tyres on the ground. As it got much closer I could just pick out a faint mechanical hum coming from within its unusual plastic-looking bodywork.

'Well I never,' said a very old man who jumped in a surprisingly sprightly way from the trailer. 'That's a Yuneec E430.'

I smiled and raised my eyebrows. No one ever knew what my plane was.

'It is indeed,' I said and the man shook hands with me heartily. 'You are the first person I've met who actually knows the plane.'

'Good landing. I've never seen one land before – it must be an extraordinary experience.'

The two people riding on the trailer, a middle-aged man and a younger woman, came and stood beside the old man, looking at me with eager smiling faces.

'That is amazing,' said the young woman. 'How did you learn to operate it?'

I smiled at her, not knowing what else to do.

'Well, I, um, I had to train as a pilot, you know, in a regular plane.'

'A regular plane,' said the middle-aged man with a broad smile. 'What's this then, an irregular plane?'

Although his statement could have been a mildly irritating criticism, he didn't seem to mean it that way. His smile seemed genuine and inquisitive.

'I'm very sorry to land in your field,' I said. 'I got a little alarmed when I saw that.'

I pointed at the blue line splitting the skyline to the north.

'Oh, the tether,' said the old man. 'Of course, that might be a hazard if you didn't see it.'

'A hazard! It's a fucking death trap!' I laughed, then stopped.

Even with my mildly stunted sensitivity I had sensed that my foul language may not have been appropriate.

'Sorry, s'cuse my French, but it gave me the fright of my life. What on earth is that thing?'

'It's the tether,' said the young woman. 'It's Didcot tether, it's been there for ...'

The older man held up his hand and the young woman fell silent mid-sentence.

'Where are you headed?' the old man asked.

'Where have you come from?' asked the young woman. 'Have you been unwell?'

I smiled. 'No, I'm fine, I've just come from Enstone airfield.'

The old man turned to his comrades. 'Up north in Oxfordshire.'

The other two nodded. The young woman said, 'I know that, Father, I have seen a map.'

'I was on my way to Basingstoke. I'm on my way to a meeting which I think I'm now going to miss,' I said as I glanced at my watch.

'A meeting. Goodness me,' said the old man.

'Is it a hall meeting?' said the middle-aged man. Again his slightly flat delivery made the question sound peculiar.

'No, no, sorry, it's a meeting of my company.'

'Your company,' said the old man. 'Goodness me, what does a company do, what do you do?'

'I'm an engineer.'

'Isn't that marvellous, an engineer,' said the old man. 'What a wonderful thing to do. Do you have an area of speciality?'

I resisted the temptation to be snide – the questions seemed so naïve and yet they didn't look stupid. They did look weird; their clothes were a bit strange, not disturbingly strange but it seemed like they'd really made an effort to look different, to look like well-dressed peasants. I wondered if they were members of some sort of cult. I answered them as best I could.

'Well, strictly speaking I specialise in mechanical engineering; it's a broad spectrum of heavy engineering products, mainly connected with ore extraction, mining, but more recently with renewable energy generation systems, large-scale stuff.'

All three people stood staring at me. It suddenly felt like I was speaking to people in Turkey or Croatia who didn't have a word of English between them.

'Mining,' said the old man. 'Ah, goodness me. Mining. Digging holes in the ground?'

'Fairly big holes,' I said. 'Not here in the UK, usually in Australia or China, and just recently South America, in Bolivia.'

They all nodded.

'I didn't know people did that any more,' said the woman. I smiled – I think it might have been a pained smile, I was really trying to be nice. However, there was something slightly hippy-ish about the woman. What she said entirely fitted the stereotype of someone who happily made use of the products I helped produce while publicly shunning the process that brought them to be, but there seemed no judgement in her voice, simply a state-ment of fact.

'Well,' said the old man after a slightly awkward silence. 'Although I'd love to stand here and chat away all the livelong day, I fear we have work to do. We are weeding the field and we still have a lot to get through.'

'Yeah, I'm really sorry mate,' I said, 'I really didn't have much choice, the sat nav's kaput and I can't get any signal on my phone. I'm a bit buggered, to be honest.'

I glanced down at the small wheels of the plane. They were dug well into the soft earth beneath the tall oil seed stalks.

'I don't think I'm going to be able to take off from here. I had to make a slightly unorthodox landing. I got very confused when I was looking for somewhere to safely put down.'

The three people glanced at each other. 'Well, allow us to help get your machine to the edge of the field,' said the middle-aged man. 'You see we need to go through here to pull weeds.'

They immediately busied themselves by unhitching the large trailer from the back of the tractor-like machine, then the middle-aged man expertly manoeuvred the machine to the rear of the plane.

He climbed off and unwound what looked like cotton thread from a small spool mounted on the rear of the machine. It had a tiny steel clip attached to the end, which he looped around the rear tow coupling and clipped it together. I started laughing – it was like watching a child with a toy plastic spanner trying to undo the wheel nut of a fifty-ton earth-mover.

'I don't think that's going to do much mate, you need more than a cotton thread to haul it. I mean, it's not that heavy but . . . '

I stood motionless, my mouth hanging open as the silent tractor pulled the Yuneec backwards without any perceivable effort. The thin thread did not break.

I followed on foot accompanied by the old man and the younger woman.

'I'm a little confused as to where I am,' I said. I looked around, trying to spot a landmark on the horizon. One thing was certain, the Didcot power station chimney was huge; surely I should be able to see it.

'You are just beside Goldacre Hall,' said the old man. 'My name is Halam, by the way. Sorry, with all the excitement of your wonderful flying machine, I have completely forgotten my manners.'

'Gavin, Gavin Meckler,' I said and we shook hands again. The old man's hands were strong and thick-skinned.

'This is my daughter, Grace.'

I shook hands with Grace – small, elegant hands which again had clearly experienced hard manual labour.

'How do you do,' she said with what could have been a slightly suggestive smile. For the first time, I noticed that Grace was a rather attractive young woman. I quickly put the thought out of my mind; things were bad enough with Beth already.

We approached the edge of the field, where a strip of unplanted land ran along beside a high hedge.

'Ahh, this is a little more hopeful,' I said, trying to assess the length of the open strip of grass. I grimaced because at either end of the strip was a standing of very mature Ash trees. 'Or maybe not.'

'Oh dear, is there a problem?' asked the old man Halam. He was scratching his head and looking slightly uncomfortable.

'No, no, well, I am only trying to find somewhere I can take off.'

'Take off what?' said Grace, she was still smiling broadly.

'Sorry, the plane, get airborne, take off, fly,' I said. Maybe this slightly attractive woman was also slightly stupid. Take off what? What a bloody stupid question.

'Oh, I see.' Grace nodded and looked at her father. I thought she was about to say something and then the old man gently interjected.

'I think we need some help here,' said Halam. 'Why don't you go back to the house with Grace and have a nice cup of tea. I will go and see a good neighbour who is far better informed than I and we can try and sort something out.'

I shrugged. 'Okay, not much else I can do at the moment. Maybe I can make a few calls on your land-line,' I said.

The old man put his hand on my arm. 'Just go with Grace, have a cup of something warm, relax, I'll return in no time at all.'

I watched as the man on the tractor pulled to a halt. I walked up to the plane to inspect the damage. The Yuneec looked fine, a few stalks of oil seed plants wrapped around the undercarriage, possibly a little paint damage to the propeller tips where they'd scythed their way through the foliage, but thankfully nothing disastrous. I turned and looked at Grace. She was standing in the bright sunlight with one hand on her hip, staring at me.

'When you're ready,' she said. I followed her and we walked towards a small gate in the hedge.

4

EALLY NICE HOUSE,' I SAID AS WE ENTERED the garden. It was incredibly well managed: row after row of vegetables, soft fruit bushes, nut trees, all neat and clearly the result of some very dedicated horticulture.

The house itself was unusual, a simple box-like design with a large sloping roof covered in something silvery; it glittered slightly as the sunlight hit it.

'That is a cool roof. What is it?' I asked as we approached the house.

'The roof?' said Grace. She glanced up to look at it. 'It's a roof; it keeps the rain out.'

'But the material,' I said, trying not to rise to the bait – she clearly had a bit of a chip on her shoulder this Grace. She reminded me of some of the antsy women Beth had been at college with, the ones who always put me down when they came to visit. The ones who could never find a bloke prepared to put up with them.

'I just wondered what it was – I've never seen anything like it,' I said slightly defensively.

Grace sighed. 'I'm sorry, I have no idea what it's made of. Roof. That's all I know.'

I followed her through the door, which also surprised me; it was made of a dark material that I would have expected to be wood, but as I entered the house I put my hand on it. It didn't feel like wood. I tapped it as I passed.

Grace turned to look at what I was doing. I smiled.

'I just wondered what the door was made of,' I said. She shrugged again and entered a spacious kitchen. Most of the contents of the room were familiar, although I did glance at what looked like a matt glass panel set into the ceiling.

Grace filled a round metal pot with water from a tap over a large metal sink. I watched her carefully as she put the pot down. There was a low throbbing noise and then she poured what was clearly boiling water into a rather ornate tea pot.

'Wow,' I said.

'What?' asked Grace.

'How does that work?'

She stared at me, clearly nonplussed.

'The kettle. How the hell does it boil that quickly?'

'How long should it take?' she said.

I stood and moved towards her; she looked mildly uncomfortable which made me stop. 'Sorry, I've never seen one before, not like that. Who makes it?'

Grace picked the kettle up and looked at it. 'It was Gustav I think.'

'Never heard of that make. German is it? May I?' I said, holding out my hand.

She placed the kettle down on the counter and stood to one side. 'Help yourself.' There was a slight intonation in her voice, revealing that she clearly thought I was the mad one.

I looked at the simple steel vessel, at least I thought it was steel. It was lighter than I expected. I held it under the tap-like device above the sink; water immediately flowed. As I moved the kettle away the tap stopped flowing – not a drip fell once it was off. I put the kettle down on the surface and waited. Nothing happened. Grace leant past me and put her finger over a slight indentation on the handle; the indentation glowed a gentle blue and the kettle boiled instantly.

'Incredible.'

'It's just a kettle,' said Grace.

The door opened and Halam the old man entered. He sat down at the large table and smiled at me.

'I have been speaking with one of our elders,' he said. I felt my
eyebrows flicker; they always give me away apparently, that's
what Beth told me. Halam must have been in his eighties at the
very least. How old was an elder?

'He is coming over to visit.'

'Oh, so we're having a houseful again, are we father?' said
Grace.

The old man smiled. 'My daughter likes things to be very
orderly, which, my dear, I assure you they will be. William is
coming alone. He wishes to speak with our guest.'

'I hope William can explain kettles,' said Grace. 'Gavin is very
interested in the kettle for some reason.'

'The kettle?'

I shrugged. 'I've never seen water boil that quickly.'

The old man nodded. 'Let's wait for William, shall we? He
will be here shortly. I trotted ahead because I just wanted to
explain to our guest that William is, well, he can be a little
abrupt.'

'A little!' said Grace with a big smile. 'He's a wicked old man.'

'But you must not take offence,' said Halam. 'I assure you, he
means no harm by it.'

I was still trying to imagine this old man 'trotting ahead' when
almost on cue there was a tap on the large door and a seriously
ancient-looking man entered. Thin and drawn, his face was heavily lined but his white hair surprisingly thick.

His eyes were sparkling and he was grinning from ear to ear.
He looked at me with almost disturbing intensity.

'Well, well. How extraordinary,' he said. 'Suddenly having all
these years under my belt is a very good thing.' He glanced at
Grace briefly. 'Hello Grace, you wanton hussy. You're looking
even more extraordinarily attractive today.'

'Thank you,' said Grace with no obvious offence. 'I take it you
are feeling well, William.'

'I am indeed. To be woken from my midday snooze with news

like this, well, it makes it worthwhile waking up just one more time.'

Halam pulled a chair out for the ancient man, but he ignored it and stood in front of me.

'So, I hear you arrived in a flying machine.'

I smiled. Who the hell was this, an ancient man who referred to planes as flying machines?

'Yes.'

'A Yuneec E430 no less,' said Halam.

'A Yuneec E430, from around 2010 I would guess,' said William.

'It's the 2011 model,' I said.

William nodded, looked at the floor and muttered something inaudible. He glanced up at me, then gestured towards the seat that had been put out for him.

'Take a seat, Gavin.' He turned to Grace. 'Give him a cup of sweet tea. Have you got any honey?'

Grace nodded.

'I don't generally have honey in my...'

'Have some honey in it – it's from our own bees, wonderful stuff.'

I sat in silence, feeling uneasy as I watched Grace spoon a healthy dollop of honey into a large steaming mug of tea.

'Gavin, allow me to explain as best I can. The tether, that's the blue line you saw from the window of your flying machine, well, they do, very occasionally cause an anomaly,' said old man William. 'And although we knew it might happen, we didn't know, well, we still don't quite know why it happens.'

Grace was standing beside me now, holding the mug of tea.

'Drink this,' she said.

Suddenly I didn't feel safe. These charming people, obviously kind and without a hint of threatening behaviour, made me feel uneasy. Why did they want me to drink the tea?

'Let me explain,' said William. ' About eighteen kilometres

above us is a solar kite; it's about four hectares. It's just a simple
kite, held aloft by the jet stream, and its upper surface contains
many billions of primo cells.'

'Primo cells?'

'Oh yes, sorry, a form of voltaic collector – it's a gigantic solar
array. A solar panel may be a better term for you. Do you understand that?'

'Well, yes, I know what photovoltaic cells are, but not on a
bloody great kite eighteen kilometres above the earth.'

'Well, that's what it is,' said William.

'Okay, I've read a paper suggesting such technology. I didn't
know it had been implemented,' I said. I looked at my tea. It
looked quite harmless, though very dark; I did consider asking
for milk but thought they might be all vegan and holier than
thou and then I'd have to hear about bloody cows and cruelty. It
looked harmless but I still felt uneasy. Maybe the honey had
some weird psychotropic drug in it.

'Yes yes, please let me finish,' said William. He stood firmly
before me, his voice clear and calm.

'So, the voltage coming down the tether, well, during daylight
hours it's very high, about 600 gigawatts.'

'Down that puny line!' I said. '600 gigs, surely not.'

William nodded gravely. 'Hence the blue light, visible even
in bright sunlight. Well, we have noticed that as the line
passes through certain cloud formations it um ... Well, we have
observed effects, anomalies if you like.' William stopped. He
glanced around at Halam. 'Maybe I will have a chair if that's
okay, Halam.'

'By all means,' said Halam, who gently moved a chair into
position. William sat down facing me. This was all getting very
weird.

'So, the area around a tether is kept clear – it can have a peculiar effect between 1,000 and about 5,000 metres above ground
level. At ground level, obviously there is great danger from

electrocution should you approach the tether mounting station, but that is well known and people stay well away.'

'When was this installed?' I asked. 'How come I've heard nothing about it?'

'No, you won't have, because, well, because you've come through a fold.'

'A what?'

'It's so hard to explain. You are here, but you should, in the course of nature as we know it, not be here. At least, not in your living physical body. It is an unfortunate collection of events, a power surge due to strong sunlight and very high thin clouds, plus we imagine the weather conditions, when... where you started from.'

I felt my eyebrows furrow; I couldn't stop them. 'I'm sorry, this is making no sense.'

'Nor will it for some time I fear,' said William. 'The quickest way for me to explain is to quickly get, um, Grace...' William turned swiftly to look at Grace who was leaning on the kitchen unit holding her own cup of tea. '... to tell you today's date.'

'It's the sixteenth of May,' said Grace. 'Tuesday the sixteenth of May.'

'I know that,' I said.

'That's fascinating,' said William. 'It was the sixteenth of May when you got up this morning.'

'Yes, but it's not a Tuesday, it's a Friday.'

The old man pursed his thin lips. 'I'm sorry to sound shocking, Gavin, but it truly is a Tuesday. Here, where we are now. Tuesday May the sixteenth, twenty to eleven.'

I couldn't help glancing at my watch.

'Hang on,' I said. 'It's the sixteenth of May, but I make it four forty five.' I shook my wrist and listened to my watch – it was working.

'No no,' said William slightly curtly. 'Not the time, the date. It is May, twenty-two eleven. The year is 2211.'

I sat still for a moment. I felt normal; I could sense my body sitting on the simple wooden seat, in a sort of olde worlde farmhouse kitchen, in a wood in Berkshire. I knew I'd once driven nearby in a silver Audi TT. I was in a room with what looked like normal human beings, but things were steadily and relentlessly going out of whack.

I simply didn't believe anything I'd heard. I couldn't quite understand why the people I'd just met would create such an elaborate hoax. There must be some other explanation.

What they were saying was nonsense – I'd simply been knocked unconscious in the landing and this was some sort of fantasy I was having. Or I was dead and this was some sort of inexplicable heaven, not that I'd ever believed in any form of afterlife. I wanted to tell Beth, who did for some even more inexplicable reason believe in God and the afterlife and spiritual things; I wanted to admit to her that maybe she had been right. Maybe this William bloke was actually God and this was how I was perceiving the almighty.

I didn't feel alarmed because nothing I'd experienced was real. It couldn't be. It was fairly bloody obvious I could not have flown into a weird-looking cloud near Didcot power station and emerged into clear blue sky two hundred years later.

5

FOR SOME TIME AFTER I'D BEEN INFORMED OF the date, there was much discussion among the people in the kitchen as to where I should stay. I didn't pay much attention. I eventually took a risk and sipped the tea. It was a bit too sweet for me but it was delicious. It wasn't tea as I know it, it was some kind of herbal stuff, the sort of thing Beth had boxes and boxes of. I'm a bit of a builders' tea type of person, well, I was.

I sighed quietly. If the weird herbal tea was spiked I may as well go with it, I was probably dead anyway.

I looked around the room hoping to spot a phone, but there was nothing phone-like on view. I was about to ask when old man William turned to face me.

'Gavin, what do you think?'

'Sorry mate, I was miles away,' I said. 'Nice tea by the way.'

'I have suggested you come to Goldacre Hall, the house I live in.'

I shrugged, no point fighting against it. 'Yeah, whatever's good for you,' I said. 'I'll try and sort things out. Really sorry to land on you like this; it wasn't my plan.'

'We quite understand, it's all very distressing.'

William was standing by the open door and beaming at me. I eventually got the message and stood up.

'Thanks for the tea,' I said to Grace. She gave me a smile, quite a nice smile.

I set off through the dusk with William, following him along a narrow but well-kept path through quiet woodland until we emerged in the large field I'd landed in. The plane sat forlorn next to the thick hedge.

'What a wonderful machine,' said William. 'Although it does look a little unsafe.'

'It's proved very reliable,' I said, noting a familiar feeling I'd had before when people criticized my choice of aeroplane. I was a bit defensive. Get over it, the bloody thing works, I was thinking. 'It's clocked up over five hundred hours without a hitch.'

William nodded; he was smiling but his eyes looked pained. He turned and pointed in a north-easterly direction. I looked up and there was the blue line, but it wasn't quite as intensely blue as it had been. I rubbed my eyes – it just seemed too unreal to be there. I looked up again into the clear, steadily darkening sky.

'If there is something huge at the end of the line, why can't I see it?'

'Oh, you can just about see it, on a very clear day. It is but a speck to the naked eye. It is gently skimming high, high above the earth.'

I shielded my eyes and tried to stare beyond the thin wisps of high-level cloud. I could see nothing; the blue line just disappeared.

'The old power station was indeed just over there,' said William. 'The tether station has been constructed on the old site. The power station was demolished before I was born, but I have seen pictures of it. A large structure with a very tall chimney.'

I grinned and shook my head. 'I'm sorry if I don't believe you when you say it was demolished before you were born. I mean, it's there, somewhere, we just can't see it from here. I saw it just before I went into the cloud.'

'Mmm, when you went into the cloud. Tell me, was it generally a clear sky?'

I nodded; there was something ominous in his accurate description.

'And did you notice that the cloud cast no shadow on the ground?'

Then I felt a rush of disquiet. How had the old man known that?

'Yes, yes, I did notice that.'

'I am so sorry, Gavin. I feel partly responsible for this. My father was part of the original group that designed and installed the tethers. I have spent many years studying their effects; we have often been troubled by some of the things they seem to do. As with most technologies there are side effects, things we could not imagine could possibly take place. I can only ask that you rest and take time to understand what has happened to you.'

'What has happened to me?'

'You are the unwitting victim of an anomaly; the fold in the curtain caused by the tether has allowed you through, that is really all I can tell you.'

'Hope you'll forgive me if I don't buy this bull— nonsense.'

William smiled and shook his head. 'That is why I am suggesting rest and reflection. You are very welcome to stay with me. I live in a large house with many other people, but I am sure we can find space for you.'

'You mean to tell me I can't go? I can't leave and return to my wife, my home, everything?'

The old man dropped his head; I felt concerned for him. When he raised it there was a tear rolling down his cheek. 'I am so sorry, Gavin. Goodness me, what a calamity. Something has to be done to stop this happening yet again.'

The old man seemed so genuinely upset, and so utterly non-threatening, that I couldn't stop myself slowly beginning to believe what I was hearing.

'To stop what happening? Where am I really?' I asked. I was beginning to feel a little nauseous. 'How am I supposed to believe it's 2211?'

William put a gentle hand on my shoulder. 'Please come with me.'

So saying, he started to walk along the side of the field. I

followed simply because I had nothing else to do. As we passed
the plane I stood next to it for a moment.

'If I could take off again, I could see where I am and I could get back home.'

William turned. He nodded. 'Let us see what we can arrange in the morning. I believe the machine needs considerable space in order to get airborne?'

'A runway, yes, or at least a clear strip of ground with no huge trees at the far end.'

'I am sure we can find a way,' said William. 'Let us decide in the morning. There are many people close by who would be happy to help, if for no other reason but to see a genuine flying machine in action.'

I snorted a little but felt embarrassed – he was such a sweet old fellow. An old man standing in the beautiful early evening light talking about 'genuine flying machines' was so absurd it was comical. I scratched my head to try and cover my reaction, then I retrieved my iPad, phone, jacket and wallet from the cockpit and followed the old man.

We walked in silence along the side of the field and through another narrow gate. On the other side of the thick hedge was a large orchard, row upon row of well-tended fruit trees with narrow tracks between each row. I noticed a rabbit scurry across our path, heading for a very well-tilled field with neat rows of vegetables to our right.

'This is an amazing farm; is it yours?'

'Mine?'

'Oh, sorry, I mean, do you live here?' I asked.

'I do indeed,' said the old man.

'Rented is it?'

'No, no, not rented,' William said and smiled at me. 'I have lived here most of my life and I've worked these fields most of my life too.'

I was surprised; due to what William clearly knew about the

tether I had assumed the man to be some kind of academic or high-level engineer.

'Oh, sorry, I s'pose I assumed you were something other than a farmer.'

William shot me a look, not hostile, more surprise.

'Oh, I'm not a farmer, I just live here.'

'Right, yeah, I'm with you,' I said, feeling no better informed. 'So whose farm is this?'

'Well, dear me, where does one start? Let me see. It's not a farm in any way you would probably understand it, and, well, we all own it.'

'Oh, right,' I said, 'And who are "we"?'

'Well, everyone, the commonwealth.'

'What, the Queen?'

'The Queen?' He chuckled more this time, seeming baffled by the suggestion. 'No, there's no Queen. I'm sorry, it seems every answer I try to give you raises another hundred questions.'

'So you don't own it, the Queen doesn't own it, the commonwealth do: who are they then?'

William opened another sturdy gate at what looked to be the entrance to a garden. I followed him through.

'I think you have to take in the information step by step. It really isn't that complicated, but I dare say our time is very different to the world you know.'

I followed William through the gate and into a well-tended garden. An old woman was sitting on a seat under an ancient apple tree, her head bowed as if she had nodded off to sleep.

'Evening, Marga,' said William. 'We have a guest.'

'How lovely,' said the old woman, raising her head to look at me. 'A very young guest, how delightful.'

I smiled. It wasn't altogether unpleasant being referred to as very young – being thirty-three years old didn't feel young.

'You are very welcome,' said Marga, offering her hand to me. I shook it. Her hand was like a small bird, tiny and so delicate I could barely register it.

'Gavin arrived by flying machine. He's left it in the bow field,' said William.

'How very exciting!' said Marga. 'A flying machine?'

'Oh it's a wonderful thing; you must go and see it in the morning.'

'How exciting,' repeated the old lady. 'I would love to hear all about it.'

I considered the possibility that the old bird was a bit batty. Not knowing what a plane was didn't seem to cause her any alarm at all.

She gazed up at me with piercing and clearly intelligent eyes that didn't look in the least bit batty. 'I dare say you are tired and hungry. An evening meal is being prepared; I hope you will dine with us and then rest for as long as you wish.'

I looked at my watch. It was seven thirty in the evening, the meeting was blown, I couldn't ring and apologise due to having no signal, no one seemed to have a land line and I couldn't even seem to send an email.

'That would be great, but I am a little concerned about my schedule. I kind of need to get in touch with people. D'you have broadband here?'

Marga looked puzzled and glanced at William, who looked equally nonplussed.

'Broadband,' I repeated. 'Internet.'

'Internet,' said William. 'Well, we have, not quite what you are talking about, but...'

'Maybe I can use your connection on my iPad,' I said, holding up the device.

'Isn't that gorgeous? Paula would love to see that – she loves the old gadgets,' said Marga as she placed a delicate hand on my forearm. 'She's my middle daughter. A historian, she's a lovely girl, but she wasn't overly blessed in the looks department.'

'Marga!' scolded William. 'She is a perfectly delightful woman.'

I smiled painfully; I didn't want to be rude but the jolly chitchat seemed to have an undercurrent I found increasingly disturbing. Something bad really had happened, something calamitous, and they weren't telling me the truth, well, not the whole truth. Everyone I was meeting seemed to know something and they were keeping this information from me.

The old lady put her arm through mine and gently led me towards a large old Victorian-looking house at the far end of the garden. As we approached, I noticed the house didn't look quite as I would have expected: it had some sort of slate-grey cladding on the walls. The roof, while the usual shape for a neo-Gothic house, was of a smooth material of a similar colour.

It was old and familiar and yet weirdly new, and unrecognisable, like a house in a dream.

6

HE INTERIOR OF THE OLD HOUSE WAS IN-
stantly familiar and reassuring, like my granny's house.
The faint smell of cooking with a gentle undertone of
beeswax furniture polish was the first thing I noticed when we
entered.

The low lighting made the house seem snug and homely
although the lighting system built into the ornate plaster ceiling
was something I'd never seen before. It looked very tidy, with a
beautiful table on one side of the entrance hall, on which stood a
massive flower arrangement in a big pot. Above that was a painting of a group of people standing in a field – at least I thought it
was a painting until it slowly dissolved and turned into another
painting of a group of children in a field. It didn't look like a
digital hoarding you might see in a big city; it really looked like
a painting, an oil painting on canvas.

I walked with Marga towards a large door, opened it for her
and she smiled gracefully at me. I was then shown into a very
large brightly lit kitchen. Maybe a better description would be a
canteen, but not an institutional eatery – it was far more homely
than that – just a very big room containing a great many people.

There were three long tables running down the centre of the
room with loads of people already sitting and eating. It was
lively and noisy; a few young children ran around at the far end
of the room, but something I noticed immediately was that most
of the people looked well over fifty.

In the hustle of people moving chairs and arranging plates and
cutlery on the long table, I was left alone. The old lady Marga
hugged an equally old lady and they sat down together. I wasn't
sure what I was supposed to do. I didn't exactly feel unwelcome

but then no one seemed the least bit surprised by my presence.

I stood next to an enormous old dresser covered in decorative plates and unusual-looking bottles, leaned back and relaxed a bit. It was good to have the time to just look around and have a good old stare at them all. There was so much to look at, so much to learn. I could now see that behind a long counter was a fairly large kitchen area with an incredibly ancient old bloke in a white apron holding a big ladle.

Right in front of me a young woman picked up a small toddler and placed him in a high chair next to the table. Another old bloke with a long beard placed a bowl of steaming food in front of the child, then the kid picked up a small wooden spoon and started to feed himself. I watched with fascination the speed at which this old bloke moved; he flitted. You expected a shuffle – he looked a hundred years old – but he darted about like a teenage girl.

'I realise this must be a little confusing. It's always very busy at this time of day,' said William, who I now noticed had been standing beside me all the time.

'Do all these people live here?' I asked.

'Yes,' said William.

'Is it, like, a religious community?'

'A religious community?' William repeated slowly. 'Goodness me, what makes you think that?'

I smiled back at him. 'I don't know,' I said. 'A large group of people all living and eating together – I'm just trying to understand what's going on.'

'It's meal time; we live here.'

'Oh, I see, is this, well, a commune then?' I asked.

'Well, we are a community, I suppose. It's just called a hall if we call it anything.'

'But are some of the people here your, well, your blood relatives, your family?'

'My son is over there,' said William, gesturing to a group of

people talking away merrily on the other side of a long table. I
couldn't pick out which particular man he meant but everyone in
the group looked to be fairly old.

'My sister is over there,' he continued, pointing to the other
end of the table. Here I saw a large group of much older women,
slender and elegant but clearly engaged in some fairly raucous
laughter.

'Allow me to introduce you to everyone. Don't be alarmed,
they are all very friendly.' He picked up a spoon and a rustic
metal jug and rattled the two together.

'I am sorry to interrupt your pleasure, everyone.' The noise
level dropped a little and most of the people in the room glanced
towards us. 'But we have a guest at our table this evening.'

I felt the attention of the entire room suddenly and it's fair to
say I didn't like it. Move along now, nothing to see here.

'His name is Gavin and he's come down from Enstone in a
flying machine.'

There were gasps from the crowd; some of the people looked
mildly concerned. I smiled, probably badly so I ended up looking a little demented. I wanted to reassure them that I was fine
and not a threat.

'I would ask that we all behave gently with Gavin; he's had a
confusing and tiring day. If it's okay with you, Roger, I suggest
he rests in the end room of the long barn.'

'No problem,' said a very tall gangly man who was standing at
the far end of the room. I noticed that the man was very tall. I
then realised that everyone I'd met, except for Marga, was rather
taller than normal. I also noticed at that point that no one was in
the least overweight. In fact, they all looked rather gaunt.

I smiled as best I could and followed William to the far end of
the nearest table, where I was shown a seat. The man with the
long white beard placed a steaming bowl of what looked like
some kind of Mediterranean vegetable dish on the table in front
of me.

'Welcome, friend,' he said with a soft smile.

'Thanks.'

The old man then poured what looked like wine into a glass for me. William took a seat next to me and was similarly served with food.

Until I sat in front of this bowl of food, I hadn't realised how hungry I was. When the smell of it hit my nostrils I was surprised at how ravenous I had become. As soon as I tried some I was equally delighted by the taste; it was utterly delicious. I nodded as I chewed.

'I take it the food meets with your approval.'

'It's bloody amazing,' I said. 'I've never had anything like it. What on earth is it?'

William gave a little smile. 'It's just a vegetable conglomeration,' he said. 'Nothing special.'

I shook my head and took another forkful. 'Believe me, where I come from, this is something special.'

As I continued to eat, I took the opportunity to stare at the people around the table, all of whom it seemed were stealing inquisitive glances back at me. When I smiled they smiled back.

I was starting to notice things I hadn't seen when I first entered the room; it was as if I was waking up from a hangover or a blow to the head.

I considered that maybe that was what was happening. Maybe I really had been in a plane crash but had survived with some sort of head injury and this was my way of finding my path back to consciousness.

It just wasn't quite real. I would classify the clothing some of the diners were wearing as slightly hippyish, but then some others were quite smartly dressed.

On closer and more detailed inspection I realised the cut and styling of the cloth was something I didn't recognise. Sort of Middle Eastern, but not in any way stern or religious. However, this was such a layman's assessment – I know less than nothing about clothes.

The old man who had given me the bowl of food was wearing classic bib and brace denim work clothes, worn and carefully patched. In fact, all the clothes looked old but well cared for.

A man sitting opposite me on the long table leant forward. He looked a little older than me, but not much – it was really hard to tell. His hands were large and capable looking.

'What type of flying machine have you been in?' he asked. 'I've seen some in a museum, quite extraordinary technology.'

'It's a Yuneec E430,' I said. 'Electrically powered.'

'So, early twenty-first century.'

'Yes, 2011.'

The man nodded.

'Have you really never been in a plane?' I asked, hoping I wasn't being offensive.

The man shrugged and shook his head. 'I've podded about, but never in a winged craft,' he said. 'I quite fancy having a go.'

'I heard that,' said a rosy-cheeked woman sitting beside him. She was smiling and she punched the man's upper arm playfully. 'I'm not standing on the ground watching you go to your doom in some fancy-pants flying contraption, young man.'

The man grinned at her and looked back at me. 'It's not likely though.'

I nodded, took a sip of what was evidently crisp apple juice in the glass before me, again raising my eyebrows because it was so delicious.

'I'm fascinated about how this all works,' I said, making a small gesture around the room with my fork. 'I mean all of you here, living together.'

'How should we live?' asked the woman with the rosy cheeks.

'I don't know,' I said. 'How long have you been here? I mean, this isn't just a kind of holiday thing?'

'I was born here,' said the man. 'I met Celine when I travelled south, I stayed with her family for a few years and then we moved back here four years ago.'

'Five years ago,' said Celine.

The man glanced at her. 'Was it?'

'Yes, dearest.' She sighed as if dealing with an infant. 'Harold is six, remember? He's your son. He was born with my lot, but we moved here when he was young.'

The man raised his eyebrows and nodded. 'I think my brain has turned to useless mush since I fathered my son.'

'And where are you from?' I asked Celine.

'Winchester,' she said. I nodded and continued eating. So that was down south. I supposed it was, although for some reason when he said down south I was imagining Spain or North Africa. She looked sort of North African, but then most of the people in the room had very olive skin; there were certainly no blonde people in the room.

William leant towards me. 'I think what will help you is to speak with Paula, the woman at the far end of the table.'

I looked at the heavyset woman William was nodding toward; she was reading a large book as she ate. She was big boned – I think that's the kindest way of describing her. She wasn't fat by any means, but she was a solid-looking lass.

'Is that who you were talking about earlier?'

'Indeed, Marga's youngest daughter. She is very well read and knows a great deal of history. I hesitate to describe to you the events that have taken place since, well, since your era. I get my dates confused and that won't help you at all. I will talk with her in the morning and see if she is willing. She has, well, I don't quite know how to put it . . . a slightly unusual manner.'

I nodded. Out of all the people around the table, she certainly stood out, not having the same lean look as everyone else.

The old man cleared away the empty bowls and soon returned with large baskets of fruit. Plums, oranges, apples, bananas, peaches, all large and very fresh looking.

'Please help yourself,' he said as he placed a basket before William and me.

'These are all grown here,' said William.

'Are they?' I asked incredulously.

'Indeed, we have large glass houses to the east of the house, we grow a great deal of produce in them year round.'

I bit into a ripe plum. It was so full of flavour I couldn't speak for a moment.

'Amazing,' I said, plum juice running down my chin.

'Although of course we have plum trees in the outdoor orchards too, they won't be ready for harvest for a few months yet.'

I nodded and took another plum. There was no question: I had never eaten fruit this fresh or delicious. Never.

'The old man with the beard,' I said, 'does he do all the cooking too?'

'Oh no, that is Bal – he likes to serve, although he's not as quick as he was in his youth.'

'He seems pretty fast on his feet to me. How old is he?'

William had to think for a minute. 'Bal, he's, well, he must be a hundred and thirty I think. I'll ask him.'

I chewed with my mouth open. One hundred and thirty – that was simply not possible. The old man was so energetic, still on his feet serving people and carrying piles of empty bowls to the large kitchen units at the far end of the room.

'There are so many questions buzzing around my head,' I said. 'How can anyone live to be a hundred and thirty years old?'

'I agree it is very old. Not everyone is so lucky, but there are people living who are older than Bal. I believe there is a gentleman in Italy who recently had his one hundred and fiftieth birthday.'

I shook my head and toyed with taking another plum but I didn't want to appear greedy.

'So tell me as briefly as you can,' I asked. 'You all live here, in one big house. Is that common?'

'Do you mean does everyone live together like we do? If so, certainly not, not everyone would choose to live like this, I would guess, and I have no figures to back this up but plenty of experience. I would suppose that maybe half the people in the land live in halls like this. There are some people who choose to live alone, some families who only live with their immediate relatives and they generally occupy smaller houses. We are always changing the houses we live in; we have rendered many thousands of older houses.'

'Rendered?'

'Yes, we have adapted much of what we inherited from, I suppose, from your time and even older. We have effectively thinned out the large urban areas, reduced the density of houses, and sometimes, if the buildings are of interest historically, we have moved them apart.'

'I don't understand.'

'Well,' said William, pushing his chair back and adjusting his sitting position, 'there were many old rows of houses, all joined together.'

'Terraces,' I said.

'Indeed, a terrace of houses. Well, this became very inconvenient, so quite often we would renovate one house and remove the two neighbouring houses in the terrace, creating a garden area between the remaining houses. This would also allow us to re-engineer the house, install sufficient insulation and support systems, rainwater capture, ground heating, composting facilities and such like. It was simply not possible to do that when they were all crammed together.'

'I noticed this house had a peculiar grey finish on the walls and roof.'

'Oh yes, of course, you wouldn't know what that is. It's a carbon composite covering, very common now. We've been using that for over a hundred years. Bal is probably the only person here who can remember houses without it.'

'What's it for?' I asked.

'Well, protection, insulation mainly, and it strengthens the

older structures like this house, but I'm afraid we don't know
how long it lasts because we haven't been using it long enough. I
think the idea was that it would stand firm for many hundreds
of years.'

I shook my head in wonderment. 'Carbon composite.'

'You have heard of this? I didn't think it was around in your
era.'

'I've not heard of it, but I sort of understand what it might be.
But isn't it a very expensive material?'

William nodded, saying nothing, as if I had just mentioned
something no one spoke of, almost a taboo.

'May I ask why you are reticent to talk of the cost?' I asked.

William smiled. 'I suppose I don't wish to burden you with too
much information on your first day here. There is so much for
you to learn and I don't want your mind racing with questions
and keeping you awake all night.'

Now it was my turn to smile. I did feel utterly knackered. The
noise in the kitchen was intense: so many people talking and the
clattering of dishes, the clouds of steam coming from beyond a
crowd of people in the food preparation area.

A gentle wave of nausea overtook me, I felt a little dizzy, I
took a deep breath to try and regain my composure. It was almost
like taking a sudden dive in a plane, I felt my stomach turn over,
the shock of what was happening to me was almost too much to
comprehend.

'I think you might be right,' I said, hoping that talking would
quell the disquiet. 'I'm half expecting to wake up in my own
home, with my wife, in my house. Maybe with a bandage on my
head and an explanation for this absurd dream I'm having.'

William stood up and looked down at me with a slightly concerned expression.

'It's not a dream, Gavin. I almost wish it were, but I fear that
is not the case. You really are here.'

7

WOKE UP IN A BEAUTIFUL ROOM. MY EYES opened and I lay on my back for a moment just staring upwards. Was I alive? Was this heaven? Was I still dreaming?

It all seemed very real – the bed felt like a bed, the air was cool and smelled delightful.

I turned my head slowly, taking in the room. It was gentle and reassuring, nothing bizarre or threatening anywhere I could see.

The building I was in was obviously old, a converted barn maybe. I could barely remember it from the night before. The events of the previous day slowly re-emerged. When I had finally been shown across the courtyard beside the old house, a very tall man led the way; it was dark and I was exhausted.

Above me large oak beams supported a huge vaulted ceiling, heavy drapes covered the small windows, and there were wide polished boards on the floor. Beth would have loved it.

It was a new experience for me to wake up and not be sure where I was. Even though I have travelled a great deal, spent time in many different countries, I had never before woken in a place and not been quite sure where I was. I suppose I'd led an orderly and predictable life up until the point I flew into the cloud. Now it seemed new and disturbing experiences rained on me without falter.

The walls were panelled in some kind of old pine. Even the smell in the room was unusual, not unpleasant and it did remind me of something, like a lost history, like a reassuring smell of calm and contentment. I guessed it was some sort of herb smell or some kind of polish. I sniffed deeply; whatever it was it smelled good and clean.

I lay motionless in bed, trying to remember everything that had happened. There was still a background feeling of anxiety because I'd let so many people down without so much as a text. I should have contacted the company I was due to visit in Basingstoke, I should have rung Beth, I should have done so many things. Surely people would be worried about me.

Unless. I rolled over in the large comfortable bed. Unless what I had been told was really true. If it was really true, everyone I had ever known, Beth, my mum and dad, my brother Timothy, my nephew Jack and his mum Louise, they were all long dead.

I felt slightly nauseous and sat up, trying to remain calm. It was nonsense – there had to be another explanation.

I climbed out of bed and could sense by the light coming around the curtain that it wasn't very early. I found my phone, which said 8:30 A.M. The battery was still full, even though I hadn't recharged it. There was still no signal. There was no 3G, no Wi-Fi, nothing.

I stood on the bed and looked out of the window. It was a beautiful May morning, the sun already high, the sky clear. Through the trees that were close to the building I was in I could see a small field, a school playing field maybe as there were numerous children running about – some suddenly stopped and spun around on the spot, others ran around them in circles before dashing off in another direction. It all seemed so normal, and yet at the same time it made no sense.

I found my clothes and had started getting dressed when there was a light tap on the door.

I looked around. The wood-panelled walls gave no clue as to where the door was.

'Um, come in,' I said. One of the panels opened to reveal Grace, the young woman I'd met in the field the day before.

'Good morning, Gavin,' she said with a broad smile. She had a large pile of folded clothing in her arms. 'I hope you slept well.'

'I did, thanks. Yeah. Slept really well,' I said, feeling a little exposed; I was only wearing underpants and my T-shirt and I started to dart about looking for my trousers.

'You seem a little anxious. Is everything okay?' said Grace kindly.

'Well, I don't know. I didn't expect to wake up here. I expected to wake up at home, or in a hospital, but I'm here aren't I?'

'You are definitely here,' said Grace. 'What are you anxious about? Is there anything I can do?'

'I don't even know where to start,' I said. I sat down on the bed with my head in my hands. Somehow the appearance of Grace made everything worse. If she was real and in the room, it made it more apparent that this was all really happening. You wouldn't dream of some slightly stern but beautiful woman one day and then dream she came into your room the next.

'Please don't be upset,' said Grace. She stood by me and I felt her hand rest softly on my shoulder.

'If what William told me is true, yesterday, in your kitchen, I mean, if none of you are lying or making fun of me, then my wife is dead.'

'You have a wife?' said Grace, she said the word 'wife' hesitantly, it was as if she wasn't used to the word.

'I don't know. I did yesterday. We had a row before I left home. I want to ring her and say sorry, you know, tell her I'm okay, but I can't.'

Grace sat next to me, keeping a respectful distance.

'No, you can't. It's very sad indeed.'

I looked at her. She seemed genuinely concerned but also very matter of fact. I couldn't call Beth: she knew it, I knew it. I also heard the sentence I had just uttered repeat in my head. Suddenly it made no sense, 'I want to ring her and say sorry.' It was so archaic, it was like saying, 'I must send a telegram at once.' I felt like a Victorian standing in an internet café, no, worse, a man who had seen an early steam engine standing by the Japanese bullet train.

We sat in silence for a while.

'The most likely explanation I can come up with is that I am dead, or in a coma,' I said eventually. 'Because nothing else makes sense. For a start, this is all too nice.'

'What d'you mean?'

'Well, here, now. You all seem so happy and healthy, there's plenty of food, there's what seems like ubiquitous energy. I mean, my phone's battery has been fully topped up ever since I came out of the cloud.'

'I won't pretend I know what you're talking about.'

I picked up my phone and showed it to her.

'Oh, isn't that lovely,' she said. 'What is it?'

'My phone,' I said. I was almost annoyed – as if she wouldn't know what a phone was! 'Never mind that,' I snapped, trying to keep my temper. 'Look, the battery indicator. A hundred per cent.'

'Is that good?' asked Grace.

'Well, yes, it's bloody amazing. That's what I mean. Everything here seems pretty bloody amazing.'

'Well, it's not all a bed of roses, Gavin.'

'Okay, I'm sure you're right, but the future looked pretty grim to some of us back in, well, what do I call it? My day? The old world. All the films and books about the future were always full of mass extinction and destruction, wars, Armageddon, the machines taking over, massive meteors slamming into the earth, the human race coming to an end, invasions by aliens, endless nuclear winters, no food, no fuel, it was all really depressing.'

'Well, I'm not the person to ask, but I think the last two hundred or so years haven't been exactly easy, and we've still got plenty of problems now.'

I looked at Grace and smiled. 'Have you? Blimey, it's almost a relief to hear that.'

Grace smiled back at me. 'Nice to see you smile.' She patted the clothes resting on her lap. 'Good. Well, let us tackle the practical problems first. I thought to myself this morning, seeing as you found my kettle so impressive, you might be interested to wash your clothes.'

I couldn't make an immediate connection but I smiled and nodded.

'And I knew you'd need something to wear while they were being washed, so I brought you some fresh clothing.' She carefully placed the folded clothes on the bed beside her.

'Oh, great, thanks.'

I picked up the neat pile; it was heavier than I expected. Grace stood up and looked at me.

'Try them on then?' she said with a smile, a smile that contained no hint of either malice or flirtation.

'Oh, right. Um, okay.'

I felt slightly confused as to what was going on. I turned my back to her and stripped off my T-shirt and pants and pulled on the clothes she'd brought. I could feel her staring at me the whole time I was dressing; it wasn't obviously sexual or even intrusive, it was maybe just a little bit creepy.

I pulled up the weird trousers she'd given me – maybe breeches would be a better description. Heavy, possibly woollen cloth, good quality but cut in a way I didn't quite understand.

'Let me assist you,' said Grace. She knelt down in front of me without hesitation and tied together two strong tapes that were sewn into the waistband of the trousers. No buttons, zips or belts on these clothes – it seemed everything tied together with strong tapes.

I pulled on a soft slightly creamy-coloured shirt and a short, boxy cut jacket made of the same cloth as the trouser things.

'There, that looks much better. Do they fit you well?' asked Grace.

'Fine,' I said. I glanced around the room for a mirror. I don't think I'm a vain man, but I felt a little as if I were going to a fancy dress party. I suppose I was very used to my chinos and polo shirts.

'What do you need?' asked Grace. I was trying to ignore the
fact that everything this young woman said sounded a bit like a
come on. I wasn't in the market – at least, the day before I hadn't
been in the market.

I stood in silence for a moment wondering if I did have a wife.
However, it was becoming increasingly possible my wife had
been dead for something like one hundred and fifty years. I
shook my head. It was nonsense; things like this didn't happen.

'I was looking for a mirror. I'm just not sure how, well, how
weird I look.'

'You look perfectly normal to me,' said Grace. 'If anything,
you look rather more handsome.'

She didn't seem to be flirting when I looked at her; she looked
as if she was just stating a simple fact: it's daytime, or it's raining.
I could discern no more emotional subtext. Mind you, according
to Beth, who may or may not have been dead for over a century,
that would be nothing new.

I picked my clothes up and followed her out of the room and
into a long, whitewashed corridor, down a flight of stone steps
– I could recall none of this from the night before – and through
a heavy door into another room. This one was noisy. Large
machines lined the walls, and Grace opened a steel door in one
of them.

'Put your clothes in here,' she said and I did so. Inside it looked
like a black drum, obviously some kind of washing machine
although I'd certainly seen nothing like it before. There was no
company logo, no markings or obvious controls on the machine
so I watched carefully to see what Grace would do.

'Light wash please,' she said as if talking to a ticket seller at a
train station.

A small, dull red light appeared above the door and the
machine throbbed a little. A high-pitched whine emanated from
within the smooth exterior and the dull light went out. Grace
pulled out the clothes.

'Don't tell me they're done already!'

'I have only washed them. I like to hang things on a line to dry if the weather is suitable, and it's a warm day today. Follow me.'

Grace opened the door and an ancient-looking woman entered.

'Morning, Grace darling,' she said as she walked in.

'Good morning, Francesca,' said Grace.

I turned around as I was following Grace, and saw the old woman open a door on the opposite wall and start hauling out some sheets.

Outside the building the sun was already high and bright, a beautiful English summer's day. We walked along a neat path, through another hedge and into a small paddock. A series of lines was strung up and most of them were festooned with laundry, drying in the sun.

'Solar drying,' said Grace with a smile. 'Low carbon.'

'Oh, so you know about carbon?' I asked.

'No, I don't know anything about carbon, I've just been reading some old records from your day. Everything had to be low carbon.' She laughed a little as she pegged my clothes up on the lines.

'They'll be dry in no time. Go into the kitchen and get yourself some breakfast. There's someone waiting there who wants to talk to you.' Grace gave me a kiss on the cheek. 'I'm working in the bow field, where you landed your flying machine yesterday. I'll see you later!'

She ran off. I watched her go and realised immediately that I didn't want her to.

8

STOOD ALONE IN THE GARDEN OF THE OLD house staring up at the oddly coloured cladding. It wasn't exactly pretty – no natural stone in evidence. However, it was very well looked after and the garden was an enchanting place.

In some ways it was like a dream, and yet I was so aware of the freshness of the air, the slight wind in my hair, the non-existence of background man-made hum, that odd sensation of being unable to discern any mechanical noise.

I looked around the garden. There was just the sound of the wind in the trees and birdsong. So much birdsong. It was unquestionably beautiful, not something I normally noticed. I realised, as I stared around the blossoming, richly verdant garden, that I quite wanted to stay.

However, as I contemplated this, imagining myself as an old man pottering around in this garden, I knew this was absurd. I wanted to see the world; I wanted to see what had happened to the world I had been so familiar with.

From the sound of people's reactions to my 'flying machine' I would have the sky to myself, if only I could take off again.

I could fly back to Kingham and see what had happened there. I could fly over London. I worked out that due to the lack of planes, there would be no air traffic control and nothing in the sky other than the very obvious tether lines to worry about.

'Mr Meckler,' said a voice behind me. 'There's hot tea and fresh cakes in here.'

I turned around and saw the heavyset woman that the old man William had pointed out to me the previous evening. She held out her hand; it was enormous. I shook it. Her hand was not only enormous, it was clearly very strong.

'I'm Paula,' she said. Her voice was deep, not quite like a man's but very deep for a woman.

'Hello,' I said. 'Nice to meet you.'

'Mmm. So, Mr Meckler, tell me, you were born when exactly?'

'June the seventh, 1979,' I said.

'1979. Indeed. That is an awfully long time ago.'

'Well, yes, I suppose, if what I've been told is true, it is.'

Paula smiled briefly. She seemed a little impatient. 'William suggested I give you a brief rundown of the historical period you have, well, you have not . . . '

'The bit I missed,' I said, trying to help.

'Indeed, indeed.' Paula entered the large kitchen and I followed her. I almost sighed with relief as at last I was in a place I recognised. It was almost familiar except there was no crowd of people in the room. It was very clean and tidy, and only Bal, the very old man with the white beard was in evidence; he was sitting at a table with a cup of tea in front of him. He appeared to be asleep.

Paula walked to the kitchen area and on top of an old wooden serving table was a tray containing two cups and some small pastries. She carried the tray to the large table, placed it down very carefully and pulled out a chair.

'Please take a seat,' she said. She pulled another chair out and sat opposite me.

'Not surprisingly,' she said, 'a great deal has happened in the period between the time you went into the cloud and the present day.'

'Right,' I said. I was feeling very confused now. More convinced that something utterly inexplicable had happened, which could only end up in lots of feelings. Weird unfamiliar feelings. Not all bad, but basically a little bit terrifying. 'It certainly looks very different.'

'In what way?'

'Well, from the glimpses I got yesterday when I was still flying, the whole place looks like a forest.'

'Ah, yes of course. That must be very different from your era. We have been busy planting trees for about a hundred and fifty years.'

'How do you grow food then?'

'We grow food everywhere, either in small highly cultivated plots or in our glasshouses. More or less everyone grows food. That's what we all do.'

'What, everyone?'

'Everyone who is physically able.'

'So are you all farmers?'

'No, not farmers. I don't think that is how we see ourselves. Gardeners primarily.'

'But you can't all do that. I mean, everywhere I look there are signs of what seems like highly developed technology. Your lighting systems, the tether thing, the power grid that seems to be everywhere. Someone is busy doing things other than bloody gardening.'

'There are certainly some who don't do any garden work. Not many though.'

'But aren't there, I don't know, like, specialists, like doctors, scientists, engineers, that kind of thing, people who are too busy doing other things?'

'There are many people who have other interests. For example, I am a historian, but I also work in the gardens every day.'

'Blimey,' I said, 'every day! But what about, I don't know, politicians, trade union bosses, bureaucrats, PR people, civil servants?'

Paula smiled. 'That is very amusing, Mr Meckler. We don't...' She paused for a moment and I assumed she was gathering her thoughts for some kind of shocking revelation.

Maybe I really was dead and she was trying to find the nicest way to tell me.

'How shall I explain?' she said eventually. 'There are no people who specialise in those sort of areas now.'

Okay, so maybe I wasn't dead and maybe she wasn't some kind of weird heavy-duty angel.

'None?' I said incredulously.

'No, not really. Oh, there are people with those kind of tendencies certainly, but they are tolerated, never encouraged.'

'So, does that mean...' I scratched my very slightly thinning hair. 'Does that mean there's no prime minister?'

'This is precisely why William wished me to discuss this with you. Most of the people here would not necessarily know what the term prime minister meant. It's not a term we are familiar with. It is only my knowledge of history that furnishes me with such information. No, there is no prime minister, no central government, no banking system, no army, navy, air force, no police or judicial system and no civil service.'

I stared at her. I was now very worried. It sounded like the whole system I'd known, in fact the whole country, had broken down into some sort of anarchist semi-medieval subsistence-farming backwater.

'Blimey. And this isn't just here, in this house; you're talking about the whole country.'

'Pretty much the whole world,' said Paula. 'Certainly there are countries who still insist on having governments and armies, but they are few and far between. North Korea is a good example. They still have a government apparently, and an army. Then there's Midwest, what you would have known as America, at least the central geographic area; they have declared themselves an independent Christian democracy, but all the reports indicate they are anything but Christian and anything but a democracy. This, however, is hearsay; no one I know has actually been there. We don't hear much about what goes on.'

'So what happened? I mean, when I entered the cloud, the world was full of anxiety about the future. We had over-population, we had energy shortages looming, we had pollution, climate change, corruption in corporate and government circles, we had powerful forces of reaction growing, racism, fundamentalist religion on the boil.'

Paula was nodding patiently as I spoke. My thoughts were tumbling over each other like rocks falling down a quarry face, I couldn't seem to stop myself.

'But we also had incredible global communication systems,' I said. 'We knew what was going on in the world, or we could find out instantly. We had the web, the internet, we had incredibly well connected peer review systems in the world of science and engineering, we were developing technology at an amazing rate, surely that hasn't all just stagnated. You can't tell me all that stopped overnight.'

'Certainly not,' said Paula. She leant down and picked up a small canvas bag. From it she extracted a rather beautiful leather-bound book.

'I decided this would help you. It is a volume of contemporary history I helped to create. It's also on The Book if you wish to access specific topics in more detail, but I thought you might be more familiar with this format. Many very well read people from around the world contributed to it.' She pushed it towards me. It looked very old but was of course produced many years after I should have died. It felt weird holding it, but it was a printed, paper book, not a bit of floppy-touch screen plastic.

'I thought this paper version might be more familiar to you. A woman in a nearby community is very keen on making these old volumes.' Paula smiled at me. 'However,' she continued, 'to précis the events, about fifty years after you, well, you left your time, around the mid 2050s, there was a crisis which did lead to much strife, many small but terrible wars and a great deal of suffering.'

'Right. I suppose that was bound to happen,' I said, realising that if I'd stayed where I belonged I might well have experienced this calamity.

Paula leant forward and rested her substantial arms on the table. 'It was not a single thermonuclear war as I believe was often expected, but many hundreds of small conflicts. It was a very dark period. The wealthy nations suffered just as much as the poor, the whole supply system collapsed, the oil extraction industry finally disintegrated – they were simply unable to supply the demand. The price of crude oil went so high it choked itself and the global industrial sector ground to a halt. Governments became unable to govern.'

Paula sat looking into her tea for a while. I realised then that I was sitting on the edge of my seat, concentrating with more effort than I could remember doing for a long time.

'So who did govern?' I asked impatiently.

'Sorry, yes, well, the big three took over the running of the countries they were most interested in.'

'The big three, who were they?'

'Moshchnost, BipTic and Greywater. The big three corporations. I suspected you might have heard of them. All incredibly wealthy and powerful.'

'Wow, I've heard of Moshchnost, the Russian gas people. Who are the other two?'

'Well, let me see. BipTic was a company that started here originally, although it was said to be owned by a Chinese corporation. British Independent Parking Tickets was the original formation; it was a Christian fundamentalist corporation made up of a great many previous companies – there is detail about its formation and ethos in the volume,' she said, patting the big book on the table between us. 'I didn't write that chapter so my knowledge is limited. I do know they slowly expanded and took over all forms of transportation, not only the management but even the production of transportation systems.'

'BipTic,' I said. 'What a rubbish name.'

Paula smiled briefly. 'Greywater was a corporation that started out in security but took over banks, financial institutions, several countries and just about all the energy supplies that BipTic and Moshchnost didn't control. They had their own armies, their own private systems of administration. They wanted to govern the world and for a while they succeeded. But instead of nations going to war, the corporations did. Moshchnost started a corporate invasion of Western Europe, not a military one, but it eventually descended into a para-military situation. This resulted in total chaos and a further breakdown of international relations. After a few years of sponsored governance as it was called, corporations proved themselves uniquely unable to cope, and in 2079 they rapidly collapsed in a mire of debt and dysfunction.'

'2079,' I said with a smile. 'A hundred years after I was born.'

Paula smiled at me and nodded. 'I won't pretend to know what that must be like,' she said gently.

I shook my head for a moment, slowly leafing through the pages of human history I had somehow skipped. I wasn't reading anything in particular; my eyes just skimmed over the dense text. I looked up at Paula.

'It doesn't feel possible that this is history,' I said. The text on the page went blurred and, being as unconnected with my emotions as I must have been, it was only when I rubbed my eyes that I realised I was crying.

'So much suffering,' I said. 'Over such a long time.'

'Indeed, there were many hard years and many people suffered unenviable fates.'

I sniffed and Paula handed me a linen handkerchief. I looked at it for a moment. It was beautifully clean and pressed. I'd never blown my nose on a piece of cloth before; I'd only ever used tissues. I took a deep breath and had an impressive blow.

'So how did you get to this?' I gestured around the kitchen.

'Well, I suppose once again we saw how human beings, when

under pressure, are remarkably resourceful. Small communities had sprung up all over the world, operating outside the corporate system, effectively off the grid so to speak. People started producing their own energy on a large scale, partly due to being unable to obtain it through the big three.'

'Sounds like it was total chaos.'

'Oh, it was, but there are always pockets of peace, and the technology was well known by then. Cellular solar, wind, tidal and geo thermal plants came on line. In this country, the people took over the new grid as no one else was looking after it. BipTic, who had owned and controlled it, had disappeared, and it was rapidly falling into disrepair. They were lucky in that many of the former employees of BipTic shared the vision and used their undoubted expertise to reinvigorate the system. Slowly the power spread, the infrastructure was gradually increased and improved, and the crucial thing was that they distributed this energy free of charge.'

'Free of charge! Why on earth did they do that?'

'Well, they didn't really have much choice. There was no economy to speak of – all the previously existing structures of banking, finance and corporate governance had slowly melted away. It is important to remember that we create energy without burning any form of fuel, Mr Meckler, which I know is a big change from your era. We capture energy that already exists, so other than the energy expended in creating and maintaining the capture systems, there is no other cost involved as such. I imagine understanding a nonecon model is very hard.'

'Nonecon?' I asked. The word just popped out, almost hidden in the flow.

'That is what the system we live in has been dubbed. Nonecon, you aren't familiar with the term?'

'Um, no,' I said.

'Essentially it is a system of non-centralized governance which bases all transactions on energy expenditure. I suppose it's an energy economy, but with the understanding that all forms of activity, human, biological, mechanical, either absorb or generate energy.'

'Wow,' I said. Something in this sounded vaguely plausible.

'So,' continued Paula, 'some brave and far-seeing individuals gave away their power. This in turn meant that any last vestige of profit-making from power supply simply became impossible. I suppose people turned their attention elsewhere. It is now generally accepted that this supply of free power undermined what was left of the fiscally based exchange systems. People concentrated on supplying themselves with food to such an extent that the gardens grew. The gardens took over everything, not through some grand political strategy, just basic human need. We needed to feed ourselves.'

I laughed. 'Are you telling me there was a gardening revolution and the gardeners won?'

Paula didn't laugh, she didn't even smile, she ignored my comment completely and continued.

'No, there was no revolution, but when people are hungry and they see they can supply most of their own food, gardening becomes a very attractive option. So it was about a hundred years ago that this place, the place you knew by so many different names, the United Kingdom, Great Britain, England, this place became more commonly known as Gardenia.'

Paula waited for my response. I wanted to laugh: Gardenia? I managed to just smile. They renamed the country after a flower.

'I considered you might find the name rather crass. I don't think anyone named it thus; it just somehow came to be. While I might agree the name is a little immature, this country became a beacon in a blighted world. People travelled from all over the globe to study here, to learn our skills.'

I smiled. 'You'll hopefully forgive me if I say this all sounds a little ridiculous. Truly, people came from all over to see how the British did something?'

Paula nodded and smiled gently.

'Sorry, I mean the Gardenians, blimey. Maybe it's just me,' I continued, 'but I was always under the impression that we had become uniquely rubbish at doing anything innovative. All the skilled people I knew who came from here had to work elsewhere, unless they were bankers.'

This time Paula's smile broadened and she raised her large eyebrows a little. 'That may well once have been the case, but I think you'll find that has changed now. There is no question that we do hold a very special place in the world. We've had no wars, no strife or social unrest for over one hundred years. We are completely self-sufficient for food, energy and all the resources we need to maintain our lives.'

'How can you be? I mean, this is England. The weather is lousy, what about oranges, what about, I don't know, out of season strawberries?'

'Well, there's no denying we are very blessed; we have adequate rainfall in the northern half of the country. The southeast is mainly arid, but here we grow a lot of subtropical plants, plus we have the infrastructure to conserve water. We have a temperate climate most of the time although our summers are now much hotter than you would have known. We grow oranges. All along the south coast are very large orange groves, and grapevines of course. But even here, in our glasshouses we grow pineapple, kiwi and many other types of tropical fruit. We have large nut groves, hardy fruit orchards, berry groves as well as more common root vegetables, grains and pulses. We grow anything and everything here.'

I sat looking out of the window in silence for a moment. Eventually I shook my head and said, 'Wow.'

'One hundred years, Mr Meckler,' said Paula seriously. 'That's how long we have been struggling to make this frail system work. It won't last for ever, we all know that, but for now, we have reached a sustainable equilibrium between people and nature. We garden the whole country, we look after it, we waste nothing, we hoard nothing, we take nothing from people less well off than ourselves. A little different from your era, I would suggest.'

'You're not kidding,' I said. My mind was racing with questions; I didn't know where to start. It sounded bonkers but from what I'd seen of the new world I was in, it seemed to be plausible. But then I shook my head. How could it possibly work? People are stupid and greedy and they mess things up.

'But when you say you have no government, no army, no police, I mean, what about crime?'

Paula smiled at me again, which was becoming mildly annoying.

'What about a murderer or rapist, what about bloody paedophiles, or is that all cool now in your hippy-dippy liberal laissez-faire world? I mean, what about basic human nature, what about prisons?'

'I admire the way your mind works, Mr Meckler. In one sentence you connect the concept of basic human nature with prisons. Again, the word prison would not be commonly used today and many people you might speak with would not know what you were referring to. However, I think we could agree, human nature encompasses such traits as co-operation, tolerance, empathy, kindness, the desire to be accepted. Now, it would be idiotic not to also state that under the right circumstances human nature can lead to violence, selfishness, cruelty and brutality, but we have now discovered beyond all argument that if the society a person grows up in functions well, if children are raised well within a loving supportive community, people are very unlikely to commit a crime. I'm not saying this as some kind of intellectual theory; this is proven by practice. And after all, there is nothing to steal, there are no impediments to ownership because fundamentally there is nothing to own.'

I stared at her. I picked up a spoon that was beside my cup.

'Well, whose is this?'

'It doesn't belong to any one individual, Mr Meckler,' smiled Paula.

I put the spoon in my pocket. 'Okay, so now it's mine.'

Paula laughed richly; this was the first time I'd seen her so much as chuckle.

'Is it?' she asked. 'Very well. From now on, that spoon is yours.'

'But I've stolen it. I've taken it from the community or whatever this is. Now no one else can use it. Doesn't that fact make a mockery of the whole thing?'

'Not in the least,' she said without alarm. 'For a start, one of the people that lives here is a dab hand at making cutlery and she enjoys doing it, so she'll make another. Secondly, I know you will feel bad about the spoon sooner or later and you will give it back. No one is going to do anything about it. You aren't going to be confined because you put a spoon in your pocket; it's just not important enough.'

Paula sipped her tea. She pushed the plate of pastries toward me.

'Steal one of those; they are delicious.'

I smiled. I took a pastry and bit into it. It was of course utterly delightful and clearly very freshly baked.

'Now,' said Paula, 'it is entirely possible that someone of a disturbed disposition could come into this kitchen, someone from outside our immediate community, and they could steal all our spoons or cups, or walk out with all our chairs. There are no locks on the doors, so it could easily be achieved. However, there isn't a house in the land that has no cup or no chair, and many people, especially the younger generations, would prefer to make their own cups and chairs, so there really is no incentive to steal. I'm not saying serious crime never happens; people still get emotionally stressed, we have murders, rapes, violent assault, but looking at the statistical data from your era, nothing like to the same degree.'

'So there really are no prisons?'

'No, we do have secure houses for people to live in who have
made mistakes in their lives, but the numbers held within these
places are very small.'

I was shaking my head all the way through this explanation,
not so much in disagreement, more in disbelief.

'It's very hard for me to understand how this kind of non-
system can work. And you also said there's no banking system?'

'No, not for many years.'

'How do you pay for stuff then? I mean, who works out
money, savings, borrowing, all that stuff.'

'The simple answer is we don't have money. We no longer use
money.'

'Okay, but do you have, kind of, online payment systems, a
chip inserted in your forearm which keeps tabs on your accounts?'

Paula smiled. 'Even with my extensive knowledge of your era
of history, I barely know what you're talking about. I don't know
how else to explain it other than there is no money. It strikes us
as a most complicated and fraught way to conduct your life,
being dependent on a belief system.'

'What, like religion?'

'Well, that as well. But no, I meant a belief system that encour-
ages you to feel safe if you have some pieces of printed paper
in your pocket, and unsafe if you don't. We don't have money,
no one does, we don't have chip inserts, and we don't have
wealth, not in any way you would understand it. We clearly are
wealthy in our lives, and we are all very grateful for that. We are
wealthy with time, the time we have to live. I would suggest that
longevity is our new wealth. Time, Mr Meckler, time to really
enjoy life and explore its wonders.'

Time. The wealth of time. Without question, time was one
thing I'd always felt short of. I never had enough time to do
anything; I was constantly in a rush, desperately trying to catch
up, to do everything that needed doing. I suddenly realised at
that moment I'd always been time poor.

'We have time, like now. I have planting to do, weeds to pull out, compost to turn over, a book to write, messages to respond to, and yet I find time to sit and talk with you.'

I smiled. 'I'm glad I've got time too. I need a lot of time.'

Paula put her enormous hand on mine. 'That is one thing we can offer you, Mr Meckler. An abundance of time.'

9

WOUND MY WAY AROUND THE SOUTH SIDE of the house, at all times surrounded by incredibly well-tended gardens. It seemed there was no corner unkempt, no pile of rubbish waiting to be cleared. It was obvious to me that people spent a lot of time looking after the place.

Time, that was the biggest difference – time and silence, no machine noises and no pressure to be somewhere, to do something, to meet a deadline imposed from outside.

I had spent most of the morning talking, well, mainly listening to Paula; she was a very good communicator, very calm and reassuring. I ended up with a thousand more questions than when I'd started, but I agreed to let her get back to her weeding and I'd save my questions up for later.

I passed through the gate I was sure I'd walked through the night before, and was mildly relieved when I realised I had entered the orchard; I remembered walking through that. As I passed by the neatly trimmed fruit trees I could hear a chattering noise, a pleasant tinkling of happy voices.

I saw a group of people at the end of a row of trees to my left, who appeared to be digging the soil with shovels. They were digging, chatting and laughing with each other. I noted my own rising cynicism: why were they so happy? Surely it was ridiculous. Digging dirt and laughing – what on earth was there to laugh about?

It was like they were too self-satisfied, not doubting enough. I found it mildly disquieting that they could live such obviously hard lives in such blind ignorance.

What had happened to technology? Why had these people reverted to medieval farming methods? Why didn't they have automated hydrogen powered farm machinery to do the digging for them?

I stopped and pondered for a moment. My reaction was something I'd felt had been growing inside me for the past few years. The years before I went through the cloud. It struck me when I saw people partying, laughing with each other or driving big inefficient cars that I was anxious. Not because I wanted to be at those parties, or because I wanted to own a big inefficient car, but because we were so obviously living in a fool's paradise. The thing was, calling it a fool's paradise makes it sound as if my era was a bit pokey and rubbish. But it was a kind of paradise; it was really good. Amazing things like planes that took you to the other side of the world, food from countries thousands of miles away, cheap food too. An abundance of choice everywhere you looked, amazing communications systems, films, TV, the internet. All things I'd become reliant on, all now gone, so it seemed.

I knew through my work, through the meetings I'd had with other engineers and scientists, that everything we'd grown used to was coming to an end. The party was just about over and the bill was about to arrive.

Well it clearly had arrived, and things were very different. People had been cleaning up after the party for two hundred years. So how come people were still partying, albeit partying in a field, digging the dirt?

I went through the narrow gateway in the tall hedge and into the field where I'd landed the previous day. Here I saw another much larger group of people standing in a long row across the middle of the field. They were also laughing and chatting away but they were pulling up oil seed plants and loading them onto the silent tractor and trailer.

I stopped and stared at them for a while. I scratched my head. They were removing growing plants in a long strip across the field. Young oil seed plants, their flowers still yellow. I don't claim to know much about agriculture, but I knew that oil seed

wasn't generally harvested until the yellow flowers had long
gone.

I walked forward. People I passed waved and smiled at me; they all looked so healthy and happy, and most of them I now realised looked slightly tanned, sort of Anglo-Indian or mixed race in some way.

It had occurred to me the night before that I hadn't seen anyone blonde. Everyone I'd met had fairly dark hair, quite olive skin. If their hair wasn't dark, it was grey because they were quite ridiculously old. I noticed one young woman wrenching out plants, her long lean arms muscled and taut. When she stood up I almost audibly caught my breath, she was so tall. Must have been near six foot seven, and yet with incredible grace and delicacy.

'Hello,' she said, a beautiful smile spread across her face.

'Hi there,' I said. I had to look up even though I was standing several metres from her.

'How is it looking?' she asked.

I breathed in, which gave me enough time not to say something tacky, something like 'It's looking very attractive at the moment darling – I'll find a step ladder, let's go and make babies.'

I just nodded and smiled. 'Good, very good. It's not harvest time is it?'

'No,' said the woman with a chuckle. 'We're doing all this for you.'

I felt worried – why were they doing this for me? The old man William showed up and gently held my arm.

'The sky pilot returns,' he said with a big grin. 'How do you like your new take-off track?'

I looked across the field. It was a clear strip of trampled earth at least 500 metres long. At the far end, a low hedge with no trees for at least 50 metres each side, in other words, the perfect light aircraft runway.

'Blimey,' I said. 'Have you seriously done this for me?'

'We thought it only right,' said William. 'In some ways, we've done it for selfish reasons – we all want to see this magnificent machine in the air.'

William led me down the runway strip, stamping his feet as he went. I followed, half-heartedly stamping as I went.

'Who was I just talking to?' I asked William.

'Ahh yes, that is Minda,' said William with a hint of sugges-tion in his voice. 'She's very beautiful, isn't she?'

'She is extraordinary, and so tall.'

'Oh, the young people today, they all grow so tall. Each generation seems to be getting so much taller.'

William continued to stamp as he walked. I glanced behind me again. A large crowd of people were following us, all stamp-ing on the ground, packing down the soft soil as they went.

'I can't believe this is happening,' I said. 'You all work together so well – it doesn't seem like anyone is in charge, like anyone is giving orders.'

'I suppose that's because they are not,' said William. I walked backwards for a while, staring at the small crowd following us, all talking to each other, stamping the ground like happy children.

'We chatted about it at breakfast this morning,' said William. 'To be honest we all have other jobs to do, but this seemed like a popular distraction and we knew it wouldn't take too long.'

Then I saw the Yuneec turned ready for take-off. I shook my head, turned back and looked at the runway. It was possible; it wasn't quite an open mowed field or tarmac runway I was used to but it was a slight downhill slope, fairly smooth, with a big wide gap in the trees to give me time to get airborne and pass over.

When we reached the plane I walked around, inspecting it. It all looked fine. William followed me closely.

'It might be a nice idea to thank everyone for pitching in,' he said discreetly.

I stopped and stared at William for a moment. His face twitched a little and for some reason I was reminded of Beth. All

the times she had criticized me for being so 'A.D.D.' as she
described it, of being an uncommunicative nerd. I knew it was true; I'd always found human beings and their foibles much harder to comprehend than complex engineering structures or computer algorithms.

'Yes, okay.' I glanced behind me. A group of twenty-five or so people stood in a semi-circle around the plane – that was bad enough, but they were all staring at me. I swallowed and started to speak.

'I don't really know what to say.' I scanned the group and my eyes fell on Grace, smiling at me. I rubbed my face nervously with my hands.

'Thank you for all your help. I feel a bit guilty that you've pulled up all these plants. Thank you.'

The group clapped politely. Then there was an awkward silence.

'Well, are you going to make the machine fly again?' said Grace. 'We all want to see it fly. I've been telling my friends and most of them don't believe what I saw yesterday. That's why we pulled up the plants, Gavin.'

'Oh, okay,' I said, feeling a big happy grin spread across my face. 'Um, okay, now please listen – when I start the motor, please stand well back. It's not noisy but does create quite a lot of turbulence; it'll throw up a bit of dust behind the plane. If you stand well to the side you'll be fine.'

There was a quiet exchange of glances and comments from the crowd, who duly started to move to either side of the plane.

'Would you like a travelling companion?' said William. 'I see the machine is built to take two people.'

'Well, yes, I can certainly take someone with me.' As I said this I was staring at Grace, who was grinning at me innocently. William walked up to the plane and stood next to it expectantly.

'I have to admit, I am very nervous.'

I got the point immediately. No, I wasn't going to be able to fly off to some fantasy location with the beautiful Grace, I was going to be joined by a jovial man who was so incredibly old it was almost funny.

'There's nothing to be nervous about,' I said. 'It's very safe, very reliable, and thanks to your technology I suppose the batteries won't even run out.'

I opened the cockpit canopy and held it wide open, helping William clamber aboard. William sat in the plane like an obedient child as I got myself seated and fastened my safety harness.

'Goodness me, does one have to be tied in?' asked William.

'It's just a safety precaution,' I said. 'They're called safety belts; you can undo them here.' I showed William the catch. 'There's nothing to worry about.'

Once he was safely strapped in, I pulled the canopy closed, made the prop-turning sign to the gleeful audience and booted up the plane. The cockpit, which was fairly rudimentary, pinged into life.

'How wonderful,' said William. 'Such sophisticated technology; I'm very impressed.'

'Well, it's all fairly basic,' I said, slightly embarrassed. To classify a simple electric aircraft as sophisticated technology when they had created 18 kilometre high solar kites and universal, global inductive electrical power distribution was a bit rich.

I explained the various screens on the small dashboard. 'Wind speed, altitude, orientation, auto pilot, sat nav.' I stopped there, remembering the sat nav didn't work. 'Let's not worry about that, we're not going far.'

'Sat nav?'

'Yes, short for satellite navigation.'

'Ah yes, I have read of this system – long gone I'm afraid.'

'It used to work very well in my day.'

'How very clever,' said William. He shifted in his seat a little and pulled out a small packet. He held it in his hand and it gently expanded before my eyes. It was a map, some kind of electronic map that shimmered and adjusted itself.

'Wow, that is so cool. What is it?'

'A map. I thought it might help us orient ourselves.'

'That is fantastic – so it's a sat nav then.'

'I don't think so,' said William. 'There are not satellites involved, it's just a map.'

I looked a little more closely. It didn't have roads marked on it, just a series of fields and houses from the look of things. In one of the fields marked on the map was a small blue dot that seemed to pulsate a little.

'Is that us there?' I asked, pointing to the dot.

'Yes,' said William. 'The dot shows you where you are.'

'So it is a sat nav then,' I said with a smile. 'I mean, how does the map know where we are? It must be communicating with something.'

'Well, I suppose it's communicating with the grid; the grid knows where we are.'

'The grid!' I said. 'As in the power grid.'

'Correct.'

'Blimey, amazing.' I stared at the map for a while longer, trying to work out what the communication protocol would be.

'Shall we take to the air then?' asked William.

I smiled. 'Yes, okay, let's do that.' I handed William a headset with a microphone. 'Pop this on; it'll be easier to hear each other once we're flying. The wind makes quite a lot of noise.'

I placed my headset on and William copied me.

'Can you hear me?' I asked.

William nodded, grinning from ear to ear. He didn't say anything.

'The microphone comes on when you talk – you don't have to do anything.'

'Oh, right you are. Can you hear me?'

'Loud and clear.'

I engaged the motor and the propeller slowly started to rotate. The crowd stared in awe as the propeller's speed slowly increased. The plane shook a little as it reached its maximum revolutions and I gestured to the crowd to stand back. I noticed then that Grace was staring in awe, maybe even a little terror, her hands clasped in front of her. Another slightly older woman put her arm around Grace's shoulders to comfort her. I glanced behind me – an enormous cloud of dust, stalks and leaves was whipping around the tail of the plane. I could see a few people running to get out of the back draft.

The rest of the crowd to the sides stood well back and when I could see our way was clear I released the wheel brakes. The Yuneec started to bounce slowly along the makeshift runway, gradually increasing speed, and before we were even half way along the cleared strip we were airborne.

Keeping the engine at full throttle I pulled the stick back and we climbed quite steeply. Not something I would normally contemplate as the strain on the batteries would reduce the range, but my eye kept flicking to the battery gauge – it was a habit I'd become used to. I realised then and there that it would be a habit I would have to get over. The battery gauge still read 100 per cent.

'Oh my goodness, are we aloft?' asked William.

'We are,' I said. I glanced at William – if this really was the first time the old boy had been in the air, I wanted to make sure he was okay. The cockpit was very small; I didn't want to deal with air-sickness. I glanced at the small cubby pocket by my side. There was an old Tesco bag in there, worth remembering.

'How are you doing, William?' I asked after I had levelled out the plane at around 500 metres.

'I am wondering if my poor old heart can take it. I've never known it beat so fast.'

'If you're not happy, just tell me and we'll land right away.'

'Oh no!' said William. I could see he was grinning. 'No, please don't do that just yet – this is truly wonderful.'

I banked the plane around gently and reduced the altitude a little to fly over the crowd in the field. I admit I wanted to show off – so few people had shown any interest in my plane before, I was really enjoying the attention. We passed over the field at about 100 metres, slowing the plane right down.

'Will they be able to see me?' asked William.

'Oh yes, they can see you fine; you can give them a wave if you like.'

I banked the plane over, glancing past William at the ground below. The small group could clearly be seen waving up at the plane. A few of the younger members of the group ran along the ground waving and jumping.

'Extraordinary,' said William, waving furiously. 'I never thought I'd live to see the day. Utterly extraordinary.'

Once we had circled the field I gained a little altitude and flew over the house.

'I think I can see our orchards down there. They look so small.'

I looked down to my left; there was the house and barn complex I'd spent the night in. The gardens looked incredibly neat and productive and they were far more extensive than I'd seen. I noticed that a few hundred meters from the house on a south-facing slope was a large complex of glass-houses. They must have covered a few acres. The glass didn't glint – it was coloured in some way, almost a silver metallic colour, but I could see dense vegetation inside.

I gently banked around so we could pass over again. On my left side I noticed a circular field. It had markings on the grass I didn't recognise, and there were long strips cut out of the grass in a kind of spoke pattern full of what looked like sand.

'What's that field for?' I asked.

William stared down. 'Oh goodness, look at that,' he said with a big grin. 'That's the playfield. Well I never.'

'What, you play football?'

'Oh no, we play structure.'

'You play structure? No, I don't understand,' I said, as we circled above the field.

'Of course, you wouldn't know this, well, let me see, where to start. I suppose the easy way to explain is that when the children are very young they play molecular.'

'Molecular what?' I asked.

'Well, it's a system, a game. They play molecular when they are small. When they reach something like the age of ten, they start playing atomic. Again at around twenty we start playing sub-atomic, then, when we are ready we start playing particular, then, doddery old men like me quite enjoy a game of string or quark.'

I continued to circle around the playing field. It was utterly baffling. These people seemed to play a game that somehow involved the most obscure aspects of physics.

'This is wonderful,' said William. 'Although I've seen this view of Goldacre Hall on a map, it is still an extraordinary experience to see it from the point of view of a bird. Marvellous.'

I turned once more and headed north, climbing gently. 'I'd love to see what has happened to Kingham,' I said. 'Where I lived.'

'That sounds like an excellent idea,' said William. 'Will it take us long?'

'Well, normally I would fly at the lowest speed I could in order to maximize my range, but it doesn't matter how fast we go, your wonderful grid keeps my batteries full.'

The throttle was at maximum as it had been for five minutes and the battery gauge still read 100 per cent.

We skirted around the tether, still glowing bright blue, but possibly not quite as bright as it had been the day before.

'I've just realised something: I didn't see the tether last night, when it was dark. I would have expected to be able to see it in the night sky.'

'There is nothing to see at night,' said William. 'The kite doesn't produce power without sunlight. In fact, during the hours of darkness a small amount of energy is going in the opposite direction, powering the control systems.'

I shook my head again. Everything I was hearing was a revelation.

'Fantastic, I love it,' I said with a grin.

We continued to head north-west, flying over what seemed to be an endless sea of green trees, broken now and again by the roof of a building, occasional thin strips of cultivated land.

'Tell me something, William, if you needed to go and see a friend or family member who lived far away, would you walk? I mean if they lived 200 kilometres away.'

I glanced at him. He was looking down at the landscape rolling beneath us.

'You see that,' he said, pointing down to his right. I banked over a little. 'In among the trees down there, a small stone structure.'

I could just about make out something that looked like a shed. 'Yes, what's that?'

'That is an entrance hall, to the track-way, they are just below the surface. I'm sure we'll use one in good time.'

'Track-ways, so you do have roads, like cars and trucks and stuff, only underground.'

William smiled. 'I'm not sure what you mean but I'm fairly confident our transportation system isn't quite the same as the systems you might have used. I believe you had surface tracks for machines to use.'

'Oh, we had roads, William, loads of them, everywhere. I often used them to navigate. Very easy to follow a motorway.'

'A motorway. That sounds rather lovely.'

'Believe me, they were anything but lovely,' I said. As we levelled out I could see a pattern emerging from this strange yet familiar landscape. I started to notice more and more long greenhouses dotted around. They were quite large structures, covering a couple of acres each. 'You've got a lot of greenhouses,' I said.

'What is a green house?'

'Sorry, I mean the glass houses, the big glass structures.'

'Oh, I see, yes, very good. They are not made of glass though; the exterior covering is entirely thermo cells, solar cells I think you may know them as. We use them to grow a great deal of our food.'

'So they generate power as well as protect the plants.'

'Indeed, that is correct. All our structures capture power. Oooh look!' said William suddenly, pointing to our right. 'That's Moore Hall. I've stayed there many times.'

The large building, still only two storeys high, had a very large glasshouse close by.

'That is one of the earliest communities,' said William. 'See the wind vanes.'

I hadn't noticed them until William pointed them out. A long ribbon of green material stretched between upright poles – like telegraph poles, the material seemed to go on for miles.

'Wind vanes?' I asked.

'It's a bit of a relic now, but they do still capture a lot of energy; the fluctuations caused by the wind drive actuators buried in the ground. All the energy they use at Moore Hall and more comes from the vanes.'

'Brilliant,' I said, this time trying not to shake my head.

'I'm glad you approve,' said William with a gentle smile.

In the distance I saw a familiar sight, a cluster of towers poking above the tree line.

'Wow, is that Oxford?'

William stared ahead. 'I dare say you are correct young man, your eye sight is clearly a lot sharper than mine.' He held up the map and stared at it closely. 'Yes, it must be Oxford; you may wish to fly over it.'

I banked gently to the left so the towers were directly in our path. Although the buildings were familiar, nothing else was – it was as if the forest had taken over the whole country. All I

could see beneath us were trees and as we got closer I realised the
bulk of the city had gone; it was just a series of old buildings in
woodland.

'So where are all the houses? This used to be quite a big town
in my day.'

'There are still houses, lots of houses. Look, there's one,' said
William. He was right, there was a house, and a mile or so
further on, another one.

As the tower of Magdalen College came closer, I reduced altitude and banked to the right. I could see the river, and Magdalen
bridge, and on the bridge, a building. Either side of the building
was a garden; it was clearly no longer a road. There really were
no roads anywhere to be seen in what was once Oxford. I banked
to the left and saw the Bodleian Library looking as though it was
in very good repair. It seemed most of the old college buildings
were still standing, although due to the number of trees growing
between them the whole place looked unrecognisable.

'Is it still a university?' I asked.

'I suppose you could describe Oxford as such, although it is
more a place of research. Many people from around the world
come to stay and work here. I have worked here in my youth. It's
a wonderful place to visit; I'm sure you'd be most welcome.'

I couldn't help it – I shook my head again as we resumed our
course. How could a city the size of Oxford disappear, the ring
road, the motorways, the industrial estates, the housing estates,
all the development I knew so well; where had it gone?

'I can't help wanting to know where everyone lives. It's like the
whole of England is a forest. What's happened? Does everyone
live in London?'

'Goodness no. We don't really have a London anymore, not as
you would have known it. We don't really have towns; we have
spread out.'

'But there doesn't seem to be enough housing for everyone.
Do people live underground? Where is everyone?'

'I don't think people live underground,' said William with a big grin. 'How big was the population in your time?'

'I don't know exactly, somewhere around sixty million.'

'Goodness me, we are now barely twenty million at the last census. Sixty million! Where on earth did you all live?'

'I'll tell you one thing: it was a lot more crowded than it is now. So what happened? How did the population drop so steeply?'

'I don't think it dropped suddenly, not like a plague or anything like that. People had fewer children and I suppose we generally live longer; I think that's the main reason.'

'But how did you do that, with legislation?'

'Goodness no, not in my lifetime. I believe when very few people have more than one child it just becomes the norm. I know that for a long time many people had one child, if that. Many men are unable to father a child, my parents bore only me, I have only one child, my child had only one child, so the population halves every generation. There is now some concern that we may have taken it too far – more and more people are having two children these days. There seem to be so many children about.'

'You don't approve?'

'Oh, I do, very much. I have one grandchild but I'm about to become a great grandfather for the second time. It's wonderful.'

I stared ahead. It all seemed too simple. It sounded as though, from what William and Paula had told me, the human race had steered away from the disasters of war, climate change, overpopulation, starvation and destruction of the planet by simple peer pressure, by organising themselves without some overriding authority telling them what to do. It all sounded utterly unconvincing. I felt sure there was something going on out of sight. Something was controlling these innocent, charming people. There had to be some hidden force or influence.

'There's Kingham,' said William, pointing slightly to our right.

I glanced down at his map. Sure enough, the map said Kingham Hall, but all I could see was trees.

'I can't see anything I recognise,' I said as we banked to the left
to circle where the village should have been. Suddenly a famil-
iar-looking roof caught my eye: the barn and the big manor
house were still there, although again surrounded by mature
trees. I worked out from the angle of the barn that my own house
had disappeared. What had taken its place was nothing more
than a vegetable garden by the look of things.

'This is so weird; my house has gone.'

William reached across the small cockpit and touched my arm
gently. 'Many years ago we had so many empty houses we did
remove the great majority of them. We used all the materials
again. Nothing was wasted.'

'So there's nothing left of my world,' I said as we continued to
circle around what had once been my home. 'Well, there's some
old buildings I recognise, but not much else. Let me see if my
airfield is still there.'

I banked to the right and headed towards Enstone. The midday sun reflected off the roof of an enormous glass-house, built
where Enstone airfield had once been. The rest of the field was
of course dense woodland, as it seemed was everywhere else.

I glanced at the battery level, still 100 per cent, and we'd been
flying for thirty minutes. Again I slowly shook my head.

'Are you feeling unwell?' asked William.

'I'm fine. I think it's just the endless shock of being here, of
how immediately familiar and yet how utterly different everything is.'

'I cannot begin to imagine what you are going through, my
friend,' said William sympathetically. He placed his hand on my
forearm and patted it gently. For some reason I didn't find this
move intrusive or uncomfortable, quite the opposite. I was very
grateful for the reassurance.

'If you are feeling up to it, I think we should head south until
we reach the Thames, then follow it east towards the sea. There
is something along the way that I feel will interest you greatly.'

'What sort of thing?'

'Have you heard of Heathrow?' asked William, pronouncing the name quite carefully.

'Heathrow airport?' I said in surprise. 'Is that still there? You do have aircraft!'

'Not exactly,' said William.

'Space rockets, oh wow!' I said, grinning like a loon.

'Let us head south now – the river is not far. I'm sure that's the best route to follow.'

I banked around and headed south. 'I'm finding it hard to orient myself,' I said. 'There are so few landmarks to guide me, and my sat nav is useless,' I said, tapping the dormant screen.

William passed me the map. With a brush of his finger an arrow appeared, a 3D hovering arrow that shimmered slightly above the surface area of the map. It looked so intensely as if it were floating between my eye and the map below I wanted to touch it, to feel its glossy surface.

'Follow the arrow – it is pointing in the direction we need to head,' said William.

I adjusted our direction very slightly and the arrow shimmered from blue to green.

'That is pretty bloody amazing,' I said, glancing over at William.

The old man smiled and stared ahead. 'I don't wish to build things up too much, but I feel what we are about to see will impress you.'

10

E FLEW DUE SOUTH FOR SOME TIME, OVER endless forest broken only by the occasional small field neatly planted with what could have been vegetables or ground fruits. There was the odd square of oil seed, an occasional field of what could have been wheat or barley. There were no towns, just houses dotted about here and there, and of course many more glass houses. At one point we flew over something that was a recognisable street, with rows of old houses either side of gardens.

'That's Burford,' said William. 'You may recognise that.'

I'd been for a pub lunch in Burford once when Beth and I had done an exploratory bike ride around Kingham. It was vaguely familiar except for the absence of the traffic chugging up the hill between the houses. No road now, just gardens.

After a few minutes or so, batteries still at 100 per cent, I saw the sun glint off a river in the distance.

'Ahh, Kelmscott and old father Thames,' said William. 'Let us turn to the east and follow it – there is much to see along its banks.'

I did as William suggested and followed the river's meandering path. The water was occasionally obscured by large trees but following its general direction was easy. I was concerned about landing by this time; we'd been flying for close to forty minutes. If the old fellow was caught short there wasn't much I could do about it.

'How are you bearing up, William?' I asked.

'I'm having the most wonderful time,' he said without looking at me; he was staring at the ground.

'I'm just a little concerned about landing somewhere. If you need, you know, if there's a call of nature, well, the only place I know we can land is in your field.'

William turned to me and smiled. 'Don't fret,' he said. 'I am fine, I'm having such a wonderful time the last thing I need is to have a wee-wee.'

A wee-wee. So after two hundred years of massive cultural and technological change, people still called taking a piss having a wee-wee.

After passing over Newbridge where the Windrush meets the Thames, another landmark I recognised, we followed the river past Oxford again, with William pointing out various communities along the way. No big urban development, just a series of houses surrounded by more trees.

It was only when we passed over the bridge at Henley, again a landmark I could recognise, that I realised we had already passed Reading, except there was no Reading, just a few farms.

Beyond the bridge I saw some strange-looking buildings on the bank of the river.

'What are those?' I asked William pointing to the structures.

'Heat extractors,' said William. 'They extract the naturally occurring heat from the river and turn it into energy; there are many of them all along the Thames.' Of course from that moment on I noticed these little buildings again and again.

I was very relaxed – the Yuneec essentially flew itself on auto-pilot, and I merely adjusted the direction every now and then in a lazy attempt to follow the river.

After another minute something ahead caught my eye. I was vaguely scanning the horizon when my eyes just stopped, transfixed by what was before me.

At first, the four lines made no sense to me, just four vertical lines in the sky, stretching from the land horizon into the misty blue. These thin lines were directly in our path and it was only when I saw an object rising up one of the lines that I started to blink.

'What in heaven's name is that?' I asked as the object continued to rise up one of the lines. As I was speaking another
appeared out of the misty blue and descended at much the same
graceful speed.

'That, my dear fellow, is Heathrow. That is what we have
come to see.'

As we got closer to the lines, another object started climbing
up another line, a small dark box-like shape.

'What is it?' I asked. 'I just can't work it out.'

'Pods,' said William. 'The ones that look like jewels or maybe
like tears, they are passenger pods; the cuboid ones are for trans-
porting goods, specialist goods or medicine, sometimes raw
materials.'

I looked up as high as I could. Way, way above us a small
speck on one of the lines disappeared into the blue.

'Blimey, William, this is utterly breathtaking – where are they
going?'

William turned to me and smiled. 'They go into space, Gavin.
They go out into space.'

'Seriously?' I gasped.

'Oh yes, once they have reached the required altitude, they
essentially stay motionless while the earth turns. When they
reach their destination they latch onto another line and then
descend; it's how we travel long distances.'

'Oh my Lord,' I said, trying not to swear. 'What are the lines
attached to, solar kites?'

'Goodness me no,' said William. 'No, something much larger.
They are attached to geo-stationary satellites located about 160
kilometres above us.'

'Wait wait,' I interrupted, trying to take all this information in.
'Satellites … so there's a satellite with a bit of string hanging
from it, and the boxes climb up the string. But how did the satellite get there, like, the first one?'

'Well, before I was born, I'm not sure exactly when – you'd

have to ask Paula – a very substantial rocket was sent up which carried the first tether satellite. As far as I recall this then sent a tether back to earth, and from then on the transportation of machines, support systems and people to work on the systems was much simplified. Now any new satellite is built on the ground in various parts, then transported into position, the various parts are constructed into a whole, another line is dropped to the earth, and so on.'

'So how many are there, I mean, around the world?'

'Oh, I have no idea. I would say a few hundred.'

We were soon close enough to see some detail of the objects crawling up the tethers. The more modular shape that was in front of me was moving upwards at a gentle pace. This was soon overtaken by a slightly more cuboid shape going up one of the other lines. That was climbing into the sky at about the same speed as a rocket, i.e. very bloody fast.

'Just extraordinary,' I said, staring in awe.

'The lines are around 150 kilometres long, as I recall,' said William. 'They just crawl up the tethers. The pods do have tiny hydrogen propulsion systems to steer themselves in zero gravity. You will have to add your name to the waiting list, have a trip somewhere.'

'Fuck me,' I spouted, then glanced at William a little shamefaced. 'Sorry.'

He was smiling at me. 'I thought you'd like it. You see, Gavin, we no longer need rockets to break the surly bonds of earth.'

'Wow,' I said, finally taking my eyes off the spectacle in front of me. 'D'you know who said that?'

'Said what?' William asked.

'The break the surly bonds of earth thing.'

'I have no idea. I must have heard it somewhere; it's quite poetic isn't it?'

'Ronald Reagan,' I said. 'He said it after a terrible rocket disaster.'

'Goodness, was he a poet?'

I laughed. 'No William, he wasn't a poet.'

After circling the tethers at Heathrow a few times we followed the river towards London. I had never flown in this area before – it was strictly off limits to light aircraft. I'd only ever seen the view from passenger jets. I knew that at the height we were cruising at I should be able to see the gargantuan spread of London before me. All I could see was the river winding its way through woodland.

'I cannot believe what my eyes are seeing,' I said. 'Where is London?'

Before me, the river fed into a wide body of water. At first I thought I was seeing a lake, a massive lake where London should have been.

'Ah yes, of course,' said William. 'This will have changed beyond recognition.'

The sun reflected off the water; it was huge, it wasn't a lake, it was an inland sea.

'Oh my God,' I said. I felt a chill surge through me. There really was no London, there was just a lake.

'What did you do to it?' I asked.

'Well, we didn't really do anything. Nature, I fear, did rather a lot. I don't remember the city but there are some very old folk who recall what happened. What you see there is the estuary. That's what we call it now. The present sea levels are considerably higher than in your day.'

'So the centre of the city is completely gone: the buildings, the houses, the streets, are they really all submerged?'

'Oh yes, for many, many years. I know for a fact that the centre of the city was stripped bare as the waters slowly invaded. I know the many treasures stored there were removed and saved, but the estuary engulfed everything else. When I was a very young boy I sailed around with friends in a boat and we saw many of the old buildings still standing, sticking out of the water. I imagine most of them have collapsed by now.'

It was true. I could see no sign of the massive metropolis.

I flew on for a while. The river was wider beneath us and I glanced down and saw that boats were using the waterway, some quite large barges being pulled by smaller craft.

'What are they carrying?' I asked, pointing down to the river traffic.

William craned his neck to see. 'At a guess I would say some raw materials picked up from a transport pod. Possibly metals of some sort.'

'Metals!' I said, my eyebrows raised in surprise on hearing this. 'So you are importing metals. Does that mean that in some other country there are vast mines and smelting factories belching out toxic fumes?'

William laughed again. 'No no, these are metals gleaned from all the deconstruction we've been doing for many years. There are small smelting installations dotted about, but nothing on the scale you are talking about. Metal is a very useful material, although I daresay the demand for it has dropped a great deal since your day. We are blessed in some ways that you mined and used so much; in some ways this is a benefit from your era. Again Paula would know more of this, but I believe there are ample supplies for our needs without us ever having to dig any more out of the earth.' William smiled. 'So thank you.'

'My pleasure,' I said.

In front of me, the meandering river looked familiar: Richmond, Kew, Chelsea, all essentially gone now – the housing density seemed about the same as I'd been seeing all morning. Once again the trees seemed ubiquitous, although I was beginning to notice more and more small fields, all heavily cultivated.

I'd seen enough: there was no London, there were no cities, the whole place had changed so much I couldn't take any more in. I stared down at the ground as we flew along, and then another thing struck me, made me question again how all this could possibly work.

The one thing I hadn't seen in our trip was open grassland, animals, cows, sheep, pigs. Not a sign of any livestock.

'So wait, don't you have animals?' I asked.

'Animals? Oh yes, of course we have animals: rabbits, foxes, an abundance of birdlife.'

'But livestock, domesticated animals, for meat, milk, leather?'

'Oh, I see. No, we don't eat meat. Well, I never have. We have small compounds here and there where the various breeds of animals are reared and looked after, but they are not killed for their meat.'

'Blimey. So is everyone a vegetarian?'

'I'm not sure. Do you mean does anyone eat the flesh of a dead animal? In which case the answer is no, not to my knowledge.'

I laughed. 'A nation of gardening vegetarians. That's so funny.'

'Why is that so funny?' asked William. He didn't sound offended, just intrigued.

'I don't know. I suppose there were a lot of jokes about vegetarians, which, just so you know, is the term we used for people who don't eat meat.'

'Isn't that extraordinary? I don't think we'd understand such jokes these days,' said William. He shifted about in his seat a little.

'You okay?' I asked.

'I admit I am becoming a little uncomfortable; sitting still this long is not something I am used to. My old bones get a little stiff after a while.'

I checked the time. We'd been flying for nearly two hours.

'I'm so sorry, William, we'll head back right away,' I said, banking steeply. William picked up the map, did something on the surface and placed it back between the seats. The blue floating arrow was pointing towards me, so I turned until it was pointing directly ahead and headed back to the hall.

11

E LANDED BACK IN THE FIELD NEXT TO Goldacre Hall in the early afternoon. There was no one visible as we flew over, no enthralled gathering of locals waving and jumping for joy, and I admit to being a little disappointed.

I circled around once just to make doubly sure there was no one standing in the way, then gently put down along the bumpy runway.

As we pulled to a halt my spirits lifted as we could see the farm vehicle bouncing its way towards us with quite a crowd hanging on the trailer behind it.

I unstrapped and jumped out of the cockpit as soon as I could and ran around the back of the plane, then jumped on the wing to help poor William out.

'Goodness me, I seem to have frozen up,' he said between grunts as I started to half haul him out. A couple of strong young men joined me and lifted him down and the small crowd gathered around us.

'What was it like, William?' asked one of them.

'I have to say, the ground beneath my feet has never felt better,' he said with a grin. 'But it was wonderful; we have travelled many miles, Gavin has seen many sights, and indeed, I have seen things in a way I never expected to see.'

Without anyone saying anything, the small group organised themselves, hitching up the plane, climbing back on board the trailer and towing the plane back to where we started.

I was helped into the trailer and I scanned the faces to see if Grace was among them. She wasn't. We trundled across the field and a hazy memory from my past about the smell of the oil seed,

the chatter among the people, the clattering of the trailer,
reminded me of something. I'm not sure what; it could have been
a childhood holiday in Cornwall – we stayed on a farm, a bed
and breakfast holiday, and I must have ridden on a trailer pulled
by a rattling Massey Ferguson tractor. I wasn't remembering a
specific incident, maybe a feeling of sadness, a realisation that a
whole world, a whole way of life had gone. Everything I had ever
known had more or less disappeared under an endless forest or a
flood of sea water.

I felt tired and lonely as I watched the happy people climb off
the trailer once we'd got back to the gateway to Goldacre Hall.
There was no doubting that what I had seen on the flight was
amazing, but I really wanted to go home. I wanted a shower with
my favourite shower gel; I wanted to check my emails; I even
wanted to see Beth.

The sudden realisation that this was utterly impossible was
very deadening.

I closed up the plane as the people started to drift off. I opened
the engine cover just to see how everything was holding up – the
engine had been at maximum power for more or less the entire
flight. I could see the heat shimmering off the main engine cowl-
ing, but everything looked okay and I certainly hadn't
experienced anything untoward during the flight.

'Hello you,' said a voice from behind me. I turned and was
confronted with Grace. Something had changed about her – she
looked stunning, somehow groomed but not in an obvious way.
I couldn't describe what it was that had changed, but my heart
skipped a beat. She had made an effort, and she had made it for
me.

'Oh hi,' I said, feeling a little gormless.

'How was your flying with William?' she asked.

'Amazing,' I said. 'He is amazing, but what I saw, your world,
it's...' I dropped my head for a moment. 'It's so incredibly different.'

'Is it?' she asked. I was a little taken aback. It was as if Grace didn't know what had gone on before her time. Surely, I thought, surely she must know how different the world was, even if it was two hundred years ago.

I knew what was happening two hundred years before my time, well, maybe not in great detail, but the gist. The industrial revolution, the steam engine, the development of cities, canals, all that. Then I thought for a minute. If some bloke had ridden a steam train through some sort of weird cloud and come from 1811 to 2011, I had to admit I wouldn't have known that much about what it was really like where he came from.

I smiled at Grace. 'Yes, it is. For a start there were something like forty million more people living here than there are now.'

'Forty million more!' said Grace. She stared off across the field. 'Where did you all live?'

'Well, very close to each other most of the time.'

'Forty million ... how did you eat, how did you grow food?'

'Well, I suppose most of it came here from other countries.'

'How?' She seemed genuinely not to know.

'Ships, planes, trucks through the tunnel. I'm not sure, wasn't my area I suppose.'

'You brought food here in planes, like this?' She was staring at my Yuneec.

I smiled. 'No, big transport planes, massive great things, jet liners, passenger jets – I don't know how to describe them. Same basic idea as this only much, much bigger.'

Grace was shaking her head. 'I must read more history, I knew nothing of this,' she said. 'It must have been terrible.'

'Oh, it wasn't that bad,' I said, feeling slightly defensive for my era. 'There were lots of good things about it.'

'Sixty million of you crammed together and having to wait for planes to bring you food – it must have been standing room only.'

'No, there was still countryside,' I said. 'And fields; we had cows and sheep too, and pigs. Far fewer bloody trees, I know that.'

'Cows and sheep and pigs,' said Grace. 'I'm confused. I only came to give you your clothes.'

She held up my neatly laundered chinos and polo shirt. I was a little disappointed; I suppose I'd hoped she'd come to see me.

'Thanks,' I said, taking the orderly pile from her. 'I don't quite feel comfortable in these clothes yet.'

Grace smiled. 'I think you look very nice in them. Very manly. Your own clothes, well, I don't wish to be rude but they look a little frail, a little, well, not manly.'

I put my head to one side, feeling cheeky. 'Mm, not manly you say. So, after two hundred years of human development, you're still wrapped up in your gender roles I see.' I was smiling as I said this, but Grace just stared at me blankly.

'Why did you have pigs and cows and sheep? What did you do with them?'

Knowing that they were all vegetarian, I decided to lie. I didn't want Grace to be horrified that we killed the little animals and cooked them.

'Mostly as pets, we had pets.'

'Pets?' Again she seemed confused by this.

'Yes, animals – sort of like companions, only they don't speak or ask questions. They are just, well, pets.'

'Animal companions?' said Grace. Now she smiled, and the smile turned into a laugh. 'So there were forty million more of you, you ate food from other countries which came on big air ships, and you had companions who were animals.'

'That just about sums it up.'

Grace shook her head slowly. 'I don't wish to be rude, but I am very glad I wasn't born back then. It really sounds like you'd all gone mad.'

'Well, there were a lot of things that didn't make sense, even to us at the time; it was a very confusing period I suppose. But when you're used to things, like, if people are used to wearing these clothes, or people are used to working in gardens, then it seems normal. I've never worn clothes like these before, and I've never worked in a garden, so it seems a bit strange to me.'

'You've never worked in a garden?'

'Well, I've planted some bushes in our front garden. Not that my house is there anymore. We flew over it today; nothing there.'

'Oh dear,' said Grace, looking concerned. 'Your house is gone?'

'Well, not just mine, pretty much every house in existence from my day. I suppose you don't need them now, just a waste of space and materials.'

'This all seems so normal to me,' said Grace, again staring off over the field, a field that I now realised had once been a housing estate on the outskirts of Didcot. Of course, before that it would have been a field, and before that it would have been woodland, so, in the long term, nothing changed that much. I looked at Grace as she stared off into the distance. She was a little brusque, she was maybe even a little sharp, but she was also very beautiful. Dark skinned, slim with a strong neck, broad shoulders and a slender frame. She didn't look like Beth, but there was something about her countenance that reminded me of Beth a little. Beth who had been dead for so long it was impossible to imagine.

'Can I say something, Grace?' I asked.

She turned to me and smiled. 'I'm sorry, I was kilometres away. Sorry, what did you say?'

'Oh, I just wanted to say thank you for being so kind to me. I have no idea what has happened to me and it's been very confusing to be here. It makes no sense, but I am grateful that you are being so calm and kind to me. It must be kind of odd for you too, I'm guessing.'

'It is very unfortunate, for you I mean,' she said, putting a hand gently on my forearm. 'Very unfortunate, but you are not the first.'

'Sorry?' I said. I stared back at Grace, trying to understand what she had just said.

'You are not the first to appear like you just have. It has happened before.'

'What! Someone's come here from my time you mean, some-one else in a plane?'

'Yes,' she said slowly. 'A long time ago.'

12

EFORE I FLEW THROUGH THE FREAKY CLOUD, I had regular day-mares about the end of the world. It was a bad habit and not one I shared with anyone, even Beth.

I don't know if these grim fantasies played out in my imagination because of all the information I was party to regarding the energy crisis and the increasing tension around limited global resources – it may just have been a part of those times.

And yet here I was, two hundred years into the future, and everything was fine. Well, fine-ish. It was certainly very different: strange, quiet, peaceful but somehow very disturbing.

There were signs of incredible technology, amazing developments in every area I'd seen. But there seemed to have been a catastrophic drop in population, a total lack of anything that resembled schools, hospitals, universities. They just didn't have them anymore. The people seemed healthy – I hadn't seen anyone who looked ill, disabled or even overweight. The ones that had survived could clearly live for a ridiculously long time and they generally seemed fairly happy. But it didn't add up. The more I saw, the less it added up.

This was all confusing enough, but then to find out I was not the first person to come through the cloud, from the distant past. Someone else had done so…

This piece of information was so huge I couldn't speak for some time after I heard it.

It wasn't until I was in the kitchen of the Oak House with Grace that I managed to say anything.

'Grace, please explain. I don't understand.'

She stopped still and I could see she felt awkward; she made it clear she felt she shouldn't have said anything.

'I think it is best you speak to William or Mitchell about this. I really know very little. You must be hungry.'

A clever move on Grace's part, as I was ravenous. I nodded with enthusiasm, 'Yes, I am pretty hungry.' All I wanted was a bacon sandwich with tomato ketchup splashed all over it on mass-produced sliced bread.

I knew all I was going to get was some slightly hippy vegetarian food. I mean that was fine, I often ate vegetarian food willingly – in fact Beth and I were more or less veggies, though we sometimes had chicken or fish. When I worked in the States I'd sometimes get a burger or barbecue ribs and then feel overstuffed and guilty, so it's not like I was a meat glutton. But in this world, well, they just didn't seem to have meat.

'You can cook can't you?' she asked with a look of mild concern.

'Well, yes, after a fashion. I'm no master chef,' I said. 'But I'm sure I can help.'

'Oh, I see,' she said, looking slightly more concerned. 'Well, I would like to go and work with the children for a while. We normally do some reading at this time of day.'

I pondered for a moment. 'Oh, right, you want me to cook, like, a whole meal?'

Grace looked at me with a puzzled smile. It was enchanting. 'Well, that would be very good if you could. Normally Mitchell would be cooking, but today has been a little disrupted.'

'Making my runway,' I said, nodding. 'Yeah, sorry about that.'

Grace didn't react to what I'd just said, which left me feeling a little deflated. She started piling ingredients on the table.

'I have some pulses here, some bean curd, some beautiful tomatoes, some leeks, some Jalhaffa.'

'Blimey, what's that?'

Again Grace looked at me like I was mentally deficient. 'Jalhaffa?' she said. 'Surely you had Jalhaffa?'

I shook my head. Grace sighed a little and carried on. 'There are jars of nuts in the cupboards and there is a blending machine over there.' She pointed to another stainless steel-looking device on the counter top. 'And you will find many other fresh herbs and beans in the kitchen garden outside the south door.' This time she pointed behind her to a corridor I hadn't noticed before.

There was a short pause. She was waiting for me to respond.

'Oh, I see. So you don't have, like, a recipe or anything?'

Grace put her hand to her mouth and laughed. 'I'm so sorry, Gavin, I quite forgot,' she said, waving her hands a little as if embarrassed. 'I'm so used to everyone being able to cook I rudely forgot you might need some assistance.'

She opened a drawer in the unit behind her and extracted a silvery sheet. She placed it on a table and it glowed slightly. She brushed her fingers over it and it glowed with greater intensity.

'Can you show me the Jalhaffa and nut roast recipe?' she said. The sheet changed as she spoke and a text appeared on it.

'Oh my God,' I said. 'What is that?'

Grace looked at me and then at the sheet. 'Oh, it's the house Book. I thought William would have explained it; did he not have one with you in the flying machine?'

'He had some clever gizmo he called a map.'

Grace nodded as she spoke. 'Yes, map, house Book, school Book, all much the same.' She picked up the sheet and handed it to me. 'There's a recipe on The Book.'

I stared at it and sure enough, in a fully recognisable form there was a recipe on the sheet; it didn't look like a screen as I might recognise it, it looked like a piece of quality paper. It didn't send out bright light but it did glow in some way I couldn't really discern.

Grace put a scarf around her shoulders and headed to the door. 'There are to be nine people eating this evening – just tell

The Book and it will adjust the amounts you need. If you can't work anything out, ask The Book, that's what it's for. Good luck,' she said with a smile that was at once slightly patronising and utterly beguiling.

'Thank you,' I said, and she was gone.

Yet again I sighed and shook my head. I was standing in the kitchen of a house, all incredibly normal. I was looking at a recipe on a piece of paper, the light I was reading by was a smooth rectangle set into the ceiling above me, the kettle boiled instantly, the tap turned on without any action, the power was free: everything was simultaneously the same and utterly, bafflingly different.

I started to look around the kitchen for the things I'd need to prepare a meal for nine people, wondering why I was cooking all of a sudden – who had decided that I should cook?

I stared at what Grace had called The Book. It was just a dormant piece of paper with a recipe on it, a recipe for nut roast.

'What do I need to make a nut roast?' I said to myself. The image on The Book changed – it was a plan of the kitchen I was standing in. It had highlighted the items I'd need, like a treasure map.

'Oh cool,' I said. Again the image changed and highlighted the fridge. A small text box showed the current temperature: three degrees Celsius.

I turned and worked out where the fridge was from the plan I could see on the book. I opened a panelled door and there was a fridge, very recognisable and full of all manner of produce, everything in glass jars and bottles.

'Brilliant,' I said and then closed my eyes as the light inside the fridge and the kitchen became dazzling and unbearable.

'Blimey, what the fuck!' I shouted. The light hurt my eyes; it was beyond dazzling, it was burning. I stumbled about, I suppose looking for a switch. 'Turn it down or something!' I screamed.

The light immediately dimmed. I stared around the kitchen

in amazement. How on earth was I ever going to cook when there was such fun to be had with The Book? I assumed it was The Book that was registering my speech and acting upon it – I assumed that but I had no idea. How did it all operate? I hadn't noticed the people in the house affecting anything when they spoke the day before. No one said 'boil' to the kettle when Grace had made me tea. I was getting more confused. I looked at The Book again, which had returned to the recipe page.

'Dim,' I said as I looked at the light panel in the ceiling. The light faded down. 'Bright.' And the light faded up. Simple I know, but it kept me amused for some time.

I eventually started cooking, found a large jar of hazelnuts in a cupboard that in turn led me to all the other ingredients I needed. The Jalhaffa was a kind of red jelly thing, a lump of some sort of wobbly material that I had to put in the blender with the nuts.

I turned to The Book. 'What is Jalhaffa?' I said to it very clearly. 'Jalhaffa?'

The image changed instantly to a Wiki page. Blimey, Wikipedia had lasted over two hundred years! I read the text. 'Jalhaffa is a protein rich nutripaste developed in India with a varying range of fat and carbohydrate levels. It contains over a hundred nutrient sources and every vitamin the human body requires for health and longevity.'

'Fantastic,' I said, then stood back a little as I saw a comment added to the bottom of the Wiki page. I put my hand over my mouth to stop myself saying 'fuck me' and seeing that appear too.

I started to grind everything in a brilliant grinder thing that just seemed to know how to grind. I added the other ingredients, the fresh herbs I found in the small garden area at the side of the house. I was able to identify them by taking the floppy sheet book thing with me, comparing it to the images that appeared without my asking and picking the correct herbs.

Everything in the little herb garden was so neat and well cared for, no sign of rubbish or waste anywhere. Everything was fresh and clearly grown very locally. I opened no packets, no plastic bags; there were no polystyrene meat trays, fruit in plastic boxes, yoghurt pots. Well, there was no yoghurt, no cheese, no eggs, milk, butter or meat. Everything they ate, it seemed, was made from fruit, nuts, vegetables or pulses.

I did have to spend ten minutes looking at the first glass jar that had no obvious sealing system, just a glass lid. I twisted it, tried to prise the top off with my thumb: nothing.

'Open,' I said. The glass lid made a tiny hiss and released itself. There was no sign of a mechanism, no levers or sealing rings I could make out; it just opened. I shook my head and carried on.

I set the oven to 220 degrees by telling it to do just that, then put the nut roast in, checked the recipe and said, 'Twenty-three minutes.'

'Aha, good to see the chef hard at work,' said Mitchell, his large frame filling the doorway. I did my best not to look surprised. Mitchell was the man who'd driven the electric tractor thing when I'd first landed. I didn't hear him come in, and although he didn't exactly shock me I did wonder how long he'd been watching me.

'Hi there,' I said as casually as I could. 'I'm very worried you are going to get a rather sub-standard supper. I am no chef, believe me.'

Mitchell washed his hands at the sink. 'Well, something smells very nice,' he said. 'Did Grace suggest you make a nut roast?'

I nodded. Mitchell smiled. 'That's what she got me to cook many years ago.'

I nodded, expecting to hear more. Mitchell poured himself a glass of water and sat down. There was no more.

I carried on chopping leaves for the salad as The Book had

instructed. I was desperate to ask Mitchell about whoever it was who had previously come through the cloud, but thankfully, due to his quiet demeanour, I had the opportunity and time to think it through. I didn't want to get Grace into trouble. Maybe this was a secret; maybe she had let slip something these strange, seemingly kind people really didn't want me to know.

I carried on chopping, then felt slightly angry. What the hell, I had the right to know what was going on. My life had been torn to shreds. If they had done it, I wanted to know why, and equally importantly, how.

'Mitchell, can I ask you something?' I said. 'I don't want to get Grace into trouble.'

'Why should Grace get into trouble?' There was no threat or anger in his question. It was just a question.

'No, no, she shouldn't. Absolutely not,' I blathered. 'But she told me something inadvertently I think.'

'She wishes to have your child,' said Mitchell.

Try and picture the silence. However long you may be able to imagine that silence, double it, triple it. I stood by the kitchen table with the knife I was using to chop salad leaves, utterly static. For a long, long time.

Mitchell was staring at me calmly for this long, long time. He eventually smiled. 'Is that not what she was talking about?' he asked.

'She wants what?' I said.

'It might be difficult for you to understand. I have spoken to Paula about it and she explained to me how different things were in your time. I maybe did learn about it when I was a child but I fear I may not have listened as well as I should.'

'I'm really confused – no, wait. I was already confused before you told me that. Now I'm more or less a full-on mental case. Grace wants to have my baby.'

'It is, I admit, a little complicated,' said Mitchell slowly. 'I am sorry I said anything now.'

'I don't even know what you mean. Grace wants me to give her a baby. What does that mean? Why me? I've only just met her! We've barely spoken. What is going on?'

I admit I was a little scared of Mitchell. He had just told me in effect that his wife wanted to sleep with me. If she was his wife, or his partner – I hate that term – or his reciprocating breeding benefactor or whatever weird phrase the human race had come up with.

He sat forward in his chair and rested his chin on his clasped hands, staring at the floor for a while and then slowly up at me.

'I fear I sometimes leave Grace a little bored, but I have to be true to myself,' said Mitchell with careful thought.

I allowed my eyebrows to rise.

'Yes,' I said. 'That's very important and very difficult.'

So what was Mitchell's relationship to Grace? Was he her brother, her teacher, her husband? I had no idea.

'Why difficult?' asked Mitchell.

'I mean, remaining true to yourself. I find that difficult,' I said.

'Surely only in relation to others,' said Mitchell, again speaking slowly and with care. 'The pressure you feel from others to conform to what is perceived to be the norm, yes, that pressure can be difficult, but to be true to yourself, surely that is simple.'

Now he was getting a bit too philosophical and hippy-like for me. I hadn't noticed if Mitchell had his hair tied into a ponytail but I wouldn't have been surprised.

'I say this because—' Mitchell stopped. He seemed to be looking at his feet, well, his big boots. I was holding a spatula, standing in front of him feeling incredibly aware of what was taking place. He looked up at me. 'Because I can see that although you come from another place, although the transition has been very difficult, distressing even, you have remained true to yourself. I admire that and I know Grace does too. I hope you can be true to her.'

I put the spatula on the table and shook my head.

'I'm sorry, I don't understand. Is Grace your wife?'

Mitchell smiled at me. 'I know what that means to you. In some ways you would understand it as such. The easiest way to explain is that Grace and I have made a child. Henry. He is eleven years old.'

I nodded. Things were starting to clear.

'But that was eleven years ago. Grace was a very young woman when she was with child, and she is still a young woman. I am not so young.'

'I've got no idea how old anyone is here. How old are you?'

'I'm sixty-eight years old,' said Mitchell.

'Get away!' I squealed. 'No way are you sixty-eight!'

Mitchell smiled warmly. 'I am telling you the truth; I was born in 2143.'

I stared at Mitchell without embarrassment – he looked forty. He looked like a very fit forty-year-old: a thick head of hair, lean, strong, obviously very active. His teeth were good, his eyes were bright, he wasn't stooped, and he didn't limp or grunt when he moved.

'Sixty-bloody-eight!' I said again. 'How on earth do you look like that when you're sixty-eight?'

'I have tried to live a good life,' said Mitchell slowly. 'I have tried to make things better. It's not always easy. If it were easy, I believe I would not be trying hard enough.'

'Mate, let me tell you, where I come from, you've been doing it right. Most sixty-eight year olds where I come from have more or less given up. They look thirty years older than you and they've retired.'

'What does that mean?' asked Mitchell. At first I thought he was being sarcastic, but his face told me otherwise. He really didn't know what that meant.

'Retired – they've stopped working, sort of given up. They spend their days pottering about, reading, going on cruise holidays, gardening, taking up golf or watercolour painting. I don't know what they do; I suppose they wait to die.'

'That doesn't sound very useful.'

'No, it isn't, well, it wasn't. I take it people don't retire now.'

Mitchell smiled gently and shook his head. He was staring at me rather intently. 'I would ask that you be discreet, with Grace. Maybe you could not mention what I have said to you. I have no wish to be secretive or distrustful, but for the good of all, some sensitivity might be beneficial.'

I nodded as he spoke. 'Don't worry, I'm not going to say anything,' I said, not sure exactly what I wasn't going to say.

The door from the garden opened and a young lad walked in. He smiled at me.

'Hello, I'm Henry,' he said.

'Oh, hi there. I'm Gavin.'

The boy smiled again and left through another door into the rest of the house. Grace entered through the door from the garden carrying a basket filled with apples.

'Hello, how's it going?' she asked. 'Have we got anything to eat?'

I smiled, feeling very awkward. Suddenly I was in possession of information about this woman, her relationships, her children, and I wasn't supposed to say anything.

'It's all fine, it's just about ready,' I said.

Grace smiled at me and put the basket down on the table. She didn't seem to glance at Mitchell; her eyes were on me alone. 'Well done you,' she said. 'Everyone should be here presently.'

13

FINALLY SAT DOWN AT THE ONLY EMPTY space at the kitchen table in Oak House and stared around at the small gathering. Seated directly opposite me was Grace; next to her was young Henry. He was staring at me intently and showed no sign of embarrassment or fear. Also present were Mitchell, William, Halam and Paula the historian. Sitting next to Paula was a middle-aged woman called Shazny and next to her a young and again startlingly tall young man called Tony.

'So,' I said with a big grin. 'Shall we eat?'

'Splendid!' said William. 'This all looks excellent.'

He was being kind. My nut and Jalhaffa roast was more of a nut pile; it hadn't really held together. It looked rather more reminiscent of something a dog leaves in the middle of a carpet when it's eaten something from the rubbish. A grey pile of chunky goo.

'I'm really sorry,' I said. 'This is the first time I've cooked for so many people.'

'It is delicious,' said Paula, who had already started forking big piles of grey mush into her mouth. 'Truly.'

I noticed the young boy pushing chunks around with his fork. Grace leant over to him but she was looking at me and smiling. 'Just don't look at it, Henry. Close your eyes and eat – it truly is very tasty.'

The young lad Henry did as his mother told him and a small ripple of laughter went around the room. Henry continued chewing and looked around the table; he was clearly enjoying the attention.

'Tastes good,' he said eventually.

'Horraaah!' said William.

A discussion erupted without any obvious introduction about the fruit trees in the far orchard. It was clearly something that had been discussed before; I only took a little of it in. I know nothing about fruit trees but clearly there was a problem with some kind of blight. A fungus infection of the bud tips, according to William. He knew of remedies but he was worried – it was the first time they had seen it for many years.

I carried on eating and trying to look like I was interested. I was trying not to stare at Grace, which was very difficult. I occasionally glanced at Mitchell, who seemed to be fully engrossed in the fruit tree discussion.

Halam suddenly nudged me and I jumped. I think he may have nudged me as I was staring at Grace and wallowing in her beauty like a fool.

'Gavin, I am so sorry,' he said.

'What?' I asked, trying so hard to be casual and probably failing.

'We are all sitting here chattering away about our petty day to day problems, eating this lovely food you have prepared.'

'Great nut roast,' said Tony, the young man at the end of the table.

Halam nodded. 'Indeed, it's exceptionally good, but we have been ignoring you, and indeed William has been full of stories of your flight today. Tell us, Gavin, now that you have seen more, what do you make of our humble island?'

I smiled as best I could, glancing around the table at the small group. They all appeared so benign – surely they weren't up to anything underhand – but I felt vulnerable and anxious in a way I had never experienced before.

'Well, I don't know where to start. It's all changed beyond recognition,' I said, taking a drink of some kind of delicious elderflower juice. 'I cannot begin to tell you what it was like.'

'Well, we have some idea of what it was like,' said Paula, who seemed even bigger in the small kitchen. 'We have an enormous amount of archive material, as I was saying to you earlier.'

'Yes, I suppose so. It's not so much the physical changes, the number of trees, the intensity of your agriculture, it's how you organise things, how you manage big projects. I'm baffled. I mean the space-lift stuff.'

I noticed Grace was looking puzzled. 'The tether things,' I clarified. 'The big ones at Heathrow – you can't tell me that doesn't need some kind of management.'

William turned to Halam. Halam smiled and spoke.

'We have systems in place, Gavin. Gaia systems.'

I must have sneered a little; I suppose I imagined they meant some kind of spiritual belief system, Gaia meaning mother earth and dream catchers and homemade jam and all the hippy nonsense my parents had been into which had held back development more than anything else I'd come across. My sneer was clearly registered – Paula picked up on it.

'Global Artificial Intelligence Arrangement,' she said.

'Is that what Gaia stands for?' asked Tony. For this question he received some caring looks from the older diners.

'Sorry, I–I suppose I'd never really thought about it.' He smiled, clearly a little embarrassed. 'I mean, I knew what it did, but I didn't know the letters stood for something.'

'Oh, right, what's that? Is that what it sounds like it might be?' I asked, smiling now.

William spoke. 'It's a system that was installed many years ago. As you say, a management system. It knows where every podmibus is, where every pod is, where everyone is, where power is being created, where it is being used, how much is being used, what it is being used for. Everything. It's in the grid so calling it a computer as you would have done would be somewhat misleading.'

'Okay,' I said. 'I think I can just about get my head around an intelligent management system for machines and logistics, but

Paula said you have no legal system, or government, and it just seems, well, it seems like it could all go wrong at any minute. I mean, a splinter group could organise and take over.'

There seemed to be general consent around the table. Clearly this had been discussed and was seen as possible.

William spoke first. 'It has happened, Gavin, over the years and many times. Somehow though, it has just never really caught on. We are just about surviving, and we all have to work hard to maintain what we have and feed ourselves.'

Halam joined in. 'We all know that at some point our young people will become frustrated with the settled ways we have adopted. We have to accommodate this yearning and learn from it. Sometimes our young people have a very good point to make.'

I noticed him glance at Tony, who apart from Henry was the youngest person present, although with what I was coming to understand of their longevity, he could have been thirty. I smiled at him.

'So, going to start a student revolution then?' I asked.

Tony smiled. 'I'm not sure what that is, and I suppose I could, but I don't know why I'd bother. Should I bother?'

He did seem to be asking me a question.

'Gavin,' said William. 'You remember the circular field we saw this morning, when we took off.'

'The one you play particle physics on?' I asked.

William nodded. 'Well, young Tony here plays very well, he is about to progress from Sub Atomic to Quark.'

'Congratulations, Tony,' said Mitchell. 'I hadn't heard.'

'Yeah, it's good. It's very confusing at the moment but I'm slowly getting the hang of it.'

'Amazing,' I said. 'I cannot imagine what it is you play, I'll have to come and watch.'

I sat back in my chair and stretched my legs. There was a silence around the table and I stared at my fellow diners one by one.

'I'm sorry, but I cannot understand how it works. I know you say you don't have money, but the materials you use... something you can't get here, materials that just do not exist on these islands, if nothing else, how is that, well, how do you pay for it?'

My question seemed to keep the gathered party silent; only Paula reacted.

'I think I know what you mean,' she said eventually.

'I'm glad you do; he may as well be speaking in tongues,' said Grace rather sharply.

'We don't pay for it. Not in the sense that I believe you mean, Mr Meckler.'

'Oh please, Paula, call him Gavin,' said Grace. Again, a slight snip in her tone and again I couldn't really read what was going on.

'I'm intrigued to hear what Paula has to say,' said William, grinning broadly as he spoke.

Paula nodded seriously. 'What we have now only works as part of an ongoing process. You have arrived at a period in history where, for about the last forty years, through slowly evolving technological innovation, we have essentially free abundant energy.'

I was about to sip my elderflower juice. I stopped, staring at Paula.

'Completely free?' I said eventually.

'Yes, we produce far more energy than we can use, so it has become effectively like the air. You cannot even compare it to fresh drinking water – water is not free. There are still many people in the world who do not have an adequate water supply, but energy is abundant. It wasn't of course always like this and indeed it may not continue to be like this but at present, that is the situation.'

'I don't understand,' I said. I noticed Henry was also listening intently, not fidgeting or mucking around, just sitting listening.

'I can imagine, coming from the era you do, it is hard to understand. A whole society whose very existence was built on a constantly dwindling energy source was indeed doomed to failure.'

'So, what are you saying, the oil ran out?'

Paula smiled. 'No, no, we still extract oil, a very modest amount in comparison to your own time, but it's a very useful resource. We only use it as an essential raw material, but we still use it.'

'So you really don't burn oil in any way?'

Paula smiled, again the brief and seemingly impatient smile of an old teacher at an annoying young pupil.

I noticed Henry looking at me like I was a bit mad.

'Why would people burn oil?' he asked, glancing at his mother. She was staring at me and said nothing.

'We try not to burn anything,' said Paula. 'Although every mid-winter's day we have a party at Goldacre Hall and we burn logs from fallen trees in the old fireplaces. The old folks seem to love it.'

'Oh yes, that's lovely, you've seen the mid-winter fire haven't you, Henry?'

'Yes,' said Henry, not looking at all impressed. 'It's all a bit mad if you ask me. Really dangerous in my opinion.'

I pondered for a moment and then asked, 'You said you had all this free energy for the time being, like the abundant free energy you mentioned could come to an end in some way?'

'All things come to an end, Gavin, or they change beyond recognition,' said Paula. 'We are very reliant on technology to maintain this abundance and as you know machines wear out, they decay, they need maintenance – and we have a little problem there.'

'Oh, indeed we do,' said William.

'What's the problem?' I asked.

'Well, just like your era with fossil fuel, we've grown used to it. We don't think about it or worry about it, because we spend so much of our time and energy growing food, maintaining the land and the forests. The vast majority of us focus on that activity. We come in from the fields, have a shower, eat food, turn on lights – it's all normal and we don't think about it.'

William butted in, smiling as he spoke. He was clearly aiming what he was saying at Tony and young Henry.

'Young people today barely know where the heat and light comes from; there are very few of them prepared to learn about it, to become technicians and engineers in order to develop new technologies or even maintain existing ones.'

'I see,' I said. 'Blimey, that all sounds very familiar.'

'What does blimey mean?' asked young Henry. He was asking me, not his mother.

'Oh, it means, well, it's when you are surprised. It's actually a really old term, from the olden days even before I was born. It's a short version of "God blind me". People said that when they were surprised I suppose. That got shortened to "Gawd blimey" and eventually just "blimey". You say, well, we said things like blimey, or Jesus or other ruder words when we were surprised.'

'Blimey,' said Henry. 'Blimey, Mum.'

There was a small ripple of laughter around the table. His mother smiled at him.

Paula wasn't laughing; humour was clearly not her thing. She cleared her throat and leant her enormous forearms on the table.

'I just want to explain to you that we have very serious problems and people don't seem prepared to face them.'

'I'm just fascinated as to how you, we, well, whoever did it, how they solved the energy crisis, because it was really looming when I, yesterday, whenever it was I was … you know what I mean.'

Paula nodded. 'Indeed, it must have seemed like an insurmountable problem,' she said. 'The very idea of burning oil, gas, coal or indeed radioactive material strikes us as a little insane if I may make so bold.'

I smiled – I'd sat motionless in enough traffic jams with an engine purring in front of me to ponder this notion on many occasions.

'So you get all your energy from solar kites in the upper atmosphere.'

'Oh no, not so much any more – the tethers you mean.'

I nodded.

'No, although there are plenty of them still around. They are coming to the end of their useful life and they are a problem to decommission. We've had a couple come back to earth when we weren't quite ready. They make a bit of a mess when they land.' She raised her enormous, bushy eyebrows as if to underline the problem. 'Not only of the kites themselves but any poor soul who happens to be standing where they land.'

'Right, so that's actually happened?'

I saw William nodding gravely.

Paula continued. 'Oh yes, it has happened many times, or some part of the tether mechanism fails, the kites sail away and the tether comes to earth. That's not so serious as the material of the tether itself is very light, but it gets tangled in everything. When there is no power running through it, you can barely see it with the naked eye.'

'This is all so amazing to hear,' I said with a big grin.

'I'm very glad I'm entertaining you,' said Paula's solid, unsmiling face. 'You see, it's a constantly evolving system; we have what you would have called a smart grid. A substantial amount of the energy we produce or capture is used to transport power around the grid. We use deeply buried UCC, or ultra cold cabling – that way we can transport sufficient energy to places far distant from the source. We use geo thermal to a large extent, tidal barriers in places, wind, especially off our shores and solar concentrators in the desert.'

'That's amazing. It really sounds like you've solved one of the biggest problems we're facing, I mean, we were facing.'

'No problem is ever really solved,' said Paula very seriously. 'A very basic understanding of history should have taught you that.'

I nodded as gravely as I could but I was fascinated to hear all this.

'Okay, so here's a question that's been puzzling me,' I said. 'When I flew into the weird cloud, the batteries on my plane were reading about 50 per cent.'

I noticed Henry looking very puzzled at this point, then I realised he was not alone. I explained as best I could.

'In my day, in the olden days, we stored energy in batteries, chemical packs that released the energy in controlled amounts which powered things. Okay, so the energy would run out and you would have no more power, so you had to constantly monitor the level of energy you had remaining. However, when I came out of the cloud, the batteries were suddenly completely full, and so was my iPad, and so was my phone.'

'I won't pretend to know what an iPad is,' said Paula. 'But the batteries just picked up the induction charge. That is now universal. We no longer use battery technology or wires. The lights you see on the ceiling – they are self-contained units.'

I looked up at the small flat panel in the ceiling. 'No wires?'

'There's no need. We have global induction. Any electrical device works anywhere on the planet's surface.'

'You are kidding!' I said.

'I don't think I'm kidding.'

'So, you mean to tell me, no wires, no batteries ever, anywhere. That is incredible!' I said. Again I noticed Henry looking at me. I smiled at him. 'It's incredible for me, Henry. In my time, we had all sorts of problems moving and storing energy; I s'pose you wouldn't even know those problems existed.'

Henry shrugged. I may as well have been speaking Russian; he clearly hadn't got a clue what I was babbling on about.

'Electrical induction was discovered well before even you were born,' said Paula.

'Nikola Tesla,' I said proudly.

'Indeed, without doubt, a genius in the field.'

'And that's why I could fly my plane all day, and the batteries would never run out.'

Paula nodded slowly. 'Indeed, that is the case.'

'Wow,' I said, then I looked around the table again. What was intriguing was that it seemed everyone else, with the possible exception of William, had been listening and taking everything in with just as much interest as me. It was as if they didn't know all this either.

'And so the lesson ends,' said William, and he clapped his hands once. 'Let us proceed with the day's events.' He stood up and everyone helped to clear the table. Young Henry did his share without being asked, then returned to the table with a pack of playing cards.

'Poker?' he said.

'Henry,' said Grace, 'Gavin may not wish to play.'

'I'm happy to,' I said. I wasn't really – I can play poker badly but it wasn't something I would have chosen to do right then. However, all the other members of the group were busying themselves and I felt it was almost expected of me.

Henry started to deal cards with a level of speed and dexterity that made me nervous. He'd done this before.

'Henry, do you ever watch the telly?' I asked as I tried to concentrate on playing cards.

'What's that?' he asked.

'Oh, like a movie, or a program on a screen, you know, television.'

The young lad looked at his grandfather for help, I turned to Halam, he shook his head and shrugged.

'I just wondered, only children in my day would watch what we called TV, a screen showing images or stories, movies.'

'Oh yeah, I watch stuff on my Book. I've seen old movies, I know what you mean,' said Henry with some relief. 'I think I prefer to read or listen to stories but some of the old stuff is funny. Mostly I talk to my friends who live further away than I can walk.'

While we played cards I was only vaguely aware of what else was taking place in the kitchen. I did notice Mitchell and Grace talking in the corner for a short time but I couldn't make out what they were saying. It didn't look antagonistic. They left the room together and I registered a slight feeling of annoyance, or jealousy, or maybe just a hint of disappointment. I was noticing my feelings: this was not something I was used to.

I wanted to tell Beth, explain to her that I was having feelings and I was noticing them and I was not allowing them to affect my behaviour in unpredictable ways. I sat in silence for a moment as I contemplated the apparent impossibility of this desire. Beth was very dead and I had to accept that.

I glanced up to see Halam sitting with a pad of paper and a pencil; he seemed to be drawing something. As I was losing yet another poker hand to the fiercely competitive Henry, I suddenly noticed the small drawings hanging in frames on the wall of the kitchen. I am one of those people that could be in a room for an hour with a Renoir hanging over the fireplace and not notice. The drawings were exquisite and very detailed, just everyday occurrences around the house and in the garden.

Henry was winning every hand we played and clearly this gave him great satisfaction; as he beat me yet again I threw my hand in and turned to Halam.

'Are those your drawings on the wall?' I asked. He looked up and held out his hand.

'Don't move too much – yes they are, but stay as you are for just a moment longer.'

'Oh, you're not drawing me again are you, Granddad?' said Henry with mock annoyance.

'I am indeed, young master Henry.'

Grace re-entered the room. She bent down and kissed Henry

on the forehead. He held a hand affectionately to her face.

'I'm going to bed now,' he said to me. 'Thanks for playing cards; you're really good at it.'

I laughed. I had consistently lost every game.

'You're not so bad yourself, mate,' I said as I helped Henry pile the cards together. Henry then kissed his grandfather on the cheek and left the room. Grace stood for a while looking at me.

'I am going to bed too,' she said. I didn't know where to look. Was she asking me to join her? I didn't know what to do.

'I will no doubt see you in the morning,' she said. Okay, so I wasn't meant to join her.

I nodded and smiled. 'Thank you,' I said.

'For what?'

'For letting me cook,' I said. I don't know why I said that. I wanted to say 'for letting me look at you and for wanting me to give you a baby'. I'm really glad I didn't say that; something in me understood it would have been wrong – it was as though I had finally learned how to interact with women. I went on to elaborate on my reasoning.

'It helped me calm down and concentrate on something other than all my endless questions about why I'm here and what's happened to me.'

That made sense to me. I hoped it would to Grace, and indeed to Halam, who was clearly observing this interaction with some interest.

Grace smiled gently at me; her face was so beautiful I couldn't help myself – I stared at her like a fool.

'You are welcome, Gavin,' she said. 'Henry has just suggested something to me. Maybe you might like to come along and talk to the young people in the learning hall tomorrow, tell them something about the history of your era.'

'That's a very fine idea,' said Hallam.

I was pleased that I would get to spend more time with Grace, but I couldn't help worrying. I said, 'Are you sure? Isn't it going to confuse the kids if I tell them I come from two hundred years ago? I mean, it's hard enough for me. If I'd been sitting in school and some bloke in britches and a top hat came into my class and said he was from the early age of steam, we'd think he was a nutter or a rubbish actor.'

Grace smiled. 'I love it when you talk like that – such passion, and yet I have no idea what you mean half the time. I think you're right though – don't you, father? I think you could talk about how the world worked in your day without revealing how you know. You will just appear to be very learned.'

I smiled and turned to Halam; he was nodding in encouragement.

'Okay, I'll try,' I said.

'Good, it is agreed,' said Grace, and then she slipped out of the room.

I smiled at Halam, who was looking at me.

'What an extraordinary kid Henry is to come up with an idea like that,' I said. 'And he is a truly brilliant poker player.'

Halam sighed. 'Yes, he's a bright little fellow, no doubt about that.' He looked up at me and said, 'And his mother is a wonderful woman.'

I nodded. It was awkward. I had learned that Halam was Grace's father, Mitchell was her sort of husband and Henry was her child. I did not see how I could fit into this cosy world without causing a great deal of distress. I didn't know if what Halam had just said was a sort of sales pitch for his daughter, or a warning to stay away.

Halam held up the paper pad he was holding, stared at it momentarily then handed it to me. I stared at the drawing in amazement. It was a wonderful picture: me playing cards with a young boy, both of us completely recognisable, the room picked out in great detail.

'Wow, that is extraordinary,' I said. 'What an incredible talent.'

'Just my doodles,' said Halam. 'I like to record events that take place in the house. It's mostly very quiet here, so your arrival has caused quite a stir.'

'Oh dear,' I said. 'I hope I'm not upsetting anyone.'

'Not in the least,' said Halam, looking right into my eyes. 'You must know you are very welcome at any time.'

I walked with William and Paula back along the path to Goldacre Hall. Paula used a rather wonderful glowing rod device, which created a pool of light all around us so making our way between the trees and along the hedge was not difficult. An owl squawked as we made our way through the soft darkness, other than that it was incredibly peaceful. However, inside I was full of noise, of anxiety and distress.

As we walked, I decided to go for broke and bring up the information Grace had inadvertently leaked to me. Apparently it is in my nature to be direct, some have said brusque, so without hesitation I came out with it.

'I learned today that I am not the first person to come through the cloud,' I said as we walked. I carried on walking but soon realised my two companions had stopped. I turned to face them.

'Sorry, I don't mean to shock you, but clearly it's rather important I know about it. I need to understand what has happened to me.'

William and Paula started walking again. William spoke first. 'It is true, although it was many years ago. I was a young man when it happened and was not present here at the time.'

'Oh right. Wait, you mean it wasn't recently. How? I don't understand.'

'The tether has been operating for over a hundred years,' said Paula. 'The event you are referring to took place in 2142.'

I quickly did the mental maths as we walked slowly towards Goldacre Hall. '2142, okay, so sixty-nine years ago.'

'Indeed,' said William. 'Another flying machine came through the cloud. It was controlled by a man called Reginald Peter Mitchell.'

'So the cloud thing, the weather patterns, all that happened before.'

'Yes, but unfortunately the flying machine was a much cruder but much faster model than yours. It apparently flew around for a while, many people saw it, then the loud noise made by the engine ceased and the man controlling the craft jumped out and came to earth with a large circular wing tied to him with cord.'

'A parachute?'

'Indeed, that was the term he used,' said William, tapping his forehead. 'I could not recall the term – a parachute.'

'Oh, so you met him,' I asked.

'Oh yes, I got to know him very well; he was a wonderful man.'

'And what happened to the plane, the craft, the flying machine?'

'That came to earth too, but with rather more disastrous consequences. It crashed into a glasshouse over near Cholsey and three people died as a result of the impact. There was a great fire and an enormous amount of damage.'

'Blimey,' I said. 'But that's, well, it's surely very relevant to my arrival. I'm surprised someone hadn't told me already.'

'Well, clearly someone has,' said William with a gentle smile. 'I don't think anyone was trying to keep it from you. It is more probable we felt it would only add to your confusion and anxiety.'

I took a deep lungful of the cool night air.

'It's very hard for me to comprehend what has happened to me – I'm not even beginning to understand – but the fact that I'm not the first to get here through a bloody cloud, this is just weird. Where is this guy now?'

'He is long dead,' said William. 'He was not a well man, and he sustained some injuries when he came to earth. We did what we could for him and he did live another thirty years or so, but he was never in good health, unlike your good self.'

'Oh blimey, so he lived for thirty years here. Did he get used to it?'

'I'm sorry,' said William. 'I don't understand.'

'Well, if he came from the same time as me, you know, back in history, did he manage to adjust to living here with you ... I don't know how to describe you. You lot.'

William smiled again and I wasn't sure why.

'I suppose he did. He was a great help to us. He is remembered very fondly by the people who knew him.'

William delved into his jacket pocket and pulled out the map he had used in the plane. He brushed his hand over it and said, 'Reginald Peter Mitchell.'

He stared at the sheet for a moment and then handed it to me. The first picture revealed the whole thing to me with a shiver of recognition. A clear colour picture of a slim man with bad teeth, a thick crop of hair and a small, neatly trimmed moustache. He was wearing a uniform I recognised immediately, a military uniform. It was the uniform of an RAF pilot from the Second World War.

14

AWOKE THE NEXT DAY HALF HOPING THAT Grace would enter the room and we might spend the day together, wrapped in each other's bodies, lost from the world.

I lay in bed for a while just absorbing the incredible silence, but with one ear listening for someone approaching. I could hear nothing.

I had a pee in my little bathroom; the sewage system had obviously changed a great deal from my time. You evacuated whatever it was you needed to evacuate using a low porcelain receptacle which, when you stood back from it, made a low buzzing sound. Whatever was in the small hole in the centre of the device then disappeared along with some air, a bit like the toilet in an airliner. A suck of air and it was all gone. I wondered where it went – did they still have sewage works? I hadn't seen anything like that during my exploratory flight.

I stretched, washed my face and pondered my situation. I had been very disturbed by the previous night's revelations and had a longing to find out more, to understand why I had arrived in this strange yet strangely familiar place. I went back towards my bed and noticed the large, leather-bound history book Paula had given me. It was lying beside my bed and I felt guilty. I hadn't even opened it. History had never been a subject I had any interest in.

I suddenly remembered that I had promised to be a history teacher to a load of kids and had no idea what to say, so I picked up the book hoping for some kind of inspiration.

History seemed to me to be just a series of stories told by people who claimed to know everything about what went on before they were born. It was too imprecise, too full of opinions and bias.

However, this was history that had taken place after I had technically died. This was, I suppose, a fairly unique experience for any human being who had ever existed.

I propped up some pillows and lay back on the bed to read. I skimmed down the chapter headings. 'The Russian–Chinese energy wars, 2063–69.' Blimey, so there had been wars – Paula had explained that they were all minor skirmishes, but Russia and China sounded like it might have been a fairly chunky dispute.

'Governments of Extremes' was the following chapter. I made myself comfortable and started reading.

The National Emergency Government, formed in what was still then the United Kingdom in 2050, lasted eight months before imploding in chaos and disorder. Initially an extreme cadre of activists seized control of the New Liberal Party, a political grouping that had emerged from the disastrous governments before the final 2049 collapse of the British Pound Sterling, as the currency (money) exchange and value system was once known.

This grouping removed all laws from the statute book, abolished all forms of taxation and effectively closed down government. They were convinced that government was the root cause of the financial and social difficulties besetting the country. They sold off the armed forces and police to the rapidly emerging 'BipTic' organisation (see Chapter 8, *The Big Three*).

Many of the former New Liberal government were already directly employed by BipTic so effectively the New Liberals gave the government to the company they worked for. This was deemed a good thing at the time according to many contemporary reports.

During this time many communities developed outside the control of what had come to be known as the NG (Non Government). Although these communities represented everything the zealots in the New Liberal Party despised, the party could do nothing about this state of affairs due to their strict adherence to their libertarian or laissez-faire policies. There were no laws which meant in effect no one could break a law.

As the New Liberal Party slowly tore itself to pieces, a new political force emerged: the GSF (Green Socialist Front) a revolutionary organisation whose members classified themselves as environmentalist communists; they finally seized control in 2068. It is unclear if there was a general election held around that time – the official NG line was that no such election took place, while the GSF claimed they had a popular mandate from multiple shows of hands at meetings held around the country.

The GSF immediately set up government departments and brought in many new laws. Due to the steadily worsening situation regarding the climate and the fact that the capital City was constantly being inundated by sea water, much of the legislation was to restrict the use of fossil fuels.

At this time the male birth control pill, developed in India and China, was introduced to the islands. The previous New Liberal Non-Government had managed to keep the pill away from the general population for moral reasons; BipTic claimed it would lead to more promiscuity and other non-Christian behaviour.

The GSF introduced legislation making weekly doses of the pill mandatory. Blood scans were fitted at strategic points around the country. Any male without a permit to breed had to take the drug. This eventually led to the rapidly despised VRR (Voluntary Reproduction Register).

The VRR was introduced in April 2070 and had a long lasting and dramatic effect on the population of the Islands. These specific laws were passed against fierce public opposition and resulted in the tests that were initially undertaken by pre-pubescent male youngsters.

If the young male failed this test, a basic general knowledge and IQ (Intelligence Quota) test, they would receive a minute chemical implant which made the children permanently infertile.

The youth test was quickly followed by a general test that every adult was required to volunteer for. If they failed to volunteer or

failed the test, they were not allowed to reproduce, which in effect
meant they were not allowed to remain fertile.

It is believed that upwards of 18 million men were chemically
sterilized during the seven years the legislation was in force.

By 2099 the population of the Islands had dropped from 63
million to 35 million. Due to unexpected side effects from use of
the male pill and the chemicals used in the sterilization process,
the population continued to fall until it reached around 18 million
in 2138.

I dropped the book down on the bed beside me. Every sentence made me shudder and yet this was history, events that had
happened over a hundred years before the present day. If I had
stayed in my time I would have lived through some of it.

The casual sentence 'the final 2049 collapse of the British
Pound Sterling' had left me in stunned silence for some time.

What about the £32,000 I had in my savings account? The
£120,000 I had in my pension fund? I hadn't even thought
about it since I'd arrived in the new world – the mortgage pay-
ments, outstanding utilities bills, the ISAs and bonds I owned,
the shares I had in three separate engineering companies. All
gone, probably not even languishing in some forgotten lawyer's
office – there were no lawyers and from what I had seen, there
were no offices.

Still, I had discovered why the population was so much
smaller. I tried to picture the sadness and suffering the so-called
Volunteer Reproduction Register must have caused, the thousands, no, millions of lives blighted by such arrogance. And the
stupidity of the ranting right-wingers and their absurd hatred of
government, or supposed hatred – clearly they had just handed
over the reigns of power to the private corporations for whom
they worked. However, all those people were long dead and I
was yet to see signs of such beliefs and worldview.

It was almost as if both extremes had won, against their better judgement maybe. It appeared there was no government, no tax and no obvious legal system, which would please libertarian extremists. It was also true there was clearly an innate understanding of the environment and the responsibility the human race had for it, being as we are the only animal capable of utterly destroying it.

I picked the book up again and skipped to the next chapter, 'The Rise and Fall of the Big Three'.

To understand how 90 per cent of the world's population came to be controlled and regulated by three hyper-powerful corporations for over forty years it is important to study their origins. BipTic, Moshchnost and Greywater all started out their corporate existence as normal trading companies, but through clever financing (money) structures and aggressive purchasing (acquiring control through the exchange of money) they grew in size, wealth and political dominance.

BipTic started, in what was then the United Kingdom, when an extremist Christian group with little funding and fewer followers was taken over and controlled by the then owner of a private parking ticket conglomerate called British Independent Parking Tickets. This was at a time of high car (autonomous transport unit) ownership and the storage of these vehicles during their downtime was a very large problem in the crowded cities that covered the globe. The process of storing unused vehicles was called parking, and this system was controlled and regulated by BipTic.

If an owner of one of the vehicles was seen to have broken the complex parking regulations, they were given a penalty charge notice or 'ticket'. They would then either have to pay a substantial fine or attend a religious school for a set number of hours.

This system proved to be a rapid way to swell the ranks of the particular church (specific religious meeting place) that BipTic was affiliated with. The membership went from under three hundred to 7 million in two years.

BipTic used many of the more zealous members of its religious group to work for very little and used specific people to take specific jobs in both government and private companies. It wasn't long before BipTic just became a natural part of everyone's life, gradually taking over more and more of the day to day running of the country until, in 2056, they were effectively the government, although this was at the time of the NG.

During this same period in what was then the United States of America (Midwest) a similar pattern was followed. A private security firm, Greywater, had many contracts with existing government departments and started taking over law enforcement and penal institutions.

By 2070 Greywater had taken over the entire government and through a series of military interventions, finally took over control of both the North and South American landmasses. Greywater was by far the biggest and most powerful of the big three but from its very inception was the most unstable.

It collapsed during the period of the dissolution of international trade in 2098. By 2105 it had completely ceased to exist although many adherents to its militaristic and patriarchal philosophy are still in control of Midwest.

Moshchnost started life as an extractor and exporter of fossil fuel from the tundra of what was then the Russian Federation (area east of Polska) and again followed a similar path to that of BipTic and Greywater. Through the use of its immense wealth and strategic interests it rapidly took over control of a vast area of the globe. Moshchnost was the only one of the big three that actually went to war in a way that could be compared to previous state conflicts.

Due to an ever-increasing demand for fuel coupled with an ever-decreasing stock of gas and oil, tensions quickly grew beyond peaceful control. China was the last remaining state run by a government as opposed to a private company. Although relatively self-sufficient in its energy needs, China felt it had a claim to the resources controlled by Moshchnost. It did not recognise the corporation as a state and invaded the territory in 2063.

Again I let the book drop. Reading this history was very far removed from the experience I had at school learning about the enclosures act or Cavaliers and Roundheads.

I slowly turned the pages, looking at the photographs of men in suits looking confident, the CEOs of these global giants with their corporate ethos, their energy and focus on planning and strategic conglomerations.

Strangely all three looked very similar – the Russian, the English guy and the American could almost have been brothers. Men in their late fifties dressed in dull suit and tie.

How could all that power and control have simply evaporated and left a buried mess, a tiny population and a load of trees?

I couldn't read any more; it was making me depressed. It really seemed as if my era was the seeding ground for this 150-year-long disaster as the world lurched from one chaotic attempt at order, or control, or growth, to recession, boom and bust. It seemed no one had the answer. The response, which I could see all around me, was to let it collapse, let it eat itself to death and then potter about in the garden. Ridiculous. There had to be some kind of authority, maybe benign and subtle, but I simply could not believe there was no government of any kind.

But there was no sign of it; somehow it did all seem to have stopped. It was as if the present generation, the one I seemed to be becoming a part of, was almost waiting, resting and recovering from the turmoil and madness. It was as if they had found peace at last, a way of living together that did not involve the divisive structures that had ruled the world for so long.

I climbed out of bed and pulled back the large curtains. I was greeted with a view of the orchards below, bathed in bright sunlight. It was an exquisite view: not a telegraph pole, pylon, vapour trail or chimney belching smoke in sight.

I dressed in my own clothes and made my way to the dining room of Goldacre Hall. On entering I was greeted with the sight of many people talking, laughing and eating breakfast. It was slightly chaotic and very busy, parents feeding young children, groups of teenagers sitting together sharing secrets and laughing, many faces I recognised but no one I had spoken with.

Although it wasn't quite like entering a remote rural pub when you're a stranger and everyone going quiet, I was aware that I was being stared at as I made my way slowly towards the cooking area.

After my breakfast, a young man approached me, and this time he really was young, only a teenager, but his manner was very confident.

'Good morning, Gavin. I'm Suman. I've been told to guide you to the learning hall if you wish to come.'

'I'd be delighted,' I said and stood up. I was relieved, finally, to be taller than someone. Suman was quite a short young fellow.

We left through the exterior door and I followed the young man around the house, along a path through a wonderful herb garden, through a gate in an old wall and then into a large hall, built of wood. A solid-looking building, they had actually cut down trees to build this thing, and it didn't look that old. Again the roof was a huge south sloping sheet of the same grey material they seemed to use for all their roofing. I now assumed it to be some kind of solar power collecting material although I still hadn't found out quite what.

Inside the beautiful and spacious interior of the hall were a great many people, mostly children and a handful of adults. There was a great deal of chattering, music and everywhere vibrant life. At the far end of the room some very old people were sitting with a group of small children who I guessed were listening to stories.

Many children had the transparent books on low tables and seemed to be working them diligently with just their fingertips. At another table teenage children were painting a large picture together, as in they were using paint and paper, I assumed paper made from wood pulp, and I could see in the far corner some were practising fairly impressive acrobatics on an area covered in crash mats and gym equipment.

I saw Grace sitting with a small group of young children who were reading large letters on their books. As they traced them with their fingers the image changed to something that looked like the marks made by a big, fat crayon.

'History time,' shouted Suman. 'The history man is here.'

I stared in awe as a large percentage of the children stopped what they were doing and gathered around me. No child was ushered by an adult; they just naturally congregated together. Many of them were carrying cushions to sit on and they somehow ordered themselves into a semi-circle around me, staring at me with an attention that could easily have been interpreted as adoration. I didn't know where to look.

'Um, hi, good morning,' I said. I'd done a fair amount of public speaking – I'd even given a TED talk in 2010 in California – but this was far more challenging. I just didn't know where to start.

'So, right, my name is Gavin, I'm, um, I'm staying in Goldacre Hall at the moment, and, um, I'm a historian. So, right, back in the olden days, a long, long time ago, back in 2011, this place where you all live now, this island you live on, it wasn't called Gardenia, it had a different name. Does anyone know what it was called?'

Some of the kids smiled at me, and one very young girl, who couldn't have been more than five or six, spoke up very clearly.

'It was called the United Kingdom of Great Britain and Northern Ireland.'

'Okay, yes, so you know all about that. Of course.' I was flustered now, I was talking to very well informed kids. 'Well, back then it was very different. For a start there were loads more people living on the Islands, living in Gardenia, like millions more. It's hard to imagine how many people, but about four times more than there are now. They lived very close to each other, in small

houses, all separate houses. They didn't live together in big halls
like you do now, like we do now, but all in their own little
houses. They used money all the time, they talked about money,
worried about it, saved it up and spent it on things.'

Now the faces were a little blank. I could sense I wasn't getting
through to them on this tack.

'Money was how people traded, how they swapped things. I
had some money, you had an apple, I would give you some
money and you'd give me the apple.'

Still nothing, utter confusion and it was not only the kids,
some of the adults looking at me clearly had no idea what I was
talking about.

'So that was money,' I continued. 'It's very confusing for us
now, but I've got something here to show you.'

I had a ten-pound note in my pocket – I pulled it out and
showed them.

'This is what money looked like. This was called a bank note.
It's just a piece of paper with pictures, patterns and writing on it.
People would have some of these and give them in exchange for
things, like milk and bread, newspapers or a pair of shoes.'

I handed the ten-pound note to the little girl who had spoken
about the United Kingdom. She looked at it carefully and
passed it to the young lad sitting next to her.

'So money was really, really important to people back then,' I
said. 'And because there were so many people, it was all really
complicated. Some people had lots and lots of money and they
could do anything, go anywhere, buy anything they wanted. But
most people didn't have very much money and they couldn't do
as many things, they couldn't buy as many things, that's what
swapping money for things was called, buying. Then of course
most people had hardly any money at all and they couldn't do
very much, they didn't have enough to eat and I suppose they
were made to feel like they weren't worth anything, like they
weren't special.'

This description had the effect of captivating my steadily growing audience. They were staring at me; I could see them struggling to imagine what it would be like to have none of this paper stuff when the whole world gravitated around it. I didn't want to tell them that I had been through the same struggle on many occasions, trying to imagine what it would be like to have no money. I'd always been lucky, my parents were comfortably off, I'd always worked and earned a decent amount. I'd never experienced poverty, but this lot, they didn't even know what poverty meant.

'And we, they, they also burnt stuff. I'm sure you all know about this, but almost everything people did back then required burning stuff. They burnt wood first off, but then coal, then oil, then gas, then nuclear fuel, everything was burnt and used up and then they went out to search for more stuff to burn. It might seem crazy now, but back then, they didn't know any other way to get energy and burning stuff seemed completely natural to them.'

The crowd of children certainly seemed to be taking in what I was saying, I was on a roll. I glanced at Grace at the back of the group; she was smiling, not a big grin, just a quiet, proud smile. She obviously felt confirmed in her conviction that this experience would be good for the kids, and for me. But then something happened that I really didn't expect.

'This I agree was all bad, but it's very important to remember that not everything was bad. There were amazing things too. Cars, okay, they were bad and stupid and short sighted, but they had passion. Cars that burnt stuff, they burnt oil, they made smoke and noise and they weren't efficient, but they had passion. When a powerful engine started up, it was an amazing noise, like the roar of a powerful animal, like something that was living and breathing. The roar of a powerful engine was a thing of great beauty. Planes, not like the one I fly in, huge passenger jets, they were bigger than Goldacre Hall, long sleek tubes made of metal, with enormous wings, like a giant bird, and yes they burnt stuff

to move and they were inefficient, but they were also very beautiful, the way they flew was magical. A huge plane with maybe six
hundred people inside, flying from one side of the world to the
other, way back two hundred years ago. On a clear day you could
see the trails from the fuel they were burning high up in the sky,
long white lines criss-crossing the blue sky. There were also cities
full of people, noise and life, lights, towers, traffic, which is what
they called lots and lots of cars all moving along slowly, shops
that sold things for money, brightly lit, exciting. There was television and films and music everywhere, there were clubs and
pubs and crowded places full of excited people talking and
shouting and laughing, sometimes fighting, sometimes drunk
and stupid but always exciting and vibrant.'

I stopped for a moment, I was finding it hard to talk, something felt like it was constricting my throat. I didn't know what
it was but I could hear that my voice had changed pitch and
everything I was saying took more physical effort. I took a deep
breath and continued.

'Then there was the internet. I know we have the grid now
and it's all very clever, but the internet started back then and
it changed everything, people could talk to each other from
anywhere in the world, it was still new and exciting and really
clever people worked out amazing things, so many really clever,
wonderful people who did so much. And now they're all dead.'

I stopped at that point. It wasn't as if I had decided to stop,
something stopped me, it was just like walking into a wall in the
dark. I didn't see it coming but I was stopped dead. I shook my
head trying to gather my thoughts, I wanted to tell them about
the early efforts to change the way we lived, I wanted to give the
present world some context, explain that although my era was
wasteful, short sighted, greedy and the world seemed to be run
by the most stupid and ignorant people rather than the wisest, I
wanted them to know that there were amazing people around
who did see the big picture.

It was then I saw Grace making her way toward me through

the crowd of seated children, it was then I realised there were tears streaming down my face. The little girl who was sitting in the front row stood up and held onto my trouser leg.

'The history man is crying,' she said. 'Don't cry history man, it's okay.'

I'm not sure what happened next. I remember Grace taking my hand and leading me from the hall, I remember feeling very embarrassed and I wanted to explain that I was fine, I didn't want to upset the children.

I took a deep breath as soon as I got outside the learning hall and Grace stood a little way from me, almost as if I was toxic.

'I'm really sorry,' I said. 'I don't know what happened.'

'Please don't worry,' said Grace softly. 'The children will be fine, it's all part of their learning, they will understand.'

I shrugged. 'I think I'll go for a walk,' I said. Grace said nothing, she didn't try to stop me.

I started walking down a path away from Goldacre Hall and the learning hall. A slightly winding path through the lovely woodland. I kept taking deep breaths of the slightly damp air, it felt so pure and clean.

I don't know how long I walked for, I would guess a few miles. After what may have been hours, I've no idea, I noticed a beautiful wooden bench by the side of the path a little way ahead of me, it had a small shingle roof to keep the rain off, a very simple structure which blended with the surrounding woodland in a pleasing way.

I sat down and tried to relax. It wasn't possible, my mind was racing, the true weight of what had happened to me seemed to hit me that day. Although I wasn't technically dead, I might as well have been. It was worse than being a refugee, forced to flee your homeland because of war or famine. Even if it was unlikely, it was still possible to go back home, you knew your home was still there. No such option was open for me.

I shifted in my seat and remembered I had my Book rolled up

in my back pocket. I stood up and extracted it, worrying that I would have put a fold in it and damaged the delicate workings buried somewhere inside. As soon as I released it from the thin sheath of material it was housed in, it unrolled as if brand new.

I said my name. 'Gavin Meckler, born April 15th 1979.'

The image on the screen changed to a kind of Wiki entry about me. My date of birth, my education, my list of companies, all neatly displayed. Then, clearly reported was the date of my death, May 16th 2011. There was a green button beside this piece of information, it was a hyperlink to an article in the *Guardian*.

An engineer and scientist with a great career ahead of him has been reported missing in a light aircraft somewhere over Southern England. Gavin Meckler from Kingham in Oxfordshire was last seen taking off from Enstone airfield in an experimental electric monoplane. No wreckage has been found and it is feared he may have ditched at sea. Meckler was part of the Tempus project, a multi-national effort to create large-scale renewable energy projects. Philipe LaRoche, an associate of Meckler's at Tempus, said: 'His skills will be badly missed, this is a terrible blow to the project and his family.'

I let the Book fall on my lap – so they thought I'd died, crashed into the sea and died. In some peculiar way this cheered me up – they didn't think I'd just done a runner and absconded with millions of dollars of investors' money.

I sat back and closed my eyes, allowing the filtered sunlight coming through the trees to tickle my retina. I found the patterns peaceful and I started to relax. Just as I was beginning to nod off, I felt a shock rush through me.

Beth, whatever happened to Beth?

'Beth Harris, born September 19th, 1979.'

As I was saying the nineteen, there was a listing for Beth on the screen. Immediately I saw it everything tumbled into chilling focus.

It told in one simple line that she had married Philipe LaRoche – my mate Philipe, she married him! I sat back and looked up into the canopy of beech trees above me – who'd ever have thought that was even remotely possible, Philipe and Beth? I couldn't get my head around what must have happened.

Philipe was quite fat for a start and Beth had always told me she liked me because I was thin. I don't mean to be cruel about Philipe, he wasn't like, obese, just well covered, maybe chunky, but he certainly wasn't remotely thin.

A little further down the page it stated that Beth had two children, both boys. I shook my head, two boys.

Beth died in December 2073! Blimey, she made it to 98 years old! But she had two boys. Two people who would have grown up and maybe had children.

I followed the links for her two boys – the older one was called Patrick Peter LaRoche and had got married in 2041. Beth's other son was called Rupert Gavin LaRoche. Another chill went through me, Rupert Gavin was born in 2018, so even seven years after I had 'died' she remembered me – she used my name as a middle name for her second son.

I sat back and smiled as a cynical thought passed through my spinning head – she didn't name her first son after me, she remembered me but only enough to use my name for her second son, for his middle name. For some reason this amused me and made me relax a little. Beth didn't forget her dead former husband totally.

Using my finger to follow the links, I found out what happened to these offspring.

Patrick Peter LaRoche had one child called Bernice Nancy LaRoche who was born in 2052. Rupert Gavin LaRoche also had one daughter, Samina Anne LaRoche, born in 2056.

Clearly all these people had passed their IQ tests because they must have been allowed to breed. I felt quite proud for them.

Bernice had a daughter in 2088, that was Tira, who in turn had a son in 2125 called Deven, who fathered a girl in 2153 called Mei.

Samina had two children: Mike, born in 2085, and Lali, a girl in 2096. After all the Asian and Chinese names, having a child called Mike seemed a little dull. Mike had one child called Luc, but that poor kid died at the age of ten. Mike's sister Lali had two sons, one called Daksha born in 2141, and another called Palash who was born in 2143.

Again I sat back. The sky was getting darker, my legs felt numb, but a sliver of possibility appeared in my mind. Three people alive now had a weird, tentative link to my old world. There was no mention of their passing in The Book. Mei, Mike and Palash could all still be alive.

15

Y THE TIME I GOT INTO THE DINING HALL early the next morning I was ravenously hungry, but as soon as I entered I realised something was different. I saw a group of older women weeping, being comforted by a young man and two teenage children.

I walked toward the large table on which was the lovely spread of breakfast dishes as normal, but something wasn't right. I looked around for old Bal; I couldn't see him and I think there and then I worked out what had happened.

'Bal has passed away,' said an old man I hadn't spoken to before. 'Many of the hall folk are sad.'

I nodded and tried to look concerned. Other than the fact that everyone I'd ever known had died over a hundred years before, I'd never known anyone who died. Well, I suppose my grand-dad, he died when I was a kid, but I barely remember him. Bal was the first person I could remember having seen walking around, being alive, who was now dead.

I saw a face I knew: William. He was walking slowly with some other old men by a door at the far end of the room. I grabbed an apple and a pastry, took a quick slug of orange juice and followed them.

In a long corridor I hadn't explored previously, a group of people had gathered outside a door. I saw Paula among them.

'Bal has passed on,' she said to me, having to bend down a little to speak softly near my ear. Paula had to be six four at the very least.

'I just heard,' I said. 'It's very sad, but he was seriously old, wasn't he?'

'Oh, he could have lived longer had he wished,' said Paula,

'He had decided that he'd had enough, he was one hundred and thirty-two.'

'Wait,' I said. 'He could have lived longer?'

Paula nodded.

'Was he murdered?' I asked in shock.

'Of course, forgive me,' said Paula. 'Let us return to the dining hall and I'll try to explain.'

We left the crowd of mourners in the corridor and returned to the dining hall. I was still hungry so I was rather grateful for this opportunity.

While I stuffed my face, Paula explained to me how people lived and died.

'The room we were standing outside just now, effectively that is our hospital, as you would have known it.'

'What, just that room?' I said through a mouthful of weird porridge stuff I had grown to rather like.

Paula nodded.

'It's really only used for emergencies, if someone receives a cut, or like a few weeks ago when Vikram fell out of a pear tree and broke his shin bone, he was seen to by some of the hall dwellers who enjoy medical work.'

I laughed a bit, the idea that dedicated, highly qualified professional medical staff had been replaced by 'people who enjoy medical work' was nothing short of preposterous.

Paula then extracted a small stainless steel phial from her voluminous pocket and held it in front of her face.

'We now use systems such as this, we use what I suppose you might understand as a 3D micro printer which creates curative systems.'

'Curative systems? What, like herbs and stuff?' I asked.

'No,' said Paula calmly. 'Probably the best way to describe them is micro robots, would you recognise such a term?'

I shrugged and nodded at the same time.

'Okay, well these tiny machines are printed out using a small printer we keep in that room. Harriet, she will be with the mourners and Bal's body at the moment, she has built and refined a few of these machines and she also travels to other halls where they discuss such things, so they are always trying to improve and revise them. However, we now don't suffer from many of the ailments that would have afflicted people from your era.'

Paula undid the tiny tip of the metal phial she was holding and poured a drop into a spoon.

'I take this much syrup each morning and it is slowly removing the small cancer I have on my kidney. The tiny robots work in conjunction with my body's natural processes. Had I been so afflicted in your era I would no doubt have died some time ago.'

'Blimey,' I said.

'So, I'm telling you this because no doubt Harriet suggested to Bal to take some appropriate syrup and he clearly decided not to bother. We find this happens quite often when people get over a hundred and thirty.'

'Amazing,' I said. 'So essentially, you don't get sick.'

'Oh, we still get mild infections, colds, rheumatism, arthritis and the general degrading of the human body through age, wear and tear, but we can manage all these ailments with our medical systems, plus our diet is a lot better and we are far more physically active than people from the early 21st century, from what I can gather.'

'Indeed you are,' I said.

At that point William joined us. He looked slightly less jolly than usual and sat next to me with his head bowed.

'Doesn't matter how many times you've seen it, or how you knew it was going to happen, it is always very sad to lose an old friend,' he said. 'Bal and I have known each other for well over one hundred years. I will miss him.'

'It's very sad,' I said. 'He seemed like a lovely old dude.'

William stared at me in silence for a moment, he looked like he could have been offended.

'I'm hoping that the term dude is affectionate, I'm not familiar with it,' he said.

'Oh, yeah, sorry,' I said, 'Yeah, dude is nice, it means he was, you know, a really good person.'

William clapped his hands and sat up straight. 'Well, as Bal would most certainly have confirmed, we have to carry on. I won't dwell on the loss of my friend now, I have a project you may be interested in,' said William.

'Oh blimey, a project,' I said, not sure what was going to be dumped on me next.

'Judging from what you've said of your past,' said William, 'you are a skilled mechanical engineer: is that correct?'

'Well, I am a mechanical engineer,' I said. 'But I don't know how much skill I have. Not with the technology you have here, now.'

'I'm sure you know more than enough for what I have in mind.'

I sat back – this sounded worrying. William gently put his gnarled old hand on my forearm. 'Please don't be alarmed; I think you might enjoy the challenge. You see, I've just heard from a very good friend that there is an old-style extraction machine needing a little care and attention. It's just up the way at the Wycombe plastic quarry.'

I wasn't ready for this. I'd just woken up, seen a group of mourners, discovered that the entire industrial medical system I had known had become miniaturised and localised, I'd spent the previous day mourning my lost loved ones from a distance of over a hundred years and now I was being told about a plastic quarry.

'I'm sorry, William, you are going to have to explain things one step at a time. Let's start with the term plastic quarry. What on earth is that?'

'It is just as it says. It is a place where we extract plastic. All manner of plastic and other useful resources that previous generations were kind enough to bury for us.'

'You are kidding – you actually quarry landfill?'

'I imagine that is what we are doing, although how you fill land is a bit of a mystery. But plastic is a really important resource and we use it everywhere.'

'I see,' I said, trying to understand where I might come into all this.

'So, we use rather old machinery to extract the plastic from the surrounding organic material. One of these machines has recently suffered a severe malfunction. It is of an old design that no one we know seems familiar with. I fear the skills needed to maintain such an ancient device have been lost. I wondered if you might cast a fresh eye over the problem.'

'Wait, is this a piece of quarrying machinery from my era?' I asked. Surely this couldn't be the case.

'I'm not sure how old it is exactly – I've only ever seen it from a distance – but it may well be that old.'

I agreed to go. William advised me to bring a coat as rain was forecast for later in the day. I returned to my panelled room, picked up my things and joined William in the garden.

'I only wish we could fly in your wonderful machine,' he said. 'But I know there is nowhere to come back to earth safely near our destination. We will therefore take a shuttle.'

'Is that one of the underground transport things you told me about yesterday?' I asked. William nodded and I followed him into the garden, eager to see this future transportation system in action. Again we passed very well tended allotments, vegetable gardens with rows and rows of growth, all wonderfully looked after. At the far end of one field I saw a woman pulling out bunches of carrots; I wondered for a moment if it was Grace, but when the woman stood upright I could tell immediately from her great height that it was not.

We followed a track through dense woodland. It wasn't a chaotic path through the undergrowth; this was a broad, well-used route through the woods. The air was spectacularly fresh

with a hint of mossy musk. The sunlight was filtered through
the high branches creating what can only be described as an
enchanting setting.

As we walked, we talked constantly; William explaining to me
that they had estimated there was enough plastic still buried in
various places to last another one hundred years. The only problem was extracting it.

'Which is where you come in,' he said, giving me a hearty slap
on the back. I had been listening, but I was also enchanted by the
sheer size and maturity of the forest we were walking through.

'William, these trees, surely they must have been planted
hundreds of years ago to be this big.'

'Oh yes, this lovely area was one of the first reforestation projects,' said William. 'I was involved in the development of the
forest but this was all planted before my time. Some of these
trees would have taken root not long after you left your era.'

I looked around, completely unaware of where I was and there
were no landmarks to be seen, only dense woodland. 'But this
must have been a developed area back in my day. It's so hard to
understand how such a dramatic change happened.'

As we continued to walk through the woods, I eventually
spied a small stone building set in a clearing covered in what
seemed like a dazzling display of wild flowers. The sun was pushing through the upper foliage sending shafts of light onto the
enchanting forest floor. I know nothing about flowers but these
made even me stop and look.

'That is such a beautiful sight,' I said. William smiled again
and entered a broad doorway in the small building. Inside was a
set of stone steps leading down, well lit and very clean. I could
hear sounds coming from beneath me but I couldn't quite make
them out – I could certainly feel warm air rushing up the stair-
well I was in, an experience that reminded me of the London
underground, only it didn't smell in any way mechanical from
what I could discern.

Two flights of steps later we entered an area that I can only describe as very unexpected and extremely impressive.

A brightly lit hallway, no, that does it no justice, a kind of super clean parking lot. The ceiling was not overly high, maybe four meters at most, but it was big. All manner of machines lay flat on the ground, though there wasn't a wheel in site.

Following William, I was aware that my mouth was wide open, but I couldn't do anything about it. This level of technology was way beyond anything I'd seen, it was completely hidden from the ground and it was on a scale beyond anything I had expected.

'Best not to cross the line,' said William, referring to a line painted on the floor before us.

'Okay,' I said. 'What happens next?'

'Oh, sorry, well, a podmibus is about to arrive, it is quite sudden so please don't be alarmed.'

As he spoke I noticed wisps of William's hair start to whip about and I felt an enormous rush of air, then, with very little warning, a low tubular vehicle rushed into the space we were in. It slowed up and settled right before us and a door opened.

'A podmibus,' said William as he stepped aboard. I, on the other hand, simply had to understand what I was witnessing, clearly this vehicle had no wheels and no clear contact point with the floor. The way it had pulled to a halt and then rested down gave some indication of the propulsion method.

I couldn't help myself, I bent down to try and inspect the undercarriage. No wheels, I could just see light from the other side of the vehicle but there was no physical point of contact.

'Maglev,' I said as I stood up.

'Bless you,' said William.

As soon as we had entered the cabin the door shut behind us. There were a few people in the brightly lit interior dressed in the slightly odd-looking clothing I had grown used to, although I could now tell there were variations, decorative strips and brightly coloured scarves here and there. Most of the other occu-

pants looked fit, healthy and active, but they were all quite old.
I was the youngest occupant by far.

William sat down on a plastic moulded seat that seemed to be part of the structure of the podmibus. I sat opposite him facing away from the front and as soon as I did so I felt pressure on my stomach; a thin belt of some kind of soft cloth had embraced me and it pulled me into the seat.

Then, the biggest shock, this lumbering hulk accelerated at top fuel dragster speed. I wailed in delight but no one else on board seemed the slightest concerned.

The acceleration was not only powerful but long lasting, although the vehicle itself was almost spookily quiet.

Our fellow passengers were chatting and laughing as we shot along. There seemed very little rocking or rolling but it was hard to tell as there were no windows.

'This is incredible,' I said. 'How fast do these things go?'

'Oh, I have no idea,' said William. 'They do indeed travel at great speed but very carefully. Any wandering person or indeed animal on the track can be sensed many kilometres before there's a problem.'

'But is there, I don't know, someone at the controls, even remotely?'

'I'm sorry, I don't understand?' said William. He looked genuinely puzzled.

'I don't know, a driver, a person in charge.'

William smiled gently. 'No, there is no driver person; the podmibus knows what it's doing, the grid knows where the podmibus is and supplies the power, the track is in a straight line – the whole system is very simple.'

William smiled and sat back, his eyes closed and he seemed to nod off. I spent the rest of the relatively short journey studying my fellow passengers. I soon came to realise that judging age by any of the criteria I was used to back in my own day was rather pointless: some of the occupants looked around my age, some looked ancient but most of them were anything but young. From what I was learning the younger ones were probably in their sixties, and the old-looking ones were probably double that.

I looked around at the interior of the vehicle I was travelling in. It was sort of like a train, only wider and with much greater headroom. It was very spacious and completely bare in terms of decoration. There were no advertising images or video screens anywhere to be seen. I supposed there was no need to advertise as there was no money to buy anything anyway.

The whole thing was utilitarian without being too ugly, well designed but very simple. I could also tell from the low rumble the frame of the podmibus made that it was very solid; there was no rattling or wobbling. The sidewalls must have been fifteen centimetres thick. I knocked on the wall beside me to see if it was hollow. It felt reassuringly solid.

I then felt myself pushed back into my seat as the vehicle slowed down. William opened his eyes and glanced at me.

'Here we are,' he said. The podmibus came to a gentle halt, the safety sash around my midriff came away automatically and we both stood up. A few other people were getting off and I followed them.

We climbed up a similar set of steps and entered another small clearing in the woodland. A delightful house, possibly originally Victorian, stood set back against the trees with a very busy vegetable plot in front of it. Three people were working in the garden as we passed by; we followed a narrow cinder path through the woods.

Before long we came to a much larger open space, a slightly odd-looking hill. I say odd-looking as it didn't look very real; it was the wrong shape for a natural rise in the landscape. It was obviously man made. The plant growth on top of it was mainly low-level bushes and scrub.

'Here we are,' said William as we climbed up the hill. When we reached the top I got a surprise – there was a big hole, a mas-

sive gash in the landscape. I'd certainly seen nothing like it when
flying the day before.

'Blimey,' I said. 'What a mess.'

The hole was clearly not cut in fresh rock. I was familiar enough with mines and quarries to know this was something else. It was without question a giant rubbish dump.

The ground around us, as we picked our way across this unpleasant landscape littered with the remnants of plastic bags, bottles and containers, created in me an overwhelming feeling of regret and sadness. This was what my generation had done, dumped all this stuff and forgotten about it. There was still so much of it two hundred years later that it was seen as a resource.

We approached a machine, in some ways recognisably a digger although I'd never seen one like it. The top half, above the impressive-looking caterpillar tracks which allowed the gigantic beast to shift its bulk, seemed again to be moulded out of one enormous piece of some kind of plastic.

Two men stood beside an open door in the side of the main structure and one was, in a classic portrayal of bamboozlement, scratching his head.

'Best not say anything about where you have come from,' said William discreetly as we approached them. 'Not for any evil reason; it's just I want to get the job done and go home for my nap. If they start talking and asking questions we will be here a fortnight.' He smiled and gave me a wink.

'It's okay, I understand,' I said.

The two men turned and smiled as we approached.

'Friends, I bring help,' said William heartily. They shook hands and turned to me.

'This is Gavin; he is a mechanical engineer,' said William proudly.

'Good day to you sir,' said one man, the shorter of the two, although he was a good deal taller than me. The other almost had to bend over to talk to me – he must have been nearly seven feet tall and yet not in the least disabled by this great height.

I spent a fascinating hour looking over the machine. It was a mighty earth-moving digger that used a hydrogen fuel cell to power the motors running the hydraulic pumps and caterpillar tracks. It was huge and clearly very powerful. It had a large array of other specialised equipment I wasn't familiar with, but I imagined it was a sorting system to extract plastic waste from the other material that lay strewn over the site.

It was so odd to investigate what to me was brand new technology that was now very old, dirty and battered. I could see that a lot of half-hearted repairs had been done to the machine over the years; it was very badly worn and hanging together more with hope than any technological accomplishment.

'It's in a bit of a state,' I said as I removed my head from within the drive chamber. 'I'd say the fuel cell is shot, the feed pipes from the tank look a bit worrying – it basically needs a total overhaul.'

The two tall men nodded but said nothing.

'What spares have you got?' I asked.

'Only these,' said the shorter of the two. He handed me some gasket rings in a plastic bag.

'Is that it?' I asked. 'Is that all you've got?'

They nodded and looked slightly ashamed. I turned to William.

'I don't understand. I mean, to me, this is the most incredible power plant I've ever seen; it's beautifully made but really badly maintained. The hydraulics and mechanics I can understand, but the power plant is a mystery. It's a hydrogen fuel cell isn't it?'

The very tall man nodded.

'Well, I know nothing about those. I mean, I understand the principles involved but if it's not working, that's a problem. If you really want it to work again, you're going to need to strip it right down, replace the worn parts and somehow re-configure the fuel cell and rebuild it. It's a huge job.'

William smiled. 'I thought you might say that. D'you want to do it?'

'Well, I'm going to need some help, and spare parts or at least the facilities to manufacture spare parts if you don't have any.'

'I'm sure we can sort something out,' said William. 'But you think at present, it's not going to function.'

'I'd say at the moment it's positively dangerous. You've got high-pressure hydrogen in that tank – you don't want that leaking – and the pipes all look shot to ribbons. My advice is forget it, get a new one.'

'There are no new ones, Gavin,' said William. 'No one is making such machines any more. This is an antique and much loved by these wonderful operators. Anything you can do to help would be greatly appreciated.'

I stood and looked at the massive machine. It was a giant job and I had no idea where to start: I needed so much kit to work on a machine of this size – all the components were far too heavy for mere mortals to tackle.

'It's going to take a long time. I'll need tools, heavy lifting equipment, welding and cutting gear and a lot of help.'

William shook my hand with enthusiasm. 'I had a feeling you were the man for the job. We shall return to Goldacre Hall and begin planning.'

Our return trip was made in the same way as our outward journey, although we had to wait longer for a podmibus to arrive. William had a small packed lunch in his shoulder bag and we sat in the afternoon sun in the small clearing next to the stone entrance. Even this close to the ugly scar on the landscape where the digger sat motionless, the air smelt fresh and clean.

I also started to feel a little more hopeful at that point. I had something to occupy myself; the prospect of spending my days gardening and cooking really didn't appeal. This earthmover project was something I could get my teeth into.

That night I dined in the kitchen at Goldacre Hall amid a

whirlwind of conversation about the digger. I spoke to people who knew of a mobile crane we could use, a woman who had access to what I eventually understood to be welding equipment and a man who ran a large 3D printer in a nearby hall. I took notes on my iPad and started building up a list of tasks that I could already see we needed to do. I was, in effect, giving lessons in engineering management which everyone I spoke to seemed very impressed with.

Late that night I went back to my room, once again exhausted but feeling a lot less depressed. I took a shower and was sitting in my towel when I heard a gentle, possibly slightly hesitant knock on my door. I stood up and was just about to ask who was there when I realised it was pointless – there was no lock on the door anyway.

My wallet, phone and iPad had been left in the room all day and effectively on display since I had arrived; no one had come in and taken anything. I looked down at myself, it wasn't appropriate to open the door when I only had a towel wrapped around my waist.

'Who is it?' I asked.

'Just me,' said a quiet voice, a woman's voice, a soft sounding, slightly husky woman's voice.

I opened the door and I admit my heart skipped a beat. It was Grace. She was alone. There was a brief moment when we just looked at each other, then she moved towards me and we embraced. We kissed for the first time, but not the last.

16

'GRACE, I WANT' TO KNOW MORE ABOUT THE other man who came through the cloud,' I said the following morning. The early morning light was just beginning to seep under the curtains. I had been awake a while and felt a little uncomfortable bringing it up; however, I wanted to know about this other man and people seemed a little reluctant to talk about him. I thought I might catch Grace in an unguarded moment.

Grace turned over in my bed and stared at me. Her hair, normally neatly tied back, was a mess. It was half covering her face. I gently moved it back with my left hand. She held my face in her hands, kissed me and smiled.

'Good morning, Gavin, you lovely, lovely man,' she said. She was right of course, not that I was lovely, but that what I had just said wasn't exactly a lover's morning greeting.

'I'm sorry,' I said. 'Good morning, Grace, you utterly stunning, beautiful and alluring woman.'

We stared at each other for a long time. I normally find high levels of direct eye contact disturbing but I was immensely relaxed in Grace's company. I sighed and was just about to tell her how beautiful she was again when she said, 'I only met him a couple of times.'

'Oh, you did meet him then.'

'I was very young when he died. He seemed like a very nice old man,' she said sleepily.

'So you never saw the plane he was flying?' I shook my head before she could respond. 'No, of course you didn't. I'm sorry, I'm so confused about dates, and time. What year were you born?'

'2181,' she said automatically. It sounded so natural coming from her, but it still sounded so weird to my vintage twentieth century ears.

'2181,' I said slowly. 'That is so spooky. I mean, if I'd lived to a ripe old age, say ninety years old, I would have died in 2068, more than a hundred years before you were even born.'

Grace smiled and said slowly, 'I'm glad you didn't die one hundred years before I was born.'

'I'm not sure I'm glad. I mean I'm glad because I'm here with you now, but it's so confusing. I still think I might be dead and this is heaven.'

Again Grace smiled, only this smile was a little more lascivious.

'Oh, I think we can safely say you are not dead, sweet man.'

'I suppose you're right,' I said and kissed her forehead gently. Then I lay on my back and looked up at the beautiful wooden ceiling in my weird room. The morning light was now leaking in and the day was taking shape.

'You know that the man who came through the cloud before you is Henry's Grandfather, don't you?'

'What!' I said turning to look at Grace. She was lying on her side with her eyes closed.

'He was Mitchell's father, that's where Mitchell got his name from. That's why some people think Mitchell is rather distant and maybe a little sad, because in some ways he comes from another time. I know that's not true, Mitchell has a quiet soul, he is at peace with the world in a way many hope and strive for.'

She didn't open her eyes once while she spoke.

'So let me get this straight,' I said, propping myself on one elbow, 'this RAF pilot comes belting through the cloud in a Supermarine Spitfire, crashes it into a greenhouse, bails out, parachutes to the ground, meets people, gets Mitchell's mum pregnant and then dies at a ripe old age.'

'I didn't understand some of that, but the bits I did understand are correct,' said Grace.

'He must have been even more confused by all of this than I am. It's so bizarre, I wish I could have met him.'

Grace put her hand on my chest and made a tiny sound, possibly the most intimate and sexy sound I've ever heard in my life. I was a little torn; the information about Reginald Peter Mitchell obsessed me, but so did the woman lying naked beside me. Who was this bloke, what did he make of Gardenia, of the changes to his world? Did he freak out, did he fit in, did he look after Mitchell when he was a kid?

'He's Mitchell's dad,' I said. I watched Grace nod gently. 'That is incredible. What must that have been like for him, it's so weird.'

I didn't have children. I've never known if I wanted them, I was fairly certain I didn't but I was starting to regret it since I'd been in Gardenia.

After a while I said, 'The other thing I thought about yesterday was that if I'd had children, then I'd have had grandchildren, then great grandchildren, and great-great grandchildren and if that had happened some of them might be alive now.'

'I suppose so,' said Grace softly. She kissed me again.

I was thinking about Beth and her children, but I didn't want to mention it in case Grace felt uncomfortable being reminded that technically I was married and cheating on my wife. I shook my head, such an idea was insane.

'I used The Book to find out about my wife the other day, after I freaked out in the hall with the kids.'

Grace didn't move but I could sense something. I wish I was more sensitive to such subtle changes in emotion but I'm not, and she seemed to cope.

'What did you discover?'

'Well, there are three people who could be alive now who are her direct descendants.'

Grace turned to look at me. 'Are there? Goodness me, am I one of them?'

I smiled and shook my head. 'No, don't worry. But I have to say I would love to meet them.'

'Hmm,' said Grace. 'Well, maybe you could find them. You found me after all and I'm rather grateful for that.'

Although she had exhausted me the night before, Grace was still not satisfied. I did my best to rectify this and we remained in bed for another two hours that delicious morning.

However, the remainder of that day and the ten days following was spent repairing the wretched digger in the filthy quarry. With some help from very willing workers who seemed to hang on my every word, I managed to strip the vehicle down piece by battered, worn-out piece.

I looked at the mechanical design of the mobile crane that arrived on the site on the second day. This was a very impressive piece of kit; the majority of the bodywork and chassis seemed to be made of the same plastic as the podmibus I was commuting in every day – a very thick but seemingly lightweight material that was clearly incredibly strong. The hydraulic systems and crane arm were made of steel, but it was the motor and power system that really impressed me.

The digger's motive power came from a substantial electric motor; it was big and resembled a 20 centimetre-thick circular dining table but was clearly a power plant of immense torque. My fellow engineers did know about this motor: I learned it was an old axial flux unit with 7,500 Newton metres of torque. I was suitably impressed, as they were with my understanding of this system. I had seen prototypes of small motors like this when I visited a manufacturer in Abingdon the year before. No, not the year before, two hundred and one years before.

After stripping out the fuel cell stack in the broken digger my initial fears were confirmed. The whole power system was redundant and needed replacing.

I spent many hours taking the complex thing to pieces; it was the first time in my life I was confronted with technology I truly

didn't understand. The fuel cell contained materials I was utterly
unfamiliar with, alloys and sheet material that baffled me, and it
seemed none of my fellow mechanics had the faintest idea what
it was or what it did.

'All I know,' said Tom, the very tall man who operated the
crane, 'is I fill it up over there.' He pointed to an installation on
the side of the pit. 'And then I turn it on and start work.'

After a brief inspection, I understood that the installation was
in fact a hydrogen generator, a water splitting system that
extracted and compressed hydrogen. I poked around its dusty
and battered interior for a while, remembering the engineers
I'd known who were convinced that this was to be the future.
Well, I suppose it was for a while, but not any more.

One thing was for certain though: unless we could get a
completely new cell stack the digging machine was next to useless.

We needed to get some power to the motor from some other
source. A lot of power. My experience up to that point had
shown me that there was electrical power everywhere – the grid
would supply any amount of it, so why didn't the electric motor
just work?

Clearly the electricity had to be received in some way, and
then had to be carefully controlled. With a motor as powerful as
the one in the broken digger, control was rather vital.

After asking the small crew of amateur mechanics I had
assembled, news came through of a disused surface soil transport
unit we might be able to salvage. There was much talk of the
ultra-capacitor system these vehicles contained and how they
could draw substantial power from the grid at any time.

The following day I waited in the clearing by the sweet
Victorian house and watched a small electric tractor thing like
the one that had towed my Yuneec through the field. This one
was slightly larger and was clearly straining to pull a large four-
wheeled truck, a soil transport they called it. It had no cab or

control system for a driver that I could see. It was clearly well used and a bit knackered. It had never been repaired, just left in a convenient yard somewhere.

Another day was spent isolating and removing the power unit and then using the mobile crane to carefully transport it through the woods and into the plastic quarry.

This process caused a lot of discussion as it clearly upset the people in the Victorian house to have this much disturbance to their precious woodland. The crane was a heavy piece of kit and we had to cut back a lot of shrubs and a couple of small trees to make the path wide enough. The low-pressure tyres didn't do too much damage to the ground but there was an impact. I was fascinated to watch how this was negotiated, how the long-term benefits of this disturbance were balanced with the short-term impact: we seemed to stand around talking about it for days.

All this took an enormous amount of time and was often very frustrating. I didn't have the right tools and it seemed I was the only one with any gumption.

However, each night when I got back to Goldacre Hall, I would eat in the big kitchen surrounded by the residents who seemed very keen to hear my news; this event had clearly sparked a lot of interest. I was beset with suggestions and offers of help.

I was barely aware of what I was eating as I was completely absorbed into their bizarre but essentially friendly community; I even began to feel a part of it. I no longer looked at the noisy group as an outsider, I came to realise I was part of the noisy chaos and I rather liked it.

However, in the back of my mind all the time I spent there, I was thinking, wondering, hoping that Grace would come and see me again. I would make my excuses, claim I was exhausted – which was never a lie, I was utterly knackered – then I'd retire to my room as early as I could.

Every evening I would start to read the history book Paula had given me. I must have read the first few pages many times but as soon as I started, I would hear the gentle tap on the door.

Every night Grace would arrive, eager and almost desperate for my body. At first I found it wonderfully romantic, but before long I became aware that there wasn't that much romance involved. It's not that Grace wasn't affectionate; she was. Very. However, there seemed to be an overwhelming drive to couple with me for as often and as long as possible. I would often tell her I loved her. I did – I had fallen hopelessly in love with her and would think about her all day. I missed being in her company but she had kept our meetings strictly to the hours of darkness.

She never told me she loved me, not in words, but she was obviously very passionately attracted to me – she looked at me intensely as we made love. She connected in that way only lovers can, but other than that there was no obvious affection or even desire to arrange things so we could share our lives.

It became increasingly peculiar. I had never experienced anything like this before but however peculiar it was, it was also incredibly pleasurable and rewarding. I had never experienced sex in such an intense and exhausting way. I admit that at first I felt bad, I felt I was cheating on Beth which was something I had never done or even considered doing, but without effort that feeling passed and I felt no guilt or shame.

I also didn't get the impression that Grace was being secretive – people must have seen her arrive and leave; they must have known she was there.

No one else ever came to the strange room that had become my refuge, only Grace. We didn't talk much. I didn't know if she had said anything to Mitchell or her father, or even her son Henry about this liaison. I suppose I should have asked, but I somehow knew it wasn't appropriate.

So it was ten long days after I had first seen the wretched digger that the mobile crane slowly lowered the moulded plastic cab and control systems back onto the bulky chassis of the enormous beast.

This was the single most complex and stressful part of the

operation. It was something I had come to know in my experience back in the old times. It's very easy to take something this complex to pieces, but it's very difficult to put it back together.

I lay in an uncomfortable position inside the guts of the monster for what seemed like hours, slowly reconnecting all the hydraulic and electrical connections. Thankfully, I had been given a Book, as in one of the ubiquitous sheets of plastic-like material, which contained very detailed maintenance manuals for the machine.

That said, I was still very anxious – the main body of the machine must have weighed several tons and it was dangling from the most precarious-looking thread attached to the mobile crane.

When I finally crawled out, covered in dust and grease, I was greeted with quite ridiculous cheering and applause. A small gathering of people I hadn't seen before had formed around the machine. How word got around I don't know, although some of the people standing watching had rolled up Books in their hands. It was only later I discovered they were recording this moment using the Books, which were of course also cameras.

I stood next to Tom, the very tall man, wiped my hands on an oily cloth and said, 'You'd better see if it works.'

Tom clambered up the moulded plastic steps, across the access gangway and into the large control cab at the top of the machine. A moment later the whole thing shuddered slightly as if it really were a monster rousing from a long sleep. I could hear the main motor and the two auxiliary power pumps start up, a gentle whine and the massive digger bucket lifted off the ground.

The cheer of approval was instant. I was being hugged and patted on the back, someone held up their sheet, Book, whatever you want to call it, and I assume took my picture.

Tom swung the machine into action. It took an enormous bite out of the fetid land we were standing on and in an instant swung the material over the hopper arrangement at the front of the

machine. It was then that something resembling noise started:
the separator wound into action, the grinding teeth span up and
from that moment the noise was intense. I stood back along with
everyone else. The noise of machinery was somehow shocking
– it reminded me of my world, of the old days, the days when all
machines made a lot of noise.

From my experience of rebuilding the machine I knew that the
giant rattling riddle was the truly dirty part of the operation; a
series of riddles slowly removed the inorganic material from the
contents of tens of millions of domestic bins over many decades.

I also knew that internally the machine sorted the various
materials it dug up, and the plastic material was mashed up and
ground down within the belly of the beast. The metal was again
separated and crushed into manageable blocks. On closer inspection this looked to be all manner of metal, from pram and bicycle
frames, old furniture fittings and drinks cans, bottle tops, bed
springs as well as larger industrial-looking metal trimmings.

The small crowd walked along with the giant machine as Tom
expertly worked its many control levers. As he dug up more and
more giant scoops of twentieth-century waste, a much less toxic-
looking material started spewing out of the back of the machine,
leaving a neat row of what looked like soil. It was steaming, as
the machine also heated the final organic waste material to very
high temperatures before ejecting it.

I followed the gaggle of now less amateur mechanics I'd been
working with around to the other side of the massive digging
machine. It was here I saw the plastic powder being spewed into
a large container. Once the digger had filled the container and
moved on a little, I inspected the contents. It was a dull grey
colour and seemed remarkably free of impurities. According to
William and Halam, this was the only mining or extraction taking place in the whole country. Mining the previous generations'
casually discarded waste.

Two of the crew used a couple of plastic spars inserted through lugs in the moulded container, lifted it and started to walk away across the broken landscape with it. They were headed back to the trail, presumably to load it onto a cargo podmibus.

I was intrigued by this arrangement. They had this very sophisticated digging machine at their disposal, they also had the most advanced passenger and freight transportation system I have ever seen or imagined and yet they used manual labour to cover the short distance between one and the other.

They seemed happy and willing to undertake this back-breaking task. I tried to shift another of the containers, but it was incredibly heavy and I was impressed that even with the spars, two people could move it at all.

After a while and a lot more chattering with the excited group surrounding me, without any obvious direction from anyone, we all started to move away from the digger. This was something I was only aware of during later reflection. The entire group just started to move back towards the track. I don't remember any-one suggesting it and I also don't recall thinking it odd at the time. I just knew it was the right thing to do.

How did I know? How did they know? Obviously it was the thing to do but I never understood how we knew. In the past, in my time, there would always be a manager, someone in charge who would say, 'okay chaps, time to go'. Not an order necessar-ily, just a suggestion, but in Gardenia nothing was said, we all started moving at the same time.

We arrived by the entrance to the track, there was more chattering with the occupants of the little Victorian-looking house in the clearing, we descended the stairs into the roadway, the podmibus arrived and we all got on board.

That night in Goldacre Hall there were even more people in the dining area than normal. I noticed a lot of faces I'd become familiar with at the plastic quarry. I spent the evening discussing what we'd done and hearing more and more information about drive mechanisms, energy capturing devices and advanced control systems. This was from a cross section of people; I was having the sort of conversation I'd only ever have with slightly nerdy men from my era, except I was now having it with teenage girls, hundred year-old women and men holding babies.

It must have been late in the evening that Mitchell appeared in the room. I felt very anxious, I hadn't seen him since Grace had been spending the night with me. I had managed to be swept along by the activity in the day and the passion in the night without giving a thought to the other people involved.

As soon as he saw me in the kitchen he made his way toward me. Was this going to be a confrontation? Was I going to get lynched, would all these friendly, enthusiastic people suddenly turn on me for abusing their hospitality?

'Gavin, I've just had word from William,' said Mitchell. He didn't sound aggressive, but then again, I'm not good at reading subtle emotions. He didn't look particularly happy.

'He suggests you get to bed early as you may have a long day tomorrow.'

'Oh, right,' I said. 'What have I got to fix now?' I said it almost as a joke, I think I do that when I'm nervous. Mitchell just looked puzzled.

'Yeah, okay, Mitchell,' I said. 'Yeah, I am pretty bushed, you know, tired, from all the work I've been doing.'

Mitchell allowed himself to smile.

'It's okay,' he said softly. 'Just try and get some rest.'

He patted me on the shoulder and left the room. An old lady smiled at me. I didn't know what to do, so I did a bad fake yawn and made my excuses and wandered back to my room.

17

Y ARRIVAL AT THE HEATHROW TERMINAL the following day was one of the most eye-popping experiences I had during my time in Gardenia. It was nothing in comparison to what I was about to experience, but it was still pretty incredible.

Certainly seeing the vast tidal inlet that once had been London, or even the tether to the solar array had been fairly breath-taking, travelling on a maglev podmibus going who knows how fast through the pristine tunnel network was very impressive, but standing at the foot of a puny looking cable that reached nearly 70 kilometres into space is not something you can shrug off.

William had accompanied me on an early-morning podmibus from Goldacre Hall. I had a small bag that one of the old ladies of the house had given me, a soft, beautifully made kind of ruck-sack. It contained a change of clothes and a Book. The Book – the plastic book thing.

In another neat pocket inside the bag was some wrapped fruit, nuts and berries, a small metal insulated pot with a hot meal inside and two small metal containers, one full of water, the other the old lady described as a special fruit juice. I'd tasted it on the journey to Heathrow; it was incredibly delicious and obvi-ously contained some kind of zingy substance – I felt it surge through my body in a way I've only ever experienced with power-ful drugs.

'Don't waste that just yet,' said William. 'You will want it later on, just take a small sip when you land, use it wisely.'

When I land, that's all he said, but William and many other people at Goldacre Hall had wanted this to be my surprise. I

didn't know what was going on. All I knew was we were going to
Heathrow. It was a gift that the community had organised for
me for helping restore the plastic quarry digger. It was, if you
want to look at it in cynical terms, a form of payment. I had done
something for the community and I was being paid for my
efforts. So being rewarded for your efforts hadn't completely fled
the scene, I mused.

When the podmibus arrived at Heathrow, I experienced the
first encounter with anything that could be described as authority since I had arrived through the cloud. There was quite a large
installation right by the exit from the transport tunnel, a kind of
station platform with a clear roof. What could be seen through
the roof was almost nauseating in its reach. A pod was climbing
up a barely discernable thread. This sight had been astounding
enough when we had flown around it previously, but to see it
from the ground was mind-numbing.

William spoke to a man standing by the entrance to the building before us. He wore a stark grey outfit without badges or
insignia, but there was something about his manner that embod-
ied authority. This was helped by the fact that he must have
been close to seven feet tall. He looked very strong and just a
little bit aggressive.

'This is Gavin Meckler, from Goldacre Hall.'

The stern-looking man turned to a small metal lectern beside
him. 'Gavin Meckler,' he said in a voice that in my day would
have needed a clever sound engineer to achieve the same deep
resonance. There was a low ping and two large glass doors slid
open in front of us.

'Thank you,' said William. He turned to me. 'Have a good
trip, Gavin. If you want to get in touch, use The Book.'

'Where am I going?' I asked.

William looked up into the sky.

'What, up there, in one of those!' I squeaked, a bolt of terror
running through me.

'There is a pod to New York in about ten minutes,' said William. 'You have a place on it if you wish to go.'

'New York!' I said, my voice even more squeaky this time, but I wasn't ashamed; it was a ridiculous suggestion.

William nodded. He was clearly enjoying revealing this information.

'Are you coming with me?'

'Goodness me no,' said William. 'I'm far too busy here, but you had said you wanted to experience pod transport and there may be someone at the other end to meet you.'

'Yeah but...Will there? Who?'

'It will be good, Gavin, it's someone you want to meet.'

William gave me a hearty hug and then guided me through the doors. 'Enjoy yourself,' he said as the two large glass doors started to close. 'I'll see you very soon.'

I stood in a small atrium feeling like a lost child at a railway station, except there weren't hundreds of people milling about. There was only one way to go, along a brightly lit corridor, so I walked along it. At the end was a small seating area and one woman stood by a large door on the far wall.

'Gavin Meckler, great to see you,' she said. 'How are you today?'

She was American – a tall, beautiful American woman with tightly swept back hair and a neat tunic made of some kind of material that wasn't cotton or linen.

'I'm good, thanks,' I said. I don't know what my face was doing, probably giving away thoughts that were far from subconscious; this incredible woman was wearing some sort of shiny stuff that clung to her impressive contours in a way I found hard not to stare at.

This was the first person I'd seen who looked in any way sort of sci-fi and space-age.

'I'm Kirsty. I'll be on your journey today. We are ready to go, if you'd just like to drink this.' She handed me a small metal cup.

'I believe this is your first pod trip; is that correct?'

'Um, you could say that,' I said. I sipped at the concoction in the cup. It tasted a bit like the fruity medicine you get when you're a kid. When I'd finished it I glanced up at Kirsty.

'Oh, don't worry, this is just something to keep you calm and comfortable during the journey. It only has an effect for about twenty minutes.'

I smiled, shrugged and downed the liquid in one gulp. At this point the door in front of me opened and revealed the entrance to a pod.

'Please follow me,' she said as she walked forward to the pod entrance. I followed and was soon confronted with a row of people standing around the sides of the small interior space held in place by some sort of stretchy material.

I won't say I was terrified by what was in store for me, but I was very anxious. To enter a bathroom-sized plastic box and see a dozen or so people strapped to the walls was fairly disturbing to a man of my experience. However, the faces of the people there looked anything but anxious.

I would guess that every race on earth was represented by the strapped-in people in that pod. A few of them smiled at me as I was guided to an empty body-shaped cavity moulded into the wall.

'If you'll allow me, Gavin, I'll place your bag somewhere safe. If you just stand in the cavity we can get moving.'

I handed Kirsty my bag and took a backwards step into my cavity. I was almost giggling – it was the word cavity that did it. I'm sure it was just nerves.

As soon as I was standing there the stretchy material shot in front of me and pulled me in tightly. I don't know how it got there; it just appeared and tightened.

Kirsty moved to the far end of the pod, opened a door which went hiss when she did so, placed my bag inside, the door closed, then she slid herself into another sort of deep cavity. A door then slid over the top of her head and I felt a slight shudder.

'Do not worry,' said a dark-skinned man who was in the next cavity to mine. I craned my head forward and smiled at him. He smiled back. 'The first trip is a little disconcerting, but it is very brief.'

I stared at him with a slack jaw like a dunderhead. His lips were not in synch with the words I was hearing. He had a flat, as Beth would have described it, Received Pronunciation way of speaking. But his lips were clearly saying something else.

'Oh, sorry, my name is Baahir; I am speaking in Farsi – the translator is what you hear.'

I nodded, like a dunderhead who has just been shown a yellow ball and is told it is a yellow ball.

'When I speak back, do you understand me?' I asked eventually. Baahir nodded.

'You are from Gardenia?'

'Yes, well, yes, I am. I suppose, but, um, I've lived a very sheltered life. I um, I grew up in a very isolated community.'

Baahir nodded again. 'Indeed, oh, looks like we're moving. Here we go,' he said.

I felt the pod lurch a little. I felt alarmed but my body was held in place by the stretchy material. Then I felt myself grow heavier, much heavier. I sensed that my body was tipped back slightly and I could see that the people opposite were indeed almost lying, the body shaped compartments had swung almost horizontal. There wasn't much noise. I could sense that fans were blowing cool air through the compartment but other than that it was fairly silent. An old man strapped in opposite me seemed to be fast asleep.

I then felt my weight increase quite dramatically. If I hadn't been so firmly strapped in I would have collapsed in a heap, my head felt like it weighed a ton.

'Lean your head back against the support,' said Baahir. 'You will be more comfortable.'

'Thank you,' I grunted. I managed to pull my head back and it was a great deal more comfortable. I felt a slight swaying as well as the immense increase in weight, but somehow the fact that all my fellow passengers were so calm was very reassuring.

I took a deep breath and tried to relax. It was then I noticed a decrease in the feeling of being crushed. It was slow, but I could sense the weight coming off, my neck felt more relaxed and I stretched by moving my head from side to side. Not long after that I felt a small wave of nausea and a rush of adrenalin that made me start.

'You are okay,' I heard Baahir say beside me. 'The feelings will pass soon. Be calm.'

I pushed my head forward again in order to thank him, but I felt myself go a little dizzy so I left it where it was. I took another deep breath and this did seem to calm me. Although I was very restricted by the stretchy material holding me in my cavity it was also very reassuring. A great feeling of calmness came over me and I felt very relaxed, tingling all over my body.

I smiled to myself. Whatever else had happened to me since I had arrived in this world, this was the most intense and unusual experience I'd had. I wriggled the ends of my fingers and then my toes. It was only when I did that I realised there was no weight on my feet. My feet were floating inside my shoes. If I pushed down, stretched my feet, I could feel the floor but there was no pressure.

'Oh blimey, are we weightless?' I said, not really to anyone, maybe just to myself, but Baahir obviously heard.

'Yes, you are now weightless. Nice, isn't it?'

'It's bloody amazing, fuck me.'

I could hear a chuckle come from the cavity next to me. It sounded different. I then realised that this was Baahir's actual voice I was hearing, not a computer voice.

'I imagine the translator had a little trouble with what you just said, but I'm glad you are enjoying it,' he said.

My head was now flopping around like a nodding dog in the back of a car on a bumpy road; it was as if my neck muscles didn't know what to do. I felt another slight judder in the pod, and after a couple of moments the door opened through which Kirsty had slid before we left the ground. This time she slid out and floated in mid air down the space between the passengers. She was smiling and checked small monitors beside every cavity. When she got to me she stopped; her face was almost upside down to mine and although I found this mildly distressing it clearly didn't matter to her. With a deft flick of one of her legs she turned until she was the right way up.

'Hi Gavin, how is it going?'

'It's just, it's just incredible,' I said. 'I can't believe I'm actually here. I've never been, you know, I've never been off the planet. Well, not like this.'

It was clearly taking Kirsty a bit of effort to remain stationary in front of me; she was constantly adjusting her position by holding small hand grips set into the walls of the pod.

'I'm glad you're enjoying it. I can explain the procedure if you like. I don't want to bore you.'

'Believe me,' I said, 'if you spoke about it for a year you wouldn't bore me.'

Kirsty laughed and allowed herself to float away a little – she did a full 360-degree turn looking like some kind of exquisite mermaid in deep clear water; it made my eyes roll as I watched her graceful body slide about.

'Okay,' she said when she finally lined up with me again. 'So we are presently 110 kilometres above the earth's surface, we have just unhitched from the Heathrow Tether and we will shortly attach to the JFK tether.'

'That is amazing,' I said. 'I've got so many questions, I don't know where to start.'

'Well,' said Kirsty, 'seeing as we are travelling through daylight, the view of earth from here is pretty spectacular if you

haven't seen it before. If you think you won't be alarmed I can
move you to the view port in the front.'

'Oh yes please, Kirsty,' I said. I was almost dribbling with
excitement.

'Some people prefer not to look out which is why we don't
have any ports in here,' said Kirsty as she pressed something on
the pod wall beside my cavity. She put a hand gently on my
shoulder and I moved towards her. There was no sense of movement in my body – it was only my eyes that told me this. What
surprised me was that my body stayed firmly ensconced in the
material that had been holding me in place. I was effectively
mummified, a floating chrysalis being guided by a beautiful
mermaid.

'We keep people safety draped because we don't want you to
hurt yourself. We only have a few moments now – we'll soon be
docking again.'

She gently launched me along the corridor between the other
passengers, and as we moved forward I heard a gentle hiss and a
small door slid open in front of me. Dazzling light came in
through this doorway and I could sense something blue and
immense beyond that. It was much lighter in the small space I
was entering and before I could speak I could see the reason.
Directly in front of me was a meter-wide viewing port and there,
glowing with staggering beauty, was the Earth.

I felt a lump in my throat. I actually wanted to cry. Never,
anywhere, at any time, have I seen anything so beautiful. I just
stared in rapt silence. I could clearly see the coast of North
America to my left and a breath-taking view of the Atlantic
ocean directly in front of me. Below me, above me? I have no
idea but it was there. The intensity of the colours, the formation
of clouds, the thin, delicate, life-giving atmosphere were all
clearly visible.

I felt a small tug on my shoulder and I moved away from the
viewing port and back into the main cabin. Without speech,

Kirsty manoeuvred me back into my cavity and I was held back in place. She smiled at me and floated off.

'How was that?' asked Baahir.

'I will never forget that moment,' I said.

Again, I heard a real human chuckle from beside me. I was so elated I couldn't even think. I wanted to stare at that vision all day, for ever.

18

Y LANDING IN MANHATTAN TOOK PLACE exactly twenty-one minutes after I left the ground in Heathrow. The actual journey across the Atlantic took four minutes; the rest of the time was spent either climbing or descending the tethers at either end. I only know this because Baahir explained it to me as we slowly got heavier and heavier.

'We are now sliding down the Manhattan tether,' Baahir told me in perfect, accentless English. 'At present we are travelling very fast. I don't know how fast – many hundreds of kilometres an hour, but you will feel we are starting to get heavy. The last minute is quite uncomfortable as we will be two times heavier than our actual weight as the pod slows down. Try not to be alarmed and put your head back against the headrest.'

'Thank you, Baahir,' I said. 'I love you, man.'

'That is most kind, sir,' said Baahir.

When I eventually emerged from the pod I discovered that the tether station was right in the middle of what I had known as Grand Central Station. I recognised it immediately; I could see the familiar central concourse through the impressive glass structure of the pod arrivals lobby.

Kirsty the wonderful attendant – or maybe pilot, who knows? – helped me out of the pod and into a small seating area. I sat down and watched my fellow passengers walk straight out of the lobby and off into the station concourse. A man wearing an interesting long coat with a belt around it bent down to speak to me; he said something in Farsi and shook my hand. I smiled.

'Hey, Baahir, thank you, man,' I said. He smiled and pointed to his ear and shrugged. He waved kindly and walked off.

I stared after him, feeling a little confused, until Kirsty handed me my bag and said, 'Welcome to Manhattan, Gavin.'

'Thank you,' I said. I felt all gooey and tingly and for some time I had no idea where I was. All I knew was this incredible woman had guided me through space with such charm and beauty and it obviously had an enormous effect on me.

'I think I love you,' I said, genuinely feeling that I did.

'That's very sweet,' she said, not in the least offended and, more to the point not in the least impressed or affected by what I'd just said. 'Now, you're only staying a few hours so please don't go too far.' She checked her book. 'Your next pod leaves from here and I won't be on it, and believe me, Gavin, the pod will not wait.'

She then suggested I sit for a while and drink some of the juice I had in the metal bottle.

'But not all of it,' she warned with a cutely raised finger. 'It's very powerful stuff; you just need a couple of little sips. Save some for your other journeys.'

I thanked her and took two discreet sips. It was hard not to gulp it all down as it was truly delicious stuff and it worked wonders. Very rapidly I felt a lot more grounded.

When I walked out of the Grand Central building a few minutes later, I stared at what had once been East 42nd street but was now what appeared to be a steep bank covered in woodland, more or less a huge park. I stood still as my brain tried to take in all before me. As far as I could see, New York had gone. I saw trees and a few small two-storey, modern-looking buildings on top of a hill in the distance. There was no street. Right outside Grand Central Station was a small stone path and a grass bank. The one thing I did know about New York was that Grand Central Station wasn't at the bottom of a hill. I stared around me; it truly did seem to be in a dip. Then something caught my eye, and I suddenly saw that the city I once visited two hundred and two years earlier had not entirely disappeared.

Above the line of trees directly in front of me was the top of a structure I instantly recognised: the Empire State Building. It

looked so incongruous, an enormous tower standing alone in the
forest. Then to my left I saw the shiny spire of the Chrysler
building emerging above more dense woodland.

As for steam coming out of the sidewalk, the noise, the bustle,
the yellow cabs, the glaring advertising hoardings and the crush
of a twenty first century city: all gone. I walked towards the trees
and turned to look back at Grand Central; the huge façade was
still recognisable, although the addition of two tethers going up
through the blue early-morning sky was a dizzying sight, all the
more so because I had just come down those same puny threads.

I wandered along the path and climbed the steep slope. When
I came over the lip of the hill all I saw at first was a white picket
fence. Beyond it several people were working on a garden that
stood in front of a row of wooden houses. Not old houses, modern-looking buildings with clearly some kind of solar collector
gubbins on the roof. I stood staring – I must have looked like a
right nutter but I just could not believe my eyes. No massive
hotels, department stores and corner diners, just a long row of
two-storey wooden houses with huge and very intensely cultivated gardens in front of them.

It's not as if the whole place was deserted – there were people
about. At that point someone sped past me on a kind of electric
bicycle; I wanted to have a closer look but the machine was moving too fast.

I stood glued to the spot when another person passed me, a
woman in weird, slightly punk clothing with some kind of callipers on her exceptionally long legs. She was running, but the
speed she was running at was enhanced considerably. I wouldn't
want to guess how fast she was going but it had to be well over
twenty-five miles an hour. She smiled at me as she passed and I
think she said 'Hi.'

I stood watching her run in a slow arc around me; she was
slowing down and I could hear a faint hiss from the contraption
she was running in.

She came to a halt in front of me – the leg callipers were

clearly acutely tuned as they seemed to flex and push her body constantly.

'Gavin Meckler,' she said, a big grin across her broad, tanned face.

'Yes, that's me,' I said, trying to hide my immense surprise.

'Oh jeepers, I glad to see you. I only just got message, I run here like crazy, you been waiting long?'

I laughed as I shook my head. 'No,' I said. 'I have literally just landed.'

'Jeepers I so sorry, Gavin. You must think us rude, expecting you wander around on your own, find Mike. You must think this crazy town.'

There was something about the way she spoke that sounded odd. She had what I recognised as an American accent, but she was speaking in a stilted way, sort of Chinese English, Chinglish I think people call it.

'You hungry?' asked the woman. Then she put her hands over her face. Her hands were enormous; I couldn't tell how tall she was as the leg contraptions gave her some extra height, but she had to be in the six foot six region.

'So sorry, I not introduce myself. I'm Chan.'

She held her hand out to shake mine, I did so and was alarmed to be reminded what it was like to be a child when shaking an adult male hand.

'Hello Chan, no, I'm fine thanks,' I said. 'This is all very different looking. For me. I mean, what's happened to New York?'

'What happen?'

'Yes, where has it gone?'

'This Manhattan,' said Chan, gesturing around her.

'Yes, but, well, New York. Manhattan. Here, I came here before, a long, long time ago.'

'How old you?' said Chan. I didn't understand.

'Sorry?'

'How old you?'

'Oh, right, um, well, more or less thirty-seven.'

Chan laughed. 'More or less, me like that.'

She actually said, 'me like that' but in a perfectly unaffected way. It wasn't as if she was making fun of Chinglish, she was just speaking Chinglish.

'But you mentioned Mike, who is Mike?' I asked.

Again she put her hands over her mouth coquettishly but it looked so odd. Her hands were so big they almost completely covered her whole head.

'I so sorry,' she squeaked. 'I get message, very simple, Gavin arrive on Pod, can you take him to see old Mike. That all I know.'

'Who was the message from?' I asked, feeling a little alarmed.

'From William at Goldacre Hall,' she said in a way that implied I was a bit stupid not to know. 'You know him.'

I nodded slowly, things were becoming clearer, but why had William sent me here to see some bloke called Mike? Then it hit me; this time I put my hands over my mouth. This had to be the Mike I told Grace about. This had to be Beth's great, great, whatever amount of greats, grandson. I was suddenly aware that a lot of conversations must have taken place in Goldacre Hall while I was busy re-building a digging machine. I was at the same time charmed and slightly stunned.

'Oh Mike!' I said. 'Yes, please take me to see Mike, is he far away?'

Chan looked at me. 'Not far but you run slow. I carry you.'

She turned her back, a supporting pad dropped down level with the small of her back, it seemed to be part of the incredibly intricate legging calliper things she was wearing. She squatted down in front of me. 'You jump on, I take you there fast.'

I stood motionless – was this slim young woman really going to carry me, was I really going to jump on and get a piggy back?

'Are you sure?' I asked.

She didn't respond, so I slipped my bag over my shoulders and hopped on.

'Hold tight to straps on shoulder,' she said. I saw that the top she was wearing had sturdy straps attached to her shoulders for her passengers to grip, so clearly this wasn't a one-off idea.

Suddenly we lurched upwards. The smoothness and force of the way she lifted me up was clearly enhanced by the calliper things on her legs, it was so powerful I don't even think a pumped-up muscle man could have done it faster.

Now, I haven't ridden a horse since I was a kid, but I don't think this was like riding a horse. For a start, her running gait was very smooth so it wasn't hard to grip on, she accelerated at great speed and thundered down the track. At the start I was just clinging on for dear life but it wasn't long before I realised I could relax a bit and allow her to support me with her long arms around my legs.

I glanced around as we sped along what could have been Broadway. There were more houses and buildings than I'd ever seen in Gardenia, but nothing like the old New York.

I noticed there were a lot of wooden buildings dotted along the way, not quite in the serried blocks that had once made up the streets of Manhattan. The air was tinged with the smell of the sea, something I'd never noticed when I'd been to New York in the old days. The trees were everywhere but there were more signs of intensive agriculture between the neatly planted rows of aspen.

After a while I noticed something blue through the shrubbery. I wondered for a moment if it was the East River but it wasn't the right colour blue for water, too bright. As we got closer I established that it was a kind of blue tent. I couldn't tell what it was made of, but it didn't look like a wood or stone structure. It looked like some kind of cloth but it was also solid, not like a flappy tent. Chan did the same circular run in front of this blue tent, hopping over a bush as she did so but gradually slowing down. Again the little hiss as the machinery on her legs reduced pressure in some way. As soon as we stopped she squatted back down and I stepped off.

'Thank you so much, Chan. That was amazing. Are you okay?'

She stood up again and towered over me. 'It's no problem, I like to run, my legstras help me,' she said patting the delicately made framework around her long thighs.

'Is that what they're called, Legstras?'

Chan nodded. 'Yeah, like extra legs, I run very fast, long way, no problem. This Mike's house,' she said pointing an incredibly long finger at the blue structure we were standing next to.

'You go talk to Mike, I wait over there, take you back to Grand Central in a bit, you catch Beijing pod soon.'

I nodded, clearly Chan knew a lot more than me. Beijing pod, fair enough. I thanked Chan, then turned toward the blue building. I approached it looking for something that might be a door. I couldn't see anything remotely door or window-like but then a section lifted on the side of the thing and an ancient-looking man emerged very slowly. He looked up and smiled at me.

'Hey you, how ya doin'?' he asked immediately he saw me.

'I'm very well thank you,' I said. 'I'm a visitor, from Gardenia. Are you Mike?'

'I sure am. Welcome sir,' said the old man. 'Tell me son, are you hungry?'

I hesitated, then decided it was probably best to say I was hungry. I nodded and he beckoned me into his peculiar abode. I passed beneath the flap and entered what can only be described as an enchanted palace. The light was wonderful, a soft blue colour. Everything inside was curved and comfortable looking, there were no obvious windows but somehow the daylight entered and cast a delicate hue over everything.

'My name is Gavin,' I said, feeling slightly awkward.

'Hey, Gavin,' said the old man as he lifted the lid on a wooden box mounted on a sort of slope in the floor. There was not one straight line in this dwelling – everything was curved and shaped, including the floor. Even the wooden box was shaped like a kind of timber torpedo. The old man extracted something wrapped in cloth.

'Here you go son; try one of my muffins, fresh baked today,' he said, smiling kindly as he spoke.

I took the small offering, opened the cloth and saw what Americans describe as an English muffin.

'Thank you,' I said and took a bite. I was feeling a bit like Alice in Wonderland, standing in this peculiar blue space with an ancient man and eating some weird cake. Although it was delicious – still warm and so freshly baked I was half expecting to shrink to mouse size or grow to tree size.

'How d'you like that?' asked Mike.

'Wonderful,' I said. 'This is truly delicious, sir.'

I had learned on previous visits to America, what had been America, that the use of the term 'sir' was very common.

'So tell me, Gavin, how is Gardenia going along these days?' He was studying me carefully as he spoke. This may have been because I was studying him very closely too. I was looking for something, some recognisable trait that he may have inherited from Beth. An English woman who had lived two hundred years earlier. It was a bit pointless, this man was clearly such a mixture of the various races of the world any Anglo Saxon heritage was well mixed in.

'Very well, I think. Everyone I have met there seems very happy, most of the time.' I chewed the lovely muffin for a while, feeling slightly awkward as the old man stared at me. 'I've only just arrived. I came by the pod, to Grand Central Station, but it all seems so different to me. Can you tell me what has happened here? What's happened to New York?'

'Whoah, New York! Not been called that for a long time. I think you mean Manhattan.'

'Yes, Manhattan, sorry. I came here many, many years ago.' I wasn't sure what to tell him. He stared at me expectantly, his face open and receptive despite his obvious age.

'There used to be many buildings, big ones like the few towers still here. There used to be streets and millions of people, noise, cars, trucks, lights, subways.'

'Subways,' said the old man, like he had just heard a word he understood. He pointed out of the flap we had just entered through. 'Well, we still got those – there's a subway station right over there,' he said.

I looked out but all I could see were trees and his small garden.

'How long have you lived here?' I asked, deciding on a different tack.

'Pretty much all my life, a hundred and twenty-six years I guess,' said Mike. I watched him move across the floor with energy and good balance. He did not look like a hundred and twenty-six year old.

'Sure,' he said slowly. 'There was a big city here once. I remember some of it.'

'You do!' I gasped.

'Sure, but so many people just upped and left – the water kept coming in, the sea. They built bigger and bigger walls but the sea just kept lapping over. Most people gave up and left. They've either gone north a ways, south a ways or they've gone over to Midwest.'

'Midwest, like here in America?'

'Whoah,' said Mike again. He smiled as he said it. 'You sure you ain't from Midwest, son? I'll grant you don't sound like you come from there – you sound Gardenian to me – but no one here calls this place Merica no more. It's a shame, but that's the way it goes I guess. Folk in Midwest, they still call it Merica.'

'So this isn't America anymore?'

'Not for a long time; longer than I've been alive. Midwest is very different – I don't think they'd let you in. You got the right colour on your skin and all, that bit they'd like, they're real funny about the colour of your skin, but don't take it personal: they just don't like to let people in, they don't like to let people out. It's just the way they are. They ain't bad people, just different to the rest of us. Take a seat.'

He gestured to a rolling area of floor behind me. I sat down on a curve of the floor still holding my half-eaten muffin.

'We're simple folk here, just get along fine and try not to rely on anyone too much. The young folk come and go, always moving around, but once they get a bit older, they find somewhere to settle. Been like that for years. We got lots of houses – that's what we call the buildings here, houses. Anyone can live in a house. I used to. I lived in lots of different houses, some here, some over on Long Island, some up north. Thing is, sometimes they get rowdy and noisy, and I'm an old fella; I like a bit of peace. So they set me up in this place about thirty years back. This place suits me just fine.'

'So people don't own the houses they live in?' I asked. Mike slowly took a seat on another curved bit of floor opposite to where I was sitting. It took him some time to lower himself and he grunted a bit when he finally made contact.

'I'm not sure I follow you, son. The houses get built by everyone, then folks live in them, they look after them good, sometimes they stay, sometimes they move on. We're a pretty peaceful bunch but some of the young folks like to make music and such. I don't mind music, but I like to sleep and listen to the birds more.'

I smiled and nodded. He was an extraordinary-looking old fellow, his face so lined and wrinkled, very tanned although that could have been the natural colour of his skin. Like old tea. However, unlike the very old people I'd seen in Gardenia he really looked weather-beaten and ancient.

'So how are things organised here?'

'You sure have some peculiar questions, son.'

'I'm sorry,' I said. 'Please forgive my inquisitiveness, I'm just getting used to things.'

'Hey, no offence taken here, just assumed you'd kind of know

how things shake down. I guess it's the same as Gardenia: we just
live, we grow food, some of the real clever folks help with stuff.
Like my lungs, I got new lungs back in 98. Really great lady
over on Jersey, she grew 'em for me. She grows all sorts in a
lovely house. Big white place. She is one clever lady; lots of
people go and see her.'

'Wow,' I said. 'New lungs.'

'Yep, I may be old, but I got the lungs of an eighteen-year-old.
They keep me going good.'

'Amazing,' I said. 'So there's no, kind of, well, government
here, same as Gardenia.'

'Government. That's a strange old word ain't it? Government.'
He sat staring into space for a moment. I waited patiently; I was
preparing myself for some kind of political lesson I didn't really
want.

'They sure got government out Midwest, plenty of that – they
love government those Midwest boys. They still live in the old
ways. You know, the old ways like it was way back. They all got
guns, they still use money. You know what that is?'

'I certainly do. I know all about money.'

'That is a strange old idea if ever I heard one,' said Mike. He
was smiling and I could see that he didn't have many teeth.

'Midwest got plenty of banks and money. They also got religion – you know about that?'

'Oh yes, I've heard of religion. You don't have that here then?'

'I guess not. Don't rightly know what it is. I heard folks say
religion is meant to make you happy. You know what though,
Midwest is not a happy place. I'm not saying that 'cos I been
there and felt sad. I've looked over the wall a few times. It doesn't
look like a happy place.'

'The wall?'

'You don't know about the wall?' said Mike. He shook his
head. 'Where have you been? How come you don't know about
the wall?'

'I realise I don't know a lot of things,' I said, feeling slightly awkward. 'What's the wall?'

Mike stood up and moved slowly around the wonderful blue space as he spoke. 'Well, the Midwest folks built a wall, more like a hill I guess. They still are building it. It's maybe fifty metres high, runs all the way from Buffalo next to the lake, right on down to Mobile, by the sea. Same on the other side they tell me, though I've never seen it. Like a big pile of dirt just chopping the land in two. Strange idea, like we want to go in there and mess things up. We don't; most of the folks I know are quite grateful for the wall – we hope it keeps the more angry folk out. They just sound so angry and unhappy. They hate some people so much and they always blame other folks when they've done something dumb their-selves. You ever come across that kind of notion?'

'Oh yes,' I said, 'that was very common where I came from.'

'Gardenia – folks in Gardenia don't do that.'

'No, you're right,' I said, 'but from what I know of the history of Gardenia, that used to happen in the old days, way, way back.'

'Right enough,' said Mike. 'Anyhow, all I'm saying is, Midwest sounds a kind of sad place to me. Not like here.'

'It seems lovely here,' I said, taking the last morsel of muffin out of the soft cloth it had been wrapped in. The old man gestured around himself slowly; he spoke slowly but without hesitation.

'We all live in a happy place here. On the coasts we live a simple life, we grow food and build nice houses, but we don't use no guns, we don't eat dead cows, we don't have no government, we don't have no money and lose sleep 'cos we think someone else is going to take it from us. We just share stuff and live together, nice and easy, not too fast. Here stuff happens real good and slow, Midwest is just fast, fast, fast.'

'So, when did the old city disappear?' I asked. He lifted a stainless steel-looking container, again beautifully curved,

poured some red liquid into a stainless steel cup and passed it to
me. I raised it to my nose and sniffed. It was some kind of spiced fruit juice.

'Smells good,' I said and tasted it. 'Oh wow, that is delicious. What is it?'

'You not had that before?'

'No, never.'

'That there, we call the happy berry. That is some decent shit you got there boy.'

I nodded with enthusiasm and took some more gulps.

'So, you ask about what happened to the city. How come you know there was a city once here and yet you don't know about the wall?'

'I, err . . . ' I didn't know what to say.

'Okay,' said Mike. He looked me square in the eye. His eyes were bright, contrasting quite oddly with his incredibly old-looking face, almost as if he were wearing a mask and underneath was a much younger man. 'You take your time and tell me when you're ready.'

He sat down on an enormous blue cushion facing me.

'How come you don't know? You got books. You look like an intelligent fella; you can read can't you?'

I smiled and shrugged. I may as well tell him the truth, I thought.

'I've not been here long, in your world. I've only been here twelve days. I come from the past.'

This time Mike shrugged. It didn't seem to surprise or interest him that much.

'I knew an ancestor of yours, Beth Harris. She's your great, great, great grandmother I think.'

'Well I'll be damned. That's the most peculiar thing I ever heard in all my long days. You knew my great, great grandmother. She was from Gardenia right?'

'Yes she was, although it was called Great Britain back then.'

'Shit my boots, I don't know whether to laugh or cry, that is one crazy story, you come from the past. How the hell d'you do that?'

'Well, I don't know, it just happened, something to do with an anomaly around a solar kite. Believe me, it's been very confusing.'

'Bet your butt it's confusing. I heard tell of such goings on but I sure as hell never met someone in the first person.'

Mike stood up with ease, approached me and shook my hand.

'It's an honour, sir, to meet someone from the past. That is some crazy shit if it's true. So you must-a-seen this place when it was a big old city.'

'I certainly did,' I said. 'It was an extraordinary place, it was huge, that's why I'm surprised. Where did it all go?'

'Okay, Gavin. I'll tell you how everything happened, as much as I know anyhow. It all started real slow. The city was not a happy place – often there was no power, there were many folks around and a lot of the time not enough food. This was way back when I was a small boy. Plus 'cos the sea level kept going up and up, the floods started and really messed things up. Not all the time, but during high tides, the old place was like waist deep in water. My folks started a community, not on their-selves you understand – a big group of folks got together and started looking after each other. Just small to start, maybe a hundred people. In Brooklyn, over the water yonder, you know it?'

'I've heard of it,' I said.

'Slowly people started to leave. A load of people heard Chicago was way better: no floods; they always had power; they had police and law and religion and schools and cars and roads. All the things that had kind of stopped working here. In Manhattan it had all slowly ground to a halt. It was a terrible mess – I'm not saying it was easy or pretty, it was real ugly and messy. So many people went to Midwest and just left their trash here for us poor folks to clear up. After a while, all the old buildings were empty; no one had a use for them any more. So much energy had been used building this big old city, and we used so much time and energy tearing it all down again. Seems kind of crazy don't it?'

This time I shrugged. I'd lost the ability to judge what was crazy and what was sensible ever since I'd come through the cloud.

Mike continued. 'So the house where I grew up got bigger'n bigger. That part was easy – there was no one else around saying don't do this, don't do that. We took over more houses, the ones we liked and could change into houses that was any good. Then slowly we knocked down the houses we didn't need. After a while, more people helped knock down more houses. I spent many years knocking down houses. We had so much rubble... you would not believe how much rubble we had to shift. Sure, we had big trucks – we still do – we had earth movers, rubbish pushers and boy did we use 'em. We pushed the piles all around the edge of the island to keep the sea at bay. Higher and higher we made those piles, years and years it took. There was something about this I really loved doing. When a real big building went down, not a house folk could live in, a great big ugly tower with nothing but broken shit inside, I loved to look at the clear air where it once stood. Slowly things started to change: we planted trees, we made gardens, we grew food, we'd talk about it, look at the plan, work out what we could do with the space, knock down some more big towers, leave some standing, the ones we liked. Nothing happened fast. We'd done fast – everything before I was born was fast, that's how my folks explained it to me. Everything used to be done real fast; now everything is done real slow. Everyone who might be affected by a change knows about it and can say their piece.'

He chuckled to himself and wiped his mouth with a cloth.

'Fast is not good; we do real slow.'

I shook my head in amazement. 'But you say you still have the subway?'

The old man smiled. 'Sure, we still have a subway. I like to ride the subway sometimes. See friends in Brooklyn, see friends in Harlem, in Washington Heights.'

'Wonderful,' I said. 'It's so peaceful and beautiful here.'

The old man got up slowly and walked to the flap we had entered through. He picked up a trowel that was resting on a circular table beside the opening. I followed him out into the small garden beside his house, watched as he squatted down with ease. He started tending to his neat rows of vegetables, pulling out weeds and eventually making divots to plant something – I don't know enough about growing things to know what he was going to plant, it had green leaves and was in a pot.

'After a long time,' he said as he worked, 'more people start to come back from Midwest. They say it's not a nice place to live there, a lot of very angry people, only folks with pale skin like you live there, no fellas like me. But it's a lot of unhappy people. They see us and think, "These people are happy – I'll live here." Not just here in Manhattan Island, all along the coast, all up to Maine, right down south to Florida.'

'Wow, so how many people live on Manhattan now?' I asked.

Mike stood up and stretched. He scratched his old wattle chin. 'Oooh, I don't know, maybe ten thousand, maybe twenty. I guess no more than that.'

'Wow, is that all?'

'I reckon it's come kinda crowded,' said Mike with a chuckle.

I laughed too, then said, 'So this is more like London. The city has gone, the population has dropped and you've become a small farming community.'

'Ain't no farms here,' said Mike. 'Ain't no livestock, just folks and gardens and some fishing.'

'So you do eat fish?'

'Sure, if we catch 'em, we eat 'em.'

'And what about power?'

'Power?' asked Mike. He looked a little worried.

'Electricity.'

He smiled again. 'Oh, I thought you meant power like government, like one man has power over another man. We don't like that here. They do power in Midwest – it's all about power over the wall. Sure, we have smart grid like in Gardenia. Geothermal, there's a big house down south that makes all the power we need. I remember when that baby was built, they built it on top of a huge mound of rubble, all the buildings from down there. That's a big house for sure.'

'And tell me, Mike, are you married?'

Mike laughed for the first time. 'You sure have been away a long time,' he said with a big grin. 'No, I'm not married, but I loved just one woman for a long, long time. She was called Harriet. She died last year.'

'Oh, I'm very sorry to hear that,' I said.

'Yeah. I'm sad about losing Harriet. She was a lovely woman – she come over from Gardenia many years back. We have a child who also sadly passed away when he was real young. Kind of broke both our hearts that did. So yeah, Harriet lived here, then she lived out West – you heard of California?'

'Yes, I have.'

'She loved it there, told me all about it, then she came back here, then she lived in China, then she came back here. She always came back here until she was too tired to go another place, then she died. I loved Harriet big time, no doubt about it.'

'That's a lovely story,' I said.

'Yeah, life is tough sometimes. I miss her every day,' said Mike slowly.

All the time we were standing in the garden, I was aware of Chan waiting for me a little way off.

This truly was a flying visit – I didn't have any way of sustaining myself in Manhattan. I couldn't wait for the next pod; I had no idea when it would be due and I knew I was logged in to go on the next departure.

I finally made my excuses and promised Mike I would visit for longer the next time I came to Manhattan.

He stood outside his extraordinary blue home and waved at me as I walked toward Chan. In some ways Mike was the first obviously sad person I'd spoken to in the new world; he looked and sounded sad. He'd lived all those years and yet he missed someone he loved. I found that oddly reassuring.

19

Y THE TIME I LANDED IN BEIJING TWENTY-
two minutes after Chan had dropped me off outside
Grand Central station in Manhattan, I felt I was
becoming a seasoned podder.

This time the pod crewmember was a man, a Chinese man
with whom I could only communicate when I was already
strapped in. It seemed the pods had universal language translation. The Chinaman was a little brusque and I noticed with
some amusement that his translation was in standard English,
not Chinglish. As he moved around the small cabin making sure
everyone was strapped in, I asked if I could look out of the porthole during the flight.

'No, that is not possible,' he said. It wasn't an admonishment,
it was just a simple statement of fact. Is it possible? No, it is not
possible.

'Fair enough,' I said with a sigh. I wasn't really in a position to
remonstrate with him, being cocooned in the tight elastic bandage sheet thing.

'I'm sorry about that; some of the people who travel on the
pods are not very kind.'

The voice was right in my ear, perfect slightly American
English, but I couldn't tell where it was coming from. I leaned
forward and looked to my left. A Chinese woman was looking
and smiling at me. Her lips moved and then I heard, 'I am Xui
Li, how are you?'

'Oh, hello, I am Gavin. Nice to meet you. I'm fine.'

'I am going to sleep on the journey, Gavin, but when we get to
Beijing, I will be glad to help you find who you are looking for.'

'Thanks, that's very kind,' I said, once again deeply puzzled. I didn't know I was looking for anyone but clearly other people did.

I too must have nodded off on this flight because I remember nothing until there was a slight jolt. I felt my feet firmly planted on the pod floor beneath me and knew we had come to a halt.

My weird elastic bondage sheet loosened and I stepped out of the pod, and into China.

I immediately recognised the world as I had once known it – the noise, the crowds, the huge towering buildings, the lights, the mass transportation systems and most surprisingly, the cars.

Thousands upon thousands of cars crawled slowly along the street right outside the pod station. I stood in the doorway gulping from the bottle of juice I'd been given that same day, on the other side of the world. I put the remainder back in my bag and clutched it to me. I was looking out into the chaos of a late-evening Beijing street, experiencing something close to terror. In the few brief days I had been in the new world my eyes and ears had grown used to the peace and serenity that seemed so abundant. Suddenly, here was the absolute opposite.

I then noticed a small Chinese woman standing next to me – Xui Li. She was tiny. She said something I didn't understand, holding something forward and gesturing. 'Babel, Babel,' she kept saying and pointing to her ear. I took the small round ball she was holding and pushed it in my ear and suddenly she said, 'That's much better. Now you can understand me, am I correct?'

'Yes, perfectly,' I said. I could hear a very clear voice in my ear. 'Can you understand me too?'

This time the woman gave me a brief smile and a curt nod.

I watched her speak, and through my right ear, in perfect Received Pronunciation I heard, 'I can understand English – I just can't speak well enough to express myself clearly. That is very frustrating, no?'

I agreed it would be very frustrating.

'Is this your first time in Beijing?'

Although I had been to the city in the old days, nothing I was
seeing was relevant, I may as well have come from another planet.
Going on previous experience it seemed much better to present
myself as entirely innocent.

'Yes, and this is my first time in China too.'

'I will take you to meet Mei, she will be waiting somewhere
that allows you to see the city below you.'

She started to walk along the crowded pavement and I stared
in awe at the vehicles jammed in the street. The air smelled of
food and perfume, not car fumes and there was no deafening
rattle of endless internal combustion engines. I soon worked out
that all the thousands of cars, trucks and busses crammed along
the road as far as I could see were electric, silent, just the sound
of cooling fans beneath the hubbub of the crowds of people.

'This is overwhelming,' I said. 'How many people live in
Beijing?'

'At the last census it was forty-three million, but I believe
the numbers are going down now. The property market has
collapsed – you can buy a nice apartment for a bowl of rice.' She
glanced at me with a smile. 'That was a joke, I'm saying that in
case the translation didn't make it clear. However, if you want to
buy an apartment I can get you one very cheaply, in a nice part
of the city.'

'I don't have any money,' I said.

'Of course, you are from the nonecon,' said Xui Li.

'Yes, I suppose I am, well, I'm from Gardenia.'

'You are not here long then?' asked Xui Li with a look of
alarm on her face.

'No, only a few hours. Would it be a problem if I stayed
longer?' I asked.

'I would not like to say,' said Xui Li. 'I don't know how you
would trade, you would become very hungry.'

I was starting to understand why my visits to such far-flung
corners of the world were necessarily brief. I was starting to

understand why I had been given a packed lunch. I had no way of paying my way outside Gardenia.

'So, how many countries in the world are nonecons?' I asked as we made our way along the crowded street.

'The Bicoast, the Europe, the Middle East, the Antipodes, all nonecons.'

'But everywhere else still has an economy?' I asked.

I saw Xui Li smiling. 'Look around you. What do you think?'

'It's pretty intense,' I said.

'Pretty and intense. I like that – very appropriate, Gavin.'

I followed Xui Li into a building. I did look up as we went in, but I couldn't tell what size this building was, other than mind-numbingly huge.

'You live in a small house, I expect,' said Xui Li as we walked along a seemingly endless mall. It must have been twenty storeys high, massive escalators, layer after layer of brightly lit stores, advertising hoardings everywhere, glass lifts going up and down the walls. It was at once entirely familiar, but in scale and cultural flavour it was all very new and shocking.

I saw brands advertised I'd never heard of; I was also surprised to see how much of the signage was in English. The whole thing was a blur of overstimulation and I started to long for the peace and quiet of Goldacre Hall, my lovely wood-panelled room and the calm I experienced with Grace.

This almost caustic, electric bombardment was awakening a part of my brain that felt like it had gone to sleep. I felt my pulse rate rise. I was hungry for something, maybe food, maybe entertainment. I started to feel aroused, but not in a way I was happy about.

'We'll take the elevator; it's impossible to have an idea of what Beijing is like without seeing it from a rooftop.'

We entered a lift that was already crowded with Chinese people. They all looked healthy and well dressed, they smelt wonderful – a heady aroma of spicy perfume filled the large glass box. It certainly wasn't a lift as we would have known one in the

twenty-first century; the interior was the size of a bus. There
were seats around the edge and poles to hold on to.

Then my ear filled with chatter, my translator ear-bead Babel
thing was picking up many conversations and translating them
at a mind-numbing rate.

'Don't say long nose, he has a Babel,' said a woman next to me.
She smiled apologetically. She'd been admonishing a small child
who was holding her hand. I smiled back.

Then I heard a male voice. 'I'm not going on Tuesday. I don't
care what she wants or feels is appropriate.'

I looked around the lift to see who was saying this. A man
stood with his back to the rest of the occupants; he seemed to be
talking to himself, although I soon worked out he was using
some kind of communication device, not that I could see anything.

'We take this lift to one forty, then we change to the express,'
said Xui Li. She was standing right next to me, looking up with
a lovely grin across her face.

I thought for a moment then it dawned on me. 'Wait, is that
like floor one hundred and forty?'

'Don't worry,' said Xui Li. 'The rooftop is pressurised; you
can't go outside that high up. We are travelling up to five eighty.'

We got out of the first lift at one forty, but it wasn't like some
dull lift lobby – the whole place was teeming with people, shops,
electric bicycles festooned with gadgets for sale. It was like a
street, only a street hundreds of metres up in the air. I glanced in
either direction and couldn't see the end of the corridor, or street.
Whatever it was, this place was huge beyond comprehension for
my primitive brain.

We waited a while next to another lift station.

'What about Africa?' I asked as we waited for a lift.

'Africa? You mean U.S.A.?' came the reply. It was hard to
truly understand what she meant, the intonation seemed a bit
quirky.

'No, Africa,' I said. 'You know, the African Sub Continent.'

'Yes, U.S.A.,' said Xui Li. She was looking at me with an expression that can only be described as hostile, like she was offended at my stupidity. I took a deep breath, maybe this twenty-third century translation software was a bit rubbish.

'Okay, wait, let's try and understand each other. I think I'm talking about Africa, the continent which lies south of Europe, the continent where the human race started millions of years ago. You seem to be talking about America.'

'United States of Africa, U.S.A.,' said Xui Li. 'I'm not talking about Merica.'

I stood next to Xui Li and said nothing. I could glean from this that the continent of Africa, the place that through my entire life in the old world had been one huge problem that only ever seemed to get worse, had finally transformed into a unified country. At least that's what it sounded like.

'Is the, um, the U.S.A. in the nonecon?' I asked eventually.

Xui Li shot me a look. 'What? No, of course not. You live in a little nonecon bubble in Gardenia. The U.S.A. is the richest economy in history. That is who we trade with the most. You must go and visit, but you will need money. Lots of money, the U.S.A. is a very expensive place to live, only the very rich live there.'

The lift doors before us slid open and revealed a very crowded compartment. A few people got out and then Xui Li forced her way inside. I did the same, constantly apologising – I was so much bigger than most of the people in the lift. If the peoples of the nonecon had grown much taller, the people of China clearly hadn't.

The short and quite uncomfortable ride to five eighty was brief but brutal; I felt my weight increase and stay increased for thirty seconds, then I felt my stomach turn over as my feet almost left the floor. No one else seemed to mind but I found it fairly distressing, not to mention the pressure – my ears popped quite painfully. I yawned and swallowed; I saw Xui Li watching

me. Her lips started to move and I could hear Chinese being
spoken, soon interpreted by the Babel.

'The lifts are pressurised but you will notice a drop in pressure. You'll get used to it quickly.'

There is no point denying that I was very relieved when I felt the lift finally come to a halt. The crush of people eased as everyone poured out of the door. I followed Xui Li into a huge atrium, where many hundreds of people were milling about, waiting for lifts. There was a huge kitchen to one side and row upon row of benches crowded with people eating, laughing, children running. It was chaos but not poverty – it was wealthy, well-fed chaos.

'Come this way,' said Xui Li and I followed her past the restaurants and cafés towards a huge window.

I felt myself stop before we reached the glass. The view was so spectacular it was frightening. Although we were at a height I'd only ever previously experienced on board a passenger jet, the building I was standing in was clearly not the tallest. There were dozens of towers reaching far higher than the one I was standing in, but to call them towers gives the wrong impression. Massive monoliths, colossal, mammoth structures, they were as wide and deep as they were tall, essentially whole cities in one massive block of man-made monstrosity.

In many ways what I saw out of that window was how people from my time had imagined the future: like cities we lived in, only bigger. Beijing was all of that, only more so. Not only was the night skyline a mass of well-lit towers, it was clear that they hadn't finished building. The whole place seemed to be an enormous construction site. Everywhere I looked, huge cranes and half-completed buildings dotted the skyline. It was all on such a massive scale I couldn't really take it in.

'What do you think?' asked Xui Li. 'It is very impressive on first sight, is it not?'

I was standing with my head shaking; I couldn't say anything.

'I am very used to it but I always enjoy experiencing the reaction of people who have not seen such a city before.'

'I just cannot believe my eyes,' I managed to say eventually. I continued to stare out of the huge window, trying to take in details of some of the technology I could see. 'Please explain the pipes that are being supported by the cranes,' I said. 'I've not seen that before.'

Xui Li pointed towards a massive crane-like structure on a nearby building – I say nearby, but it was very hard to tell how far away this building was, how tall it must have been and most important of all, how high it was going to be when it was finished. The structure was already higher than where we were standing and it was clearly unfinished.

'You mean the pipes over there?' she asked.

I nodded with vigour.

'Those are coming from the pumps, the material pumps. I'm not sure how you would understand ... I'm hoping I can explain a little. I know the buildings use the same PMCG that will be used for construction in Gardenia.'

'Sorry, what was that?' I asked, pushing the little Babel thing deeper into my ear to make sure I could hear what she was saying.

'PMCG, Protein mediated crystal growth: the material is pumped up and fed into position, then the protein bacteria form it into a super-strong crystal-based material along preordained design. Surely you have seen this – maybe on a smaller scale, but that is all that is happening. This building was grown in the same way.'

'Wait, so the building is growing?' I asked.

'Yes, of course. How else would it get there?'

I glanced at Xui Li and could see she looked a little concerned and alarmed.

'I'm sorry,' I said. 'Of course I know what you mean, I've just never seen anything on this scale. Everything in Gardenia is very much smaller.'

Xui Li smiled and bowed a little. I turned back to look at the massive construction, then something caught my eye. A moving light seemed to be approaching us. I was just about to ask what it was when suddenly something swooshed right past the window. It made me jump back and I heard Xui Li laugh.

'Sorry, I should have warned you,' she said. 'That was a commuter transport.'

I stared out of the window to try and take in what had just frightened the life out of me.

'I have never seen anything like it!' I said. 'What on earth is it doing?'

Xui Li smiled and patted my arm to reassure me.

'There is no need to be alarmed. You may not have seen anything as big before. Just think of it as a subway, but in the air. We have a subway system, underground, but we also have an above-surface public transportation system. This is quite new – it has become very popular in the last ten or so years. So many people now live in the upper areas of buildings that for many it's far quicker to travel on an above-surface system rather than taking an elevator all the way down to a subway, and then going all the way up an elevator at their destination building. This is how the person you are meeting is getting here, she will be with us presently.'

She gently pulled on my arm and guided me to another part of the huge window. Along the side of the building was a structure that jutted out. Whatever the thing was that had shot past me moments before had pulled to a halt and was docking alongside. It was a huge pod-like ship, with some kind of propulsion unit on the back and some interesting-looking pads beneath its bulk.

'What keeps it in the air?' I asked.

'Oh, I don't know,' said Xui Li. 'You'd have to ask my husband; he knows all that sort of thing. I think it's hydrogen, it's something to do with hydrogen.' Xui Li was already walking away. I could see she had lost interest in explaining everything to me.

I followed her through the crowd until she stopped and greeted a woman who was considerably taller than the Chinese people surrounding us.

'This is Mei,' said Xui Li. 'She will give you her Babel.'

I took the little bead out of my ear and handed it to Xui Li. She held a small cloth in her hand and I placed it here. She bowed and said something in Chinese. I bowed back as best I could and said thank you.

Xui Li left me as rapidly as she'd arrived in my life. I wanted to find out more about her but now I was faced with someone new. Mei did look rather different from her fellow countrymen; she was clearly mixed race of some sort – there was an obvious Chinese element in her features but she was tall and had a European aspect to her size and manner. She graciously handed me a Babel bead and I put it in my ear.

'How do you do,' she said. 'I am Mei. I had a message from kind people in Gardenia to come and meet you. I was told you know my family.'

'Well yes. In a strange way I do,' I said, fascinated that this woman was somehow a descendant of a history teacher from Oxfordshire.

'Are you hungry?' Mei asked. She turned and started walking. I had to almost trot to catch up with her, weaving my way through the crowds so as not to lose sight. I didn't know if I was hungry but I thought food might be a good idea. Mei guided me towards an area where a lot of people were eating.

'I'm concerned that I can't pay for food,' I said as we joined a fast-moving queue.

'Please do not worry. I have credit; this is not an expensive place to eat.'

We reached a large white box. Mei put her hand on a screen and two stainless-steel bowls of hot noodle soup gently slid into view. They were on individual trays, accompanied by a metal spoon, chopsticks and a cloth napkin.

'We can sit here,' she said and I joined her at the end of a long bench. It was crowded with people; most of them Chinese but I noticed representatives from every race on earth in that café. As I looked around I noticed that people of African descent made up the vast majority of the non-Chinese people around me. I looked at one very striking man sitting with a group of Chinese people; it was obvious he was speaking Chinese without hesitation.

The noise and bustle was intense. I didn't feel nervous about that. I certainly felt a little disoriented; for a start it was late at night in Beijing and yet it was only early afternoon for me. I had checked my phone sporadically during the day's journey. I had only been out of Gardenia for five hours and yet already I had travelled to the far side of the globe.

The noodle soup was delicious and really helped; I felt myself calm down as we ate it. A young woman came to our bench and poured something into two metal cups and placed them graciously before us.

'Tea,' said Mei. 'Do you like tea?'

I drank the green tea and grinned at Mei.

'I love tea,' I said.

I was experiencing a dizzying mixture of the familiar and bizarrely new. When I have a feeling like that, I allow my intellect and curiosity to take over, thus quelling my irrational fears. I was sitting down in a mall-style food hall in a building higher than anything I had ever imagined. It just didn't bear thinking about.

'So please tell me, Mei, were you born here in Beijing?' I asked eventually.

'Yes, my mother was Chinese,' said Mei. 'She worked in Europa when she was a young woman, she met my father there.

He was half Gardenian, half Indian, so I am a mixture of many races, like most people I suppose. What about you, Gavin, you look very Gardenian to me.'

'Both my parents were from Gardenia,' I said. 'However ... ' I coughed and shuffled in my seat. Although I had told Mike in Manhattan about coming through the cloud, I didn't know if it was appropriate to tell Mei. I swallowed and went for it.

'I think I knew your great, great grandmother,' I said. 'I come from a different time.'

'Oh, you are an anomalee,' she said, and the voice in my ear made a big deal of the elongated e at the end of the word. Her reaction was not what I expected.

'I suppose I am, but I'm very unclear exactly how many people make, well, the jump from then to now.'

Mei laughed. 'Oh, not many, but it does seem to happen every now and then. There is a man in Nanjing who I have seen. talk, he came from 1958 I believe. He was very confused at the start, kept asking what had happened to Chairman Mao. It was slightly amusing although the laughter was a little cruel.'

I was fascinated, just watching Mei talk – so people had been popping through clouds for years, and no one back then knew about it. It sounded so normal, maybe something that would make the news, but not earth shattering.

'It's very nice to meet you,' said Mei. 'I've never met anyone who has come forward in person so this is a great honour. So, you knew my great, great grandmother. Was she a good woman?'

'Yes, she was a wonderful woman,' I said. 'I was married to her.'

Now Mei looked a little shocked, I held my hand up.

'No,' I said. 'I did not have children, I left my time long before your great grandfather was even born. I have read about her children in a book. That is how I came to be here. My friends in Gardenia have arranged this trip for me.'

'I am pleased to hear she was a good woman. I try to be a good woman too. It is very important for me to be good.'

I must have looked puzzled because before I could ask why, she explained her reasons to me.

'I was a lawyer, now I am a judge, I sit in a court and pass judgement, to do this well you need to be a good person. I strive to be good.'

'So, you have a legal system here?' I asked. Mei acknowledged this with a curt smile as she sipped her green tea. 'And you have an economy.' Again she nodded. 'But I come from a country with no economy, is that correct? But you still have one here.'

'That is correct,' said Mei. I loved watching her talk, there was something of Beth there, the way she held her head as she spoke, the way her lips moved, I was convinced I could see a trace and it made me feel so happy.

'The Chinese economy is presently the second biggest after the U.S.A.,' said Mei. 'We have the strongest currency, all international trade is conducted with RMB. But...' I watched her smile broadly, her lips started to move again and moments later I heard, 'that is not saying as much as it would have many years ago, when there still was a true global economy. Now we have only four global trading partners.'

'I'm guessing India, Japan...'

'No, not Japan. Japan is a nonecon.'

'Is it?'

'Oh yes, for more than fifty years now. Our trading partners are India, Brazil, U.S.A. and Midwest. All of them are successful economies, except maybe Midwest. Doing business with them is always very difficult. They are not very trusting; they are very scared of people who are not like them.'

'Yes, I've heard that,' I said.

'However, they do import some goods and industrial equipment from us and we import some bulk grain products from them. None of this trade is easy and we are slowly reducing the amounts we buy from them. It is said that eventually all countries will become nonecons; there is certainly a big movement for

that in China. Outside the big cities small communities are starting to use nonecon methods. I personally don't have a strong
opinion about it, but I like to live in a big city. I don't want to be
a gardener like you.'

Again she smiled and looked something close to being
ashamed. She waved her exquisitely well-manicured fingers at
me.

'I value my nails too much. None of the nonecon countries
have big cities, just many houses and gardens, everywhere gardens.'

This was something I already knew too well.

'But I love Beijing. Surely you can see why. It is so vibrant and
exciting to live here, there is so much business going on; I love
business.'

'It's certainly very spectacular,' I said. 'And I can see people are
certainly very busy. But tell me this. I know from reading history
that at one time China had the biggest population on earth. Is
that still the case?'

'China, the biggest!' Mei laughed. 'No, sir, not now. Brazil
and India have far more people. China is getting fewer and fewer
people all the time. We need more babies but all the women
here, women like me, we love business, we love to work and we
don't need men to support us, we all make good money and we
don't have children. I am fifty-eight; I don't have a child yet.
Maybe one day but not yet.'

Again I had that now familiar shock with the age supposition.
I would have put Mei at around twenty-five years old, I should
have known better, I had seen her date of birth but in the chaos
and shock of being there with her it had fled my mind.

Her skin was flawless, she was radiant and her hands . . .
that's how you always could tell. Maybe in the old days a plastic
surgeon managed freaky wonders to the face, but hands gave it
away. Mei's fifty-eight-year-old hands looked so young. That

particular aspect of human biology, or genetic engineering, or
diet or medicine, whatever was the cause, had changed beyond
recognition.

'So is the population falling?'

'Oh yes, my husband is a statistician – he would tell you all
about population. All over the globe the population is falling.
One hundred years ago there were twice as many people alive
as there are now. Some see this as a big problem; some see this as
a good thing. Me, I like people. I like business, I like law, all
businesses need many people to make it fun. That's why I live in
Beijing.'

Without any warning Mei stood up and waited for me. I
followed her through the bustling throng towards the lifts.

'I must get you back to the tether port, I had very clear instruc-
tions from Gardenia. You are not staying in Beijing.'

'No, that's correct, I'm not. This is a very quick visit but I truly
wish to come again.'

'You must come and visit and say hello to my husband – he
would be very happy to meet you and talk about population. He
can talk about population for hours and hours without stopping.
I say to him, stop, no more facts about population.'

She laughed, almost like a child.

I rode down in the lift with her to the huge shopping mall on
level one forty. We stood in the massive looming atrium together;
she seemed very distracted now.

'I have to go and do business. It was very nice to meet you
Gavin, please – when you are in Beijing next time, look me up.'

'Thank you, Mei,' I said as graciously as I could. I was being
constantly jostled by the passing crowd. 'How on earth will I
find you again?'

'You have my contact details on your Book,' she said as though
it was the most obvious thing in the world. The translator even
put a nuance on the words.

'Can I have my Babel back please?' she said. I felt something move in my ear and the little bead pushed itself out, making it very easy to retrieve.

I handed it to her.

We shook hands and she walked off into the crowd. I watched her tall slim figure disappear into the chaos all around me. I needed to rest, to find somewhere quiet. The pod, the elastic restraint and the silence of space suddenly seemed very appealing.

20

ASHMI, THE CABIN CREWMEMBER ON MY journey from Beijing to Mumbai, was very kind and very accommodating. The flight was once again full to capacity although this was a slightly different design of pod from the two previous craft I had travelled in.

It was longer and thinner and I noticed as I went aboard it had two clear porthole windows at one end. As I was strapped in I asked Rashmi if I would be allowed to look out of the window when we were in space.

'I will do what I can, Mr Meckler,' she said in perfect English – no need for a translator for this conversation. It almost felt odd to converse with someone whose lips were in synch.

As we climbed the tether I started to experience the now-familiar feeling of increasing weightlessness, I worked out that I had been away from Gardenia for a mere eight hours. I had two further hours on the ground in Mumbai before getting my final flight back home. I knew I couldn't truly call Gardenia home, but I didn't have anywhere else to go.

I think something in the pre-flight drink had a soporific effect because once again I fell asleep during the journey. The next thing I remember was waking with a start and feeling quite nauseous. I could sense that I was weightless again and Rashmi was floating sideways in front of me.

'I have another passenger who wishes to take a view out of the window – would you mind if I take her first? This is her first flight and she is very excited.'

'No, please go ahead,' I said, and watched her gently float off down the passage between the strapped-in passengers. A moment later she reappeared with a young Indian girl wrapped up like a chrysalis floating sideways past me. They both acknowledged me graciously as they passed, talking in what must have been Hindi.

I breathed a big sigh. This whole experience was so intense and unusual I had to keep checking with myself that I hadn't gone mad. I'd just seen two young Indian women float past me sideways as though it was the most normal thing in the world. Except we were miles above the world.

There was very little noise, just a very faint hiss which I took to be some kind of air circulation system. I was strapped into a plastic hollow with some weird elastic material that held me in place without noticeably squashing me, and I wasn't dreaming.

I wriggled my toes and fingers just to make sure I was functioning. Somehow that made everything seem more real. I looked at the passengers opposite me, all wrapped up and all seemingly deeply asleep. A woman opposite had long hair tied back behind her head, but her dark ponytail was waving around like weeds in a slow-flowing river. How many more extraordinary sights could one simple twenty-first century mind take in during a single day before it went barking mad?

Rashmi guided the young chrysalis girl past me and took her back to her position, then returned for me.

'We are about to dock on the Mumbai tether, Mr Meckler,' she said. 'If you like, I can attach you to the view area while I dock the pod. Once we start to descend, however, I will have to return you to your travel position.'

'Oh, that would be splendid. I promise I won't be any trouble.'

With a graceful brush of her hand over the controls beside my travel position, I felt the bonds release me and I started to float free, still tightly wrapped in my cocoon of elastic material.

Rashmi gently guided me towards the two windows, much bigger than in the first pod I'd travelled in. She moved me to one side of the window and I felt my elastic bonds grip to the wall. I could see the great glowing ark of the earth's surface but in the distance something caught my eye.

'That is the Mumbai tether station,' said Rashmi, pointing towards the object. 'I will leave you now and return shortly.'

I wanted to tell Rashmi that I loved her too – the experience was so intense and yet so gentle, no sound, no rumbling or hissing, just a gentle breeze of cool air on my face, and a view out of the window which made me want to stop breathing.

Rashmi slid in through a door near the view window and then I noticed I could see her take up her position in a small transparent kind of bulb that extended from the main body of the pod. She was possibly controlling the ship or at least observing its progress. I could see her talking and flipping through screens on a console in front of her. I wanted to have a go: the screen looked amazing and I was trying to work out what the brightly lit information was telling her when I noticed the Mumbai tether station approaching with great speed. What at first glance had been a tiny speck was suddenly a looming mass. An ocean liner-sized construction, no, bigger – in fact I'd never seen anything as big that wasn't built on the ground. This was a huge, complex lump of manmade stuff, not many lights or windows as someone from my era who had seen many science fiction films might have expected. If anything it looked more like an oilrig or a large industrial installation.

As we got closer I realised we were slowing down. I could just make out the hiss of some kind of propulsion system being activated. I looked down at the earth and could make out the west coast of India below us. On the horizon I could see another landmass I took to be Madagascar, but my grasp of geography is slight – it could have been anywhere. I wasn't even sure which way up I was or which bit of planet earth I was staring at.

I then saw something moving. I strained my eyes to try and make out what it was; it certainly looked as if it was nearer than the planet's surface. Before long I could see it was another pod coming up the tether. I craned my neck to try and see the tether station, but we seemed to be turning. Just before it went out of my view I watched the pod slow down, stop and release from the tether. Moments later it seemed to shoot off at a speed that defied the eye.

Being now a very seasoned pod traveller I decided I understood exactly what was going on. In fact the pod wasn't truly moving, it was the earth that was shifting through space, we had effectively remained motionless in space while the earth and the tether stations turned beneath us at many tens of thousands of miles an hour. Hence the incredible speed of travel and the incredibly low amount of energy needed to attain this remarkable feat.

The pod I was in had now turned and I did feel a slight jolt as the pod locked onto the tether. I then had a very different view of India. We were still just high enough for me to be able to see both coasts, the great brown expanse of the subcontinent stretched before me. I could make out no details of the land save the beautiful traces of clouds above the surface.

I felt a hand on my shoulder; it was Rashmi. 'I have to return you now, Mr Meckler,' she said softly.

'I can never thank you enough for allowing me to see that. It was an incredible experience,' I said. Rashmi smiled at me. She was incalculably beautiful and I was once again hopelessly in love. As she gently guided me back to my travel position I stared at her face.

'You are without doubt the most beautiful woman I have ever seen,' I heard myself say.

Rashmi glanced at me and smiled; it was a glance I will never forget. She said nothing, just placed me back in my position and as she turned to float away, she brushed my forehead with her hand with such gentle care I felt a sob develop in my throat. I was so happy and relaxed it was ridiculous.

Once again I must have dozed off as we descended, as I recall little of the growing feeling of heaviness as we approached the ground.

I awoke when we jolted a little at the bottom of the tether. I
watched Rashmi move along the passage, releasing her cargo of
sleepy passengers.

I had now become more familiar with the feeling of being
released from the elastic body corset I had been bound in for all
of twenty minutes. I shook myself a little and walked a little
unsteadily out of the pod.

What greeted me was heat, light and utter chaos. When I
stepped out of the pod terminal, a beautiful glass and possibly
aluminium structure, I realised it was next to the old Churchgate
railway station in the centre of Mumbai.

I was in a square or open space before the old building that
reminded me of a cross between St Pancras station in London
and the Taj Mahal. It was a massive Victorian building, but now
housed under a vast modern structure, so tall I felt dizzy looking
up at it. I also felt unsafe looking up as I was immediately surrounded by literally thousands of people, the majority without
doubt Indian, but there were so many races present it was impossible to know where you were or where all these people came
from.

One thing was obvious though: the seething mass of people
were not poor. I had been in India before – a quick mental calcu-
lation told me two hundred and ten years before – although
never in Mumbai, but my overriding memory had been of abject
poverty and incredible guilt on my part. I stayed in swish hotels
and had money to hire taxis. Everywhere I looked back in the
twenty-first century I'd seen terrible human misery and poverty.

All I could see in the twenty-third century were affluent
people: happy, tall, slim, well-fed, healthy people, seemingly
millions of them – a sea of incredible movement and activity all
around.

'Mr Meckler,' said a man who suddenly appeared in front of
me.

'Hello,' I said.

The man shook my hand with vigour. 'I am Palash. I am so happy to meet you.'

'Did you get a message from Gardenia too?' I said. His grin was infectious and I felt myself grinning back.

'Indeed I did, Mr Meckler. A lovely message from a very nice man called William. He clearly holds you in very high regard and it is a great honour to meet you.'

I was still feeling fairly dizzy and disoriented and remembered I hadn't recently drunk the juice I still had in my small bag.

I extracted it and drank a little; there wasn't much left. I felt its goodness surge through me and immediately felt more grounded.

'I'm not used to pod travel,' I said.

'Oh don't worry, you never get used to it. You must be very tired but I imagine not that hungry.'

I smiled. 'No, I'm really not hungry, I've just eaten in Beijing.'

'Did you meet Mei?' asked Palash.

I laughed again. 'Yes, do you know her?'

'Of course, she is a distant cousin on my mother's side,' said Palash; he almost sounded offended.

I hung my head in shame.

'Please forgive me,' I said. 'I knew she is your cousin. I'm a little overwhelmed by this experience, and this heat.'

'Oh yes, of course, you are from freezing cold Gardenia, let us retire to a watering hole and you can cool off a little.'

I walked with Palash, who took great care of me. We turned a corner and I was greeted with a spectacle of yet more people, no traffic, just what seemed like teeming millions of people on foot.

'This is Veer Nariman Road,' said Palash. 'It's a very old road, it dates back to when the Gardenians ruled this place. So funny.'

I smiled, I wasn't sure what to say. British colonialism pre-dated even me but clearly Palash felt it was relevant.

Although there was no traffic on the Veer Nariman Road it was anything but quiet. Apart from the laughing, talking and shouting going on all around us there was music everywhere. I couldn't see a source but the quality of the sound was extraordinary – it was as if there was an Indian music group right beside me.

Palash guided me toward a large building. I say large – I cannot describe it in terms that make sense to me, probably thousands of metres high and with a footprint that must have covered many acres. It was truly massive, maybe not quite as big as the building I visited in Beijing, but clearly of a similar construction.

Once inside we were blessed with cooler air but no fewer people. We used an escalator to go to the third floor and we were soon standing in front of a wonderful recreation of a roadside eating establishment. There was an overabundance of intense decoration, bunting, flags and old wooden-wheeled handcarts covered in exotic-looking brass containers. Everywhere there were intense colours and fantastic smells of food.

'We can just have a cool lassi or maybe a beer. Would you like a beer?' said Palash.

'Maybe just some tea,' I said.

Palash entered the establishment and started talking to a man in an elaborate and oversized turban. As I got closer I realised that the man's head was also a little oversized, this was followed by the dizzying realisation that the man wasn't a man, it was some kind of creature.

Palash turned and saw my state of shock.

'Oh, you have never seen a chai wallah before, please do not be alarmed, he's very kind and helpful.'

I was staring at the chai wallah trying to understand what was before me. The grin was too wide, almost comic book in its exaggeration and when it spoke, the head bobbed from side to side in a way no human could possibly achieve.

'Good afternoon, Palash, how is your family, the little one is well?'

'She's fine thank you.'

'Happy times, and will you be eating with us today?'

'Just a refreshing drink I think,' said Palash without hesitation, even though he was talking to a machine.

'Please to follow me, sirs,' it said in comical Indian English. The body of the machine spun around on its axis but the almost ridiculous grinning face was still staring right at us. Its head bobbed from side to side as it moved swiftly through the many hundreds of seated occupants of the eatery. The noise and activity were dizzying all around me; I was desperately trying to soak it all up.

I noticed that the chai wallah machine had arms – not just two, more like ten – and they were busy picking things up and moving people out of the way as the machine moved along, but with the most delicate movements. This machine was supremely aware of its working environment.

'First time in Mumbai, Mister Gavin sir?' asked the machine, its head looming toward me.

'Y–yes, it is,' I stuttered. For a moment I pondered how it knew my name but then decided such a query was too mundane to even consider. Obviously the machines in the world, the grid, the pods, the entire place was fully aware of everything and everyone and no one seemed to mind. I wasn't carrying any form of identity that I knew of, no one had inserted a chip in my neck or squirted special ink on me.

'Happy times,' said the bizarre contraption. 'Please be seated.'

A collection of the many arms joined to the side of the vaguely humanoid and highly decorated box that served as the machine's curvaceous body made a very gracious and naturalistic sweep indicating a low wooden-looking bench at the end of a long table.

'A sweet Lassi for me and a sweet Gardenian tea for my friend please,' said Palash.

'Coming right up, Mister Palash sir.'

The machine turned and moved back through the milling crowds in the eatery, its bizarre multiple arms gently alerting people to its presence.

I spent a moment trying to relax and take in my surroundings.
Although the place I was sitting in was decorated to look like an old-style Indian roadside eatery, it had something of the fifties American diner recreated in a modern shopping mall about it. It looked very realistic but it was all too perfect. The building it was in was massive; the air-conditioning system could be seen beyond the endless fronds of banners and bunting hanging from the roof.

The establishment was truly on an industrial scale. It was obviously capable of feeding hundreds of people at a time. It also became apparent as I soaked up the mass of information around me that my plastic waiter was not alone – there were numerous bizarre figures like him helping people, moving through the place with trays held by their multiple arms. Each of them had a very different face. Some had turbans, others simple white hats, and one, for reasons I was never to learn, had a classic cowboy Stetson on his head and a polka dot neckerchief around his flexible neck.

'So tell me, Gavin, how do you like podding?' Palash asked as he sat opposite me.

'It's, well, it's quite incredible, I can't believe that just a few moments ago I was looking at more or less the entire Indian subcontinent.'

'Oh, you dared look out of a window. Brave man, very brave,' said Palash. 'You would not catch me doing that in a month of Sundays. I am out like a log for the whole trip.'

'I can imagine that if you did it regularly, that would be the best option,' I said. 'I do feel pretty weary now.'

'Oh, you are so much the weary traveller. As soon as I saw you I thought to myself, I know that feeling. Have you done multipods today?'

I grinned. 'How can you tell?'

'Oh, I have a knack,' said Palash. 'I can almost smell podshock.'

'Podshock, is that what you call it?'

Suddenly a stainless steel mug of tea was placed before me at such speed I have no idea how it didn't spill. At precisely the same time another stainless steel cup of lassi was placed in front of Palash.

'Enjoy,' said the chai wallah, who immediately spun around and moved off again.

'Amazing,' I said, grinning like a fool. 'What a cool machine.'

'Interesting you refer to the chai wallah as a machine,' said Palash. 'I suppose he is, but I think of him as a person.'

'Wow,' I said. 'How intelligent is he?'

'Intelligent, I couldn't say,' said Palash, 'but he will remember you, if you don't come back for fifty years and then drop in, he will welcome you again as if you came here every day.'

'Wow,' I said again. 'You'll have to forgive me Palash, this is all so much more than I can take in. But while I'm here, tell me about yourself and this incredible city and India? Assume I am a complete ignoramus, which I am.'

Palash laughed richly. 'I can also tell you are a very intelligent man sir, far from an ignoramus. I can certainly tell you all about my country, but then I fear you would be here for a year or two – there is so much to tell. Maybe narrow down your desires to one or two areas and I'm sure I can furnish you with any information you wish.'

'Anything would be good. I have lived a very sheltered life in Gardenia. This is my first trip around the world.'

'Okay, Gavin. Well, I am Palash, I am married to a wonderful woman called Manisha and we have one lovely child, a girl called Semina.'

'Oh, like your Grandmother,' I said. Palash froze, the cup of Lassi just below his lips.

'You know about my Grandmother?' he asked.

I realised my mistake immediately and didn't know how to get out of it without offending him, but on my trip I had learned that truth is usually the best option.

'I'm an anomalee,' I said. 'Does that mean anything to you?'

'Goodness me! Yes, it does. Oh bless my footwear, how wonderful,' Palash covered his mouth with his hand and stared at me for some time. Eventually he said: 'How long have you been with us here?'

'Only a few weeks, hence my confusion.'

'Of course, you poor man, it must be a terrible shock for you. Tell me, what era did you come from?'

'Well, I left in 2011. I'm trying to get used to it. But tell me this Palash, you've heard of other anomalees?'

'Well yes, it does seem to happen from time to time. I fear there are some who claim to be so but are really just putting on an act to receive more love and affection. I am assuming this is not the case with you.'

'No, very much not,' I said. 'I wish it were, then I would be more used to the world I now see.'

'But why did you wish to meet me?' asked Palash, his grin still enormous. 'Do we have a family connection?'

'No, well, not really, sort of,' I said. 'I knew your great, great grandmother, a woman called Beth Harris, an Englishwoman.'

'Englishwoman,' said Palash, carefully mimicking my pronunciation. It was clear he'd never heard the term before. 'What does that mean please?'

'Sorry, I mean Gardenian, she lived in Gardenia when it was still called England.'

'I am already learning far more than I expected, and you knew my great, great granny. That is wonderful!' said Palash, and he leant over the table and embraced me – it was a bit awkward, I was worried we were going to spill our drinks.

He sat back down again, a huge smile on his face. 'No wonder William, your friend from Goldacre Hall, no wonder he said I would enjoy meeting you. How exciting, tell me, Gavin, what was my great, great granny like?'

'Oh, she was, well, a wonderful, kind woman. We were once

married but then I left and came through a cloud thing.'

'You were married to my great, great granny! This is more extraordinary, but does this not make you my great, great grand-dad?'

'No, we never had children, but after I left she married a very good friend of mine, they had two children, one was your great grandfather Rupert.'

'Indeed, indeed,' said Palash. 'I can just remember him, a funny old man with no hair and no teeth, but a charming fellow. He lived here.'

'In Mumbai?'

'Yes indeed. My family has been here for generations, but great granddad did indeed come from Gardenia. How utterly extraordinary.'

We sat staring at each other for a while. I was yet again look-ing for some kind of genetic trace of Beth but I couldn't see it.

'You knew my great great granny. I still can't believe it. So did you follow the family tree?'

'Yes, it was fascinating, well, it was kind of disturbing to study a history that should have happened after you were dead. It does your head in.'

'I think I can understand what you mean, your turn of phrase is very interesting. I suppose it would have been more confusing had you been my great great grandfather, that would quite do your head in, especially as I am older than you.'

A huge grin spread across Palash's face.

'So, tell me, Gavin, did you ever visit India way back in 2011?'

'I did come here once, and let me tell you, Palash, it's unrecog-nisable. Everyone seems very affluent now, very well fed and clean.'

'I have read of our history and indeed I would imagine it is a very different country now. Like everywhere else our population is dropping which has all kinds of consequences. Not all bad but it does change things.'

'It still seems like quite a crowded place,' I said glancing around
the packed eatery.

'Oh, certainly Mumbai is a very big city, not something you
Gardenians are used to, but, if you have been in Beijing, I suppose you have seen what a big city can be like. How long were
you in Beijing?'

'About two hours,' I said sipping my sweet tea.

'Two hours, yes, long enough. I am not a fan of Beijing. Hong
Kong on the other hand, now that is a great city – of course it is:
it's full of Indians.'

'I don't understand how this place can function, how so many
people can live so close together and not grow food.'

Again Palash smiled and looked at me in a way I can only
describe as patronising, but not in a way I could take offence at.

'As you can see, we do have food, however, there are more and
more people leaving every day. The predictions are that in
about a hundred years' time the city will be a fraction of the size.
Even now many suburbs are being returned to farmland as the
population decreases. We are just a little behind the times in
India: we're not as advanced as you Gardenians.'

'Wow, I would say you are way more advanced than Gardenia,'
I said gesturing around me. 'I mean, the whole country is just a
load of trees and gardens; there doesn't seem to be much going
on there. This place is insane – there is so much going on here.
It must be an incredible place to live.'

'Oh we all love Mumbai,' said Palash, 'but we have many
problems, things that only a city can produce. If you collect this
many people in one place you have all sorts of problems. I
specialise in sewage. Believe me, I have my hands full.'

This comment was clearly overheard by the many people sitting near us, who, I was suddenly aware, were listening intently
to our conversation. It caused much raucous laughter and amusing gestures.

'So please explain to me then, Palash,' I said. 'I understand that Gardenia is a nonecon, but how do you organise things here? I assume there is an economic system working here. Do you have a job?'

'I deal with jobs, that's for sure,' said Palash. This comment aroused more groans and laughter from our immediate neighbours.

'I suppose you could call it a job. I think of it more as a calling. I have always loved waste – sewage is wonderful stuff. We have an enormous amount of it and we use it very carefully. We have wonderful facilities for treating and reusing it. However, knowing you come from Gardenia I know it is hard to understand. I have what is called a profession. I get credits for my work and these credits allow me to feed and clothe my family and have somewhere to live. I know you have none of these things and I can see a time coming when we will not have them either.'

'But all these credits,' I asked. 'How do you transfer them?'

Palash looked puzzled for a moment, then he shrugged.

'I have no idea. I just know I have them. It's all done…' he waved his hands around '… somewhere.'

'Is it the grid?' I asked.

'I suppose it is,' said Palash. 'It's not something I ever think about. There is a system in place. Fully sentient, fully aware, hasn't made a mistake in over one hundred years.'

'Does it know I'm here?' I asked.

'Of course,' said Palash. 'You have the grid in Gardenia.'

'I think so, yes, but we don't have credits,' I said.

'No, but there are arrangements in place,' Palash explained. 'We do trade with the nonecons, well, we have arrangements. I know that if I visit Gardenia, I can eat and be looked after with no stress. I suppose that's what the grid has done since your time. It has removed the stress you may have experienced when you travelled away from home. It has also removed the stress of just living. If, for example, my daughter needs some lovely shampoo to wash her hair, it is delivered to our house by a shampoo wallah.'

'What, the grid knows when your shampoo runs out?'

'Yes,' said Palash. 'It's all very simple really.'

I finished my tea and checked the time on my phone.

'Palash, it's been wonderful to meet you, but I fear I have to get back to the station, I'm taking a pod back to Gardenia very soon.'

'It is a tragedy that your visit was so short. I truly hope you can return one day soon.'

'Please, I would love to come back and meet your family. You have been very kind to take the time to talk to me.'

I stood up and another multi-armed machine approached me at speed. Palash held his hand up. The machine froze, this one had an enormous female face and a shawl over its wobbling head.

'Don't be alarmed, it's just going to assist you, it's the wipe wallah.'

Palash dropped his hand and the machine moved toward me rapidly, one hand gently held my head in position while another wiped my face with a warm scented cloth. It couldn't have been more carefully done; the feeling of the movements reminded me of nothing more than my mother wiping my face when I was a child.

'Happy times,' said the wipe wallah machine and immediately started clearing away our cups.

We made our way through the heaving streets to the pod terminal, all the time Palash pointing things out to me, explaining about the sewage system and the cleanliness of the toilet facilities.

He gave me a hearty hug and left me outside the station, I entered and sat down in the small waiting area and just breathed in, trying to somehow hold onto something of this incredible city.

It seemed to be functioning very well, however chaotic it looked. The streets were clean and tidy, there were many trees planted in orderly rows and they all looked well cared for. Unlike Beijing I didn't see signs of vehicles. Certainly in the area

I had seen, which was a tiny corner of the city, I had only seen pedestrians.

The last pod trip back to Gardenia was uneventful. I was almost bored by the procedure of being strapped in, I felt utterly exhausted and slept through the whole experience. I can't believe it now. Travelling around the globe and being weightless in space had become commonplace to me in less than twenty-four hours.

21

I HAD DRAINED THE LAST OF MY SPECIAL JUICE
stuff from the little stainless steel bottle before departure in Mumbai, and when I came out of the pod
terminal at Heathrow in Gardenia, my mouth felt like a hollow
wound.

I had a headache and my guts clearly weren't doing well. I felt
sweaty and dirty and my clothes seemed to cling to my skin like
a badly worn bath flannel. I tried breathing in lungfuls of heady
Gardenian air but it didn't seem to help.

I had lost track of time, and looking at Gardenian time on my
perpetually charged phone didn't help, 5:45 A.M. Judging by the
light in the forest clearing outside the terminal, it really was
early in the morning.

This was far more intense than jet lag, I stood motionless, my
body utterly exhausted but my brain going at five hundred miles
an hour. If I didn't have jetlag, what did I have, tether-lag?
Pod-lag? I glanced at my phone again, the battery indicator
suggested it was charging. I then started to try and work out
what had happened to it. I knew it was pointless trying to understand, but it was almost as if my brain wouldn't let the issue lie.
I deduced that when I was in orbit the phone was out of range of
the ubiquitous global induction charging, so it actually used
some power from the battery. Now I was back on the ground it
was picking up the charge. Then I realised that through all the
time I'd been in Gardenia, I hadn't yet discovered how the induction charge actually worked. Was it coming from a wire mesh
buried underground, or from power masts strewn across the
land? I hadn't seen anything like that anywhere.

I also didn't know where the pods got the power from to climb up fifty kilometres of flimsy graphene thread. That had to use some serious kilowatts, but where from?

I yawned and squinted through the haze; for every answer I'd received, I had a backlog of hundreds of thousands of questions. But then I realised that this information would only be of any use to someone if I actually got back to my own time. I started pacing around in a circle, I worked out that if I travelled back two hundred years then I could make use of such knowledge. As it was, here in Gardenia any such detailed information was more or less useless. I could fix diggers, that was about it. My cooking was rubbish, I was dreading the time I'd have to start gardening, I suppose I could teach kids, fix the odd broken gate, but my role was almost guaranteed to be dull and uninteresting.

I'd been around the world, seen that it had left me well and truly behind. I was now like a man who had just created a mechanical adding machine and I had a job as a hardware engineer at Apple headquarters.

I stood looking up the tether as the pod I had arrived in started to climb back up into space. It was normal, this is just what happened, there was nothing I could do to improve it, or come up with another system. I was useless, my whole existence back in the old world was about being useful, about coming up with things that could make the world better, more efficient, make things stronger, lighter, faster. Now I was in a world where everything already was far stronger, lighter, more efficient and faster than I could have ever imagined, and I was going to have to live out my days in a fucking garden growing spuds.

I turned back toward the entrance to the track and saw some figures emerging. Although my eyesight was good, they were a fair distance away and my eyes were almost useless with exhaustion.

I had been wondering if I could get on any old podmibus and if it would take me anywhere near Goldacre Hall when one of

the figures came into focus. A woman with a big smile. It was
Grace. She walked up to me and stood motionless.

'Well, how was it?' she asked.

I didn't say anything, she was so beautiful I just found it impossible to speak. Even though I was feeling sick and had a headache from hell I wanted to grab hold of her, I wanted to hold her more than anything I've ever felt, but everything about her slight physical distance from me and her hands clasped in front of her was telling me to hold back.

'That bad?' asked Grace, her eyes sparkling in the morning light.

I took a deep breath, held it for a moment, felt dizzy, let it out and said, 'Just totally overwhelming, just incredible, amazing, I cannot begin to take it in.' I pointed up at the pale blue sky. 'I've just been up there.'

'It is quite spectacular isn't it?'

I felt I was grinning like a village idiot. Grace handed me a bottle similar to the one I'd been carrying. 'I thought you might like some of this,' she said. I took the bottle, popped the weird top off and took some very big gulps. Within a few breaths I was feeling better, still pretty worn out but not quite as battered as I had been moments before.

'That is so kind, Grace. Thank you.'

'It was no bother. Are you happy to travel back to Goldacre Hall right now?'

I shrugged. 'I've got nowhere else to go, that's for sure.'

I touched Grace's arm gently. We had never been intimate anywhere other than my wonderful room at Goldacre Hall and I didn't know how appropriate it might be for me to embrace her, which I dearly wanted to do.

Grace responded with a kiss on my cheek and a gentle embrace.

'I've got something to tell you,' she whispered. I felt dizzy with delight that she had acknowledged our passion for each other in a public place, although to be honest where we were standing wasn't exactly Beijing or Mumbai; there seemed to be no one else around.

'What is it?' I whispered back. I was expecting to hear that she missed me, that she wanted me, that I was her man.

'I'm pregnant,' said Grace.

There is no point denying it, I froze. It wasn't unpleasant, I just didn't move or say anything. I felt Grace gently stroke my back, reassuring me.

'It's okay,' she said softly. 'It's exactly what I wanted.'

'Oh my God, oh my God,' was all that came out of my mouth. I stood holding Grace for a long time. I could smell her hair; it smelled so utterly intoxicating, such a wonderful, I suppose natural human smell that I found incredibly comforting.

I must have eventually allowed Grace to lead me down the steps and into the transport tunnel, I really can't recall exactly what happened. I know a podmibus arrived so quickly it was as if it knew we were ready to travel, which, I was beginning to understand, it probably did.

We climbed on board and chose facing seats; the podmibus was completely empty. I was confused, felt fuzzy and disconnected. The elastic safety band thing came around me and pulled me into the seat, I watched as the same thing happened to Grace. She was somehow very far away from me although in reality I suppose I could have stretched forward and just about touched her. It wasn't physical distance, it was something else. I didn't feel close. I didn't know how to describe that feeling even to myself, but it was a feeling, and not one I liked.

Suddenly and unexpectedly I was missing Beth. I had met her descendants, happy healthy people living all over the world. I wanted to tell Beth about everything I'd seen, I wanted to be with her, I wanted to experience her telling me she was going to have a baby – Beth had wanted babies and she eventually had them, but not from me.

Yet here I was, rattling around in the future with no connec-

tion to anyone, to any history, to anything at all and suddenly I
was going to be a father. I didn't even know what that meant.

I wondered if Grace was looking at me as I stumbled blindly
through my jumbled up feelings. I didn't dare check, I couldn't
look at her so I just kept staring at my hands which were not still
or calm.

I was very confused on that journey. I scratched my head for a
long time – it was something Beth told me I did when I was
anxious. I pondered what it would be like to grow up in this
world, to be a child of Gardenia. From what I'd seen, it wouldn't
be that bad. It could be a lot worse. There were plenty of periods
of history where being born was a complete nightmare. I found
myself smiling. Maybe it was a good thing. I was going to be a
father – at least I hoped I'd be allowed to be one. Maybe that
wasn't the idea. It was all so different. Did fathers have a role in
Gardenia?

I hadn't seen anyone who lived as a couple in a house with
kids, the nearest to that would be Grace and Mitchell but clearly
my role in that relationship made it very different from anything
I'd known. I'd seen nothing like families as I'd grown up knowing
them. They all seemed jumbled up.

Did people love each other? Was there still romance? I'd met
people who were clearly couples but there was something very
different in the way they mixed together, the way that such
relationships were defined was unrecognisable. Did people fall
in love at all? I'm sure one of the reasons I felt confused was
that I realised Grace didn't necessarily love me or want me – she
wanted what I could give her. Pleasure, which was fine by me,
and a baby, which was ... Well, maybe it was fine too.

We must have remained in complete silence for almost the
entire journey. As I felt the podmibus finally slow down I also
felt Grace's hand touch my arm.

'I haven't told anyone yet, so could you be kind and remain
discreet about it for a little time?'

'Of course,' I said. The pod stopped and we got off. The machine moved off with a barely audible hiss and we climbed the steps back up into the forest. When we got outside, we stood together in the early morning mist.

It was a ridiculously beautiful spot, the birdsong almost painful in its intensity. Without thought, I took a deep lungful of musty forest air and turned to Grace. I found I was smiling again, I was happy. My headache had gone.

'It's wonderful news,' I said. 'I love you and I'm really truly happy for you.'

'That's very nice,' said Grace. She kissed me gently on the lips and I was shocked at how rapidly I became aroused. I longed for Grace but there was, even with this shared intimacy and the announcement of the baby, still a huge barrier between us. I don't think it was me, I think it was all from Grace. She had barriers, unspoken but solid. I could not just grab her, kiss her, find a quiet spot in the woods and make crazy, passionate love with her.

As we walked back along the cinder path I felt rain start to fall, a wonderful summer rain, big splats dropping on the ground all around us, very unlike the rain I remember from old England. The noise of the rain on the leaves above us was becoming steadily louder, I immediately quickened my pace and crouched against the cool drips falling from the trees.

'What's the matter, are you scared of rain?' said Grace. I turned to look at her. She continued to walk at the same pace, the rain slowly dampening her clothes.

'No, I suppose it doesn't matter,' I said. 'I just didn't want to get soaked.'

'The rain is much needed,' said Grace. She stopped for a moment, looked up and let the water splash on her elegant face. 'It's been very hot lately.'

This image really didn't encourage me to maintain my distance, it was almost like a hair care product advert from the old days, a beautiful woman allowing the rain to wash her. It was, to say the least, intensely erotic and romantic. I desperately wanted to hold Grace, I was losing track of what I was meant to do. I think I wanted to somehow be her man but because there was no clearly defined role for me in this new world I'd kind of forgotten how to do it.

I wanted to be with her; I suppose wanted some kind of acknowledgement of our intimacy. I have no idea how I knew, but I just knew this was not what she wanted, and it would be seen as inappropriate behaviour. I truly hope my decision to keep my distance was correct. I'd hate to think Grace was longing for me to hold her hand and was too shy to make the first move. Somehow I don't think that was the case; she didn't come across as in any way shy, just clear about what she wanted and when she wanted it.

However, I didn't want to repeat the terrible mistake I'd made with Beth. I never wanted to take my leave from a woman I loved without making it painfully obvious that I wanted to connect with her. I wanted to make sure she knew I cared.

When we arrived at Goldacre Hall, I stood at the small gate into the rear orchard. Grace continued walking through the now quite heavy rain.

'Are we okay?' I asked.

'I'm sorry, I don't understand you?' said Grace turning to face me. The rain running down her beautiful face could almost have been tears, but she didn't look like she was crying.

'Are we, well, okay? I mean, can I, can I be with you?'

'Be with me?' she asked. 'You are with me.'

'I know, but, can I love you, hold you, can I be, you know...'

'Gavin, what do you mean?' she asked. She looked a little concerned.

'I don't know how you do stuff like this here. In my world, when a man and a woman make a baby, there's kind of a social thing, you know, everyone knows they are together, people acknowledge their relationship. They get married and stuff.'

'Married, you mean a wedding?'

'Yes, a wedding. They live together and bring up the children together and all that sort of thing.'

'Well, we all do live together anyway. I don't quite know what you want.'

I let my head drop. I watched the soft rain drip from my flattened fringe and fall on a leaf lying on the path at my feet.

'It's okay,' I said. I lifted my head to look at Grace, who was now very soaked and looking a little more anxious.

'Just put it down to pod shock. Maybe I just need a lie down.'

Grace smiled and held out a hand, my spirits lifted and I walked with her, holding hands, through the Goldacre Hall gardens, past the big back porch and into the barn. Grace walked with me to the door but stood on the threshold as I entered.

'Everyone will want to see you and hear of your adventures this evening. Why don't you have a shower and a rest now? I have many tasks today but I will come to Goldacre Hall tonight.'

'Oh, okay,' I said. I was disappointed but I was also very tired. I leant forward to give her a kiss, she allowed it briefly but too soon she delicately moved away, smiled at me sweetly and was gone.

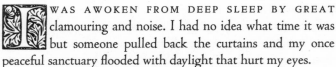WAS AWOKEN FROM DEEP SLEEP BY GREAT clamouring and noise. I had no idea what time it was but someone pulled back the curtains and my once peaceful sanctuary flooded with daylight that hurt my eyes.

I felt embarrassed as I dithered and tried to focus on what was happening. I saw there were people in my room, lots of people, it was almost full and it wasn't some kind of practical joke, they all looked very concerned. It seemed as though everyone in the crowd was looking at me, as I stared around in shock I noticed there were even more people standing in the doorway. For some bizarre reason what seemed like half of Gardenia had decided to wake me up.

William, Halam, Grace and Paula were standing right by my bed looking very concerned, their clothes seemed to be soaking wet.

'The cloud,' said William. He was breathing heavily and resting his hands on his knees. 'The cloud has formed around the tether, the anomaly.'

'It's the cloud you came through,' said Grace. 'It's back.' She looked ashen faced.

I was fairly alarmed when they woke me up. Now I was having a bit of a mental meltdown.

'The cloud?' I asked. 'What time is it?'

No one seemed to know.

'You've been sleeping for about four hours,' said Grace helpfully, 'but it's still morning. William was out in the bow field when he noticed.'

'It is exactly the same cloud formation,' said William as calmly as he could. 'We only see it rarely, but it is definitely back. It is the anomaly. Get dressed, come and see.'

I slipped out of bed and pulled my clothes on. I had been sleeping naked and no one seemed in the least bit shocked to see me in my natural state. They just waited impatiently at the door, staring at me.

I pulled on my weird Gardenian boots and tried to tie them up, fumbled and cursed under my breath. With one smooth movement Grace knelt down at my feet and did the job with no trouble.

'Let us be gone,' she said as she stood up.

I walked through the entrance hall surrounded by people who all seemed to be talking at once. I couldn't understand anything they were saying; my head was fuzzy and everything was too bright.

The anomaly, that's what I kept hearing. The anomaly.

As soon as we got outside I could see that there had been very heavy rain, but it had just stopped. The air smelt incredible, so fresh and clean, the sky was getting brighter and it was very warm. I think I registered then that the air was much warmer than I ever remember air in old England being, not tropical but definitely Mediterranean.

We walked around the side of Goldacre Hall and yet more people streamed out of the house. As we went through the orchard and into the bow field, more or less every occupant of the hall and a few more besides had come to see what was going on. I had come to know these people. I didn't know all their names, but I'd conversed with most of them, eaten with them; I felt very at home with them. But hearing about the cloud again suddenly made me feel very isolated, very different, it was a savage reminder that I truly didn't belong.

As we approached the narrow gate I couldn't help breaking into a run. I threw it open and started to run headlong into the centre of the field where I knew I'd get a view of the tether behind the trees.

The oil seed had already lost its bright yellow glow and the seedpods were forming, but the runway I'd used for the Yuneec a few weeks earlier was still very apparent. It was slightly muddy due to the recent heavy rain, but by the time I reached the centre of the field the sun was shining. I kept glancing over my shoulder as I ran to see if I could spot the tether over the top of the trees surrounding Oak House.

When it finally came into view I stopped and gasped. The cloud was there. It looked instantly familiar. It's not that it was exactly the same cloud, but it was bizarre enough. What puzzled me at that point was why I hadn't been more alarmed when I'd seen it the first time, when I was flying over familiar territory near Didcot power station. It was so obviously a weird cloud formation, it wasn't the right shape, it swirled and billowed in a peculiar way, and the interior of the cloud occasionally flashed with lightning.

'Oh fuck,' I said, my hand over my mouth. A lot of the younger people joined me in the field. Grace stood by my side and held my arm. I then held her arm. We both somehow knew instantly what this could mean.

'Does it look the same?' she asked.

'Fuck yeah,' I said.

William came stumbling across the field toward me. He was with a large group of the older folk who had taken a little more time to reach the spot we were standing in.

'It has the same basic features, does it not?' he said between gasps. 'The cloud appears to be formed by the excess energy coming down the tether. Look around us: the rain clouds have long since moved on, but this one remains.'

'Fucking hell,' I said, all notions of being polite and not upsetting people forgotten. The shocking sight of this massive cloud swirling around in what was now a perfectly clear blue sky was at once terrifying but strangely uplifting. I felt like the stereotype seventeenth century sailor who'd been stranded on a beautiful desert island where he had fallen in love with an exquisite maiden from the gentle and caring tribe he had encountered, who suddenly sees a ship of the realm on the horizon.

'I don't know what it means,' I blurted. 'What does it mean?'

'Well, it doesn't necessarily mean anything,' said William. 'It's all to do with the current coming down the tether. This time of year when the sun is fully high in the sky, the voltage coming down the tether is, well, it's enormous; the facility at the tether base will be shedding power by the bucket load.'

I grabbed William's frail old arm. 'Will it have the same effect?' I asked. 'Will it send me back?'

'I have no idea,' he said. 'No one knows why it happens. We have been studying it for years and still do not understand what is happening. It's been a noted phenomenon wherever this style and size of power tether is in use, but no one knows why it happens.'

'I've got to try,' I said. 'I don't want to upset any of you, but I don't belong here.'

'Are you really going to leave?' asked Grace.

Suddenly Grace looked different, weaker in some way, like she almost wanted me to stay.

'I don't know what to do. I'm so confused, I've only just woken up.' Again I turned to William. 'How long does the cloud normally last?'

'Oh, well, only a matter of minutes. We've got used to it. I'm not sure, I've never timed it.'

I held my head in my hands. I wanted to stay, I wanted to be with Grace, to help in the gardens, to see my child born. But it was utterly ridiculous for me to stay in this world, in this time. I'd seen what was coming and it was good and it somehow felt like my duty to go back and try and facilitate it. Maybe that was what this whole experience had been about, maybe I was destined to come here, see what could be done, then go back and make sure it did. That is how mad I was, standing in the bow field surrounded by people from the twenty-third century. Such an absurd notion actually seemed plausible.

I grabbed Grace and hugged her hard, I didn't care who saw
us.

'I have to go,' I said into her ear.

'I know,' she said into mine.

'I love you,' I said. 'I'm sorry, I can't help it.'

'That's okay, you can love me,' she said. She gripped me tightly one last time and then gently pulled away.

I turned to the gathered crowd surrounding us.

'Can you help me get my flying machine into position?' I said. Without another word the large group turned and headed back towards Goldacre Hall. The Yuneec had been stored under a large waterproof cloth at the edge of the field, an amazingly light material that had been pegged down around the plane. Within moments it was removed and I climbed inside.

'I've left all my stuff in my room,' I said. 'You can give it to a museum or something.'

'Good luck, Gavin,' said William.

'I can never thank you enough,' I shouted. 'I can never repay you. You have all been wonderfully kind.'

'You must go now if you want to catch the anomaly,' said Halam. 'And thank you, Gavin, you have made Grace very happy.'

The intensity of those few seconds, of looking into the faces of the future was too much for me. It was only when I closed the canopy that I realised tears were streaming down my face.

I booted up the Yuneec and everything sprang to life with reassuring familiarity. The batteries were naturally fully charged, I started the prop, the gathered crowd scattered, I watched Grace lead William away to the side, and she then held onto Halam.

Without delay I started bumping along the makeshift runway. The going was slow because of the softness of the ground. I increased the power to maximum and felt the plane lurch and shudder with the forces being exerted. I'd never taken off from soft mud before, and started to panic; the plane might not make it. As I started to bowl along the ground I could feel the plane starting to lift, and as soon as I felt it leave the ground I pulled the nose up as hard as I dared.

I just made it over the trees and banked hard to the left immediately. I circled over the field a couple of times, slowly gaining height – I needed to be at around 2,000 metres in order to enter the cloud. I was craning my neck to see it as I turned. I didn't want to fly too far away from it as I gained altitude but it did look like it was dispersing a little.

I glanced at the screen – 1,900 metres. I levelled out and aimed at the cloud, glancing up to see the still shocking blue tether coming out of the heavens. I aimed slightly to the right of it, hoping I wouldn't fly straight into a razor thin, unbreakable thread carrying several billion volts.

I wanted to look back at the people gathered in the field behind me, but I had to focus on the cloud ahead. I was gripping the controls like never before; I could sense the old country coming back to me, the roads, the trains, the power stations, the houses, cities and the millions and millions of people.

The cloud engulfed me suddenly and I was shocked by how dark it became. This dull grey world I had entered was suddenly and very shockingly illuminated by blinding flashes of lightning, more than I remembered on my first encounter.

I glanced down at the controls. Everything seemed okay, and it was at that precise moment the plane lurched violently, almost as if it had been grabbed by a giant. Some force threw me up and then dropped me. I was terrified. I think I may have been crying out – I can't quite recall, I was so scared. I lost all sense of direction, my eyes open in terror, at any moment expecting to see a flash of blue as the tether appeared out of the swirling grey cloud that filled my world.

Again I felt the plane utterly lose lift and I felt myself drop. The engine was wailing, red lights started to appear on the dash, warning lights for engine over-revving.

I tried to lift the nose and slowly managed to gain some con-

trol of the plane. I saw something through the cloud, light, some
sunlight.

'Fuck!' I remember shouting. 'Fuck yeah! Come on!'

The cloud started to thin and the light increased. Suddenly, I saw something through a gap in the clouds. Could it have been a building, a structure of some sort? I panicked again and tried to gain height. I didn't want to fly into Didcot power station after what I'd been through.

Then, suddenly the clouds just dispersed and I was flying level and true. I glanced at the control panel: my batteries were low, 40 per cent. It made no sense; I'd only been in the air for about ten minutes. I experienced a sick feeling seeing the battery metre drop like that – it was like going from a hydrogen fuel cell car to a wheelbarrow.

Then I looked up. If the battery level made no sense, what I saw below me made even less.

Subscribers

NBOUND IS A NEW KIND OF PUBLISHING HOUSE house. Our books are funded directly by readers. This was a very popular idea during the late eighteenth and early nineteenth centuries. Now we have revived it for the internet age. It allows authors to write the books they really want to write and readers to support the writing they would most like to see published.

The names listed below are of readers who pledged their support and made this book happen. If you'd like to join them, visit: www.unbound.co.uk

Billy Abbott
John Abraham
Geoff Adams
David Traver Adolphus
Eric Aitala
Monty Alfie-Blagg
Tracey Allen
Gareth Alston
David Anderson
Steve Angell
Judy Anthony
Brian Appel
Paul Arman
Marc Armsby
Mary Arnold
Simon Arthur
John Ash
Jon Ashton
Lucent Askew
Steven Askew
Michael Atkins
Michael Auerbach
Simon Austin

Nick Baber
Kevin Bachus
David Bafoot
Matthew Bain
Karen Baines
Kevin Baker
Lindsay Baker
Paul Baker
Emma Mim Baker-Cooke
Graham Ball
Chris Ballard
Arthur Banks
Tom Barber
Genevieve Barbieri
Stuart Barkworth
Tom Barnard
Nick Bartlett
Cat Barton
Derek Bashford
David Basnett
Brian Bassingthwaighte
Frank Baxley
Emma Bayliss

Matthew Beale
Gerald Beattie
Jennifer Beattie
Dan Beavon
Frazer Beckingham-Smith
Joseph Bell
Amanda Benson
Calum Benson
Andrew Bentley
Keith Berry
Paul Berry
Fredrik Berts
Ben Best
Rowanne Black
Rachel Blackman
Christof Bojanowski
Paul Boland
Lucy Bolton
Phil Boot
Duncan Booth
David Boston
Karl Bovenizer
Doug Bowers
Hazel Bradbeer
Simon Bradley
Adrian Bradshaw
Julian Bradshaw
Robin Bray
LTC Jon P. Brazelton US Army
Jon Briggs
Cheryl Broder
Philip Broder
Alan Brookland
Marie Brown
Oliver Brown
Scott, Sophie & Finlay Brown
P.J. Bryant
Adam Bryce
Paul Bucknell
Peter Buckoke
Geoff Bullock

Jonathan Bullock
Rob Bulmer
Adam Burke
Alison Burns
Jo Busuttil
Sally Buswell
Marcus Butcher
Gareth Butler
Siân Cafferkey
Mike Calcutt
David Callander
David Callier
Clare Cambridge
Viv Carbines
Caroline-Isabelle Caron
Alexis Carpenter
David Carrington
Richard Case
Tony Castley
Wanda Caulfield
Chris & Liz Chadwick
Rohan Chadwick
Eleanor Chalkley
Sarah Chalmers
Claire Chambers
Martin Chapman
Phil Chapman
Derrick Charbonnet
Gavin Cherriman
Benjamin Chiad
Paul Churchley
Stephen Clay
John Clayton
Deborah Clement
Robert Clements
Sam Clements
Mark Clifford
Andy W. Clift
Alison Cobby
Don Cochrane
Mark Cockshoot

Richard Cohen
Nicholas Cohn
Sean Colbath
David Coles
Stevyn Colgan
Lisa Pearce Collins
Timothy Collinson
Dave 'sircompo' Compton
Cheryl Connor
Ryan Conway
Anthony Cooper
John Cooper
Samantha Cooper
Simon Cooper
Suzy Cooper
Richard Coppen
Linda Corrin
Stephen Cosgrove
Anthony Creagh
James Cridland
Ewan Crossan
Joshua Crothers
Ann-Marie Curran
Richard Curtis
Peter Dalling
Gerald Daniels
Bruce Davenport
Shazza Davidson
Coral Davies
Glyn Davies
Graham T. Davies
Liam Davies
Peredur Davies
Jonathan Davison
Paul Davison
Tony Dawber
Belinda Daws
Amanda Dawson
Darren Dawson
Edd Dawson
Paul de Greef

Paulo Jorge de Oliveira
Cantante de Matos
Jamie De Rycke
Meriel de Vekey
Michelle de Villiers
Matt Dean
Ryan Dehmer
Andy Devanney
Gavin Dietz
J. P. Diver
Stephen Donnelly
Adam Dowden
Lawrence T. Doyle
Simon Drinkwater
Will Dron
Jonathan Dubrule
Christopher Dudman
Keith Dunbar
David Dupplaw
Justin Dykes
Cariad Eccleston
Liz Eden
Gordon Edwards
Roger Edwards
Richard Eggleston
Suzi Ellington
Brendan Ellis
Thor-Dale Elsson
Charlotte Endersby
Derek Erb
Marc-Alexandre Espiaut
Mark Faithfull
Lily-Jo Fannon
Di Farence
David Fauvrelle
Gillian Fifield
Anna Eve Figueroa
Richard Firth-Godbehere
Bård Fjukstad
James Fowkes
Craig Francis

Ian Frank
Laura Franks
Alan Freeman
Paul Freeman
John Frewin
Anthony Froissant
Stephen Frost
Tony Fyler
Christian Gaetani
David Gallaher
Hilary Gallo
James Gander
Chris Garnham
William Garrard
David Garvie
Joe Gaunt
Perry Gerakines
Saman Gerami
Simon Gibson
Stuart Gilbert
Beryl Giles
Sarah Gill
Neil Godfrey
Richard Goldsmith
Ben Goodchild
Mark Goody
Jean Graham
Neil Graham
Kerrie Caflas Gray
Jacinta Grayden
Arthur Green
Roger Green
Paul Gregory
James Griffin
Mike Griffiths
Lee Grimshaw
Emily Hopkins
Lance Haig
Andy Hall
Natalie Hall
Daniel Hallifield

Penny Hands
Michael Hansen
Marie Hanson
Pete Harbord
Paul Hardingham
Peter Harrigan
Chris Harris
Paul Harris
Vron Harris
Bryan Harrison
Kris James Harrison
Richard Harrison
Stacy Harrison
Graham Hassell
Andrew Hawkins
Paul Hawkins
Neil Hayhurst
Elizabeth Henwood
Roger Herbert
Ian Higgins
Stuart Higgins
Julian Hill
Adi Himpson
Adam Hinton
Matt Hobbs
Michal Hobot
Magnus Hoelvold
Iain Holder
Brad Holland
Andrew Holmes
Emily Hopkins
Simon Houghton
Peter Howell
Rod Howitt
Gordon Hudson
Ben Hughes
Jack Hughes
Paul Hughes
Tim Hughes
Jordan A. Hulme
Andrew Humbles

Luci Humphreys
Andrew Hunter
Leif Hunter
David Hutchinson (N5XL)
Fiona Hyde
Deb Ikin
Matthew Iles
Martyn Ingram
Tom Ingram
Marie Irshad
Richard Isherwood
Lee Israel
Ben and Izzy
Auli Jaatinen-Stock
Steve Jalim
Fadi Jameel
Fiona James
Mark Jeffrey
Paul Jewitt
Kay Johannes
Adam Johnson
Dean Johnson
Pete Johnson
Thomas Johnston
Catherine Jones
Heather Jones
Jessica Jones
John-Paul Jones
Peter Jones
Stephen Jones
Terry Jones
Deborah Jones-Davis
Richard Judd
Milan Juza
Chris Kanieski
Robin Karpeta
Katspjamas
Mike Keal
Joan Kelly
Martin, Rebecca & William Kelly
Scott Kennedy

Henry Kenner
John Kent
Matthew Keys
Dan Kieran
Andy Kiernan
John Kikkert
Meg Kingston
Steve Kirtley
Narell Klingberg
Peter Knight
Alexis Kokolski
Michael Kowalski
Arthur Kressner
Karim Kronfli
Aleks Krotoski
Steve Kunzer
Steven Laing
Lis Lambertsen
Karen Langley
Mark Larbey
Tracy Laurence
Craig Lawrence
Jeffery Lay
Gareth Layzell
Jason Le Page
Gareth Lean
Jørgen Leditzig
Holly Leeds
Steven Leighton
Masha and Klim Levene
Andy Lewis
Ian Lewis
Wendy Lewis
Ben Lindsay
Liane Linstead
Mark Lis
David Lister
John New & Deborah Lough
Tristram Love
Lisa Lyons
Abby MacArthur

John Macmenemey
Simon Macneall
Cait MacPhee
Beth Magner
Ewan MacMahon
Mark Mangano
Greg Manning
Richard Manning
Gemma Cleal & Nick Mansbridge
Andy Marczak
Shuna Marr
Karen Marshall
Andrew Martin
Colin Martin
Johnny Martin
Paul Martin
Tim Martin
Paul Mason
Rebecca Mason
Karen Masson
Brett Masterson
Andrew Matangi
Ajay Mathur
Noel Matthews
Donna Maxx
Shaun McAlister
Don McAllister
Rod McDonald
Shane McEwan
Dustin McGivern
Kathryn McGrath
Stuart McKears
Ben McKenzie
Gavin McKeown
Andy McLeod
Sarah McNair
Ian McWilliam
Jacqueline Meaney
Neil Melville
Wendy Metcalfe
Deborah Metters

Nick Middleton
Tamsin Middleton
Simon Middleyard
Miggi
Daryl Millar
Paul Miller
Nick Milligan
Richard Mills
Lindsay Mitchell
John Mitchinson
Deena Mobbs
Danny Molyneux
Tom Moody-Stuart
Lee Morecroft
Bethany, Grace & Morgan
David Morgan
Paul Morriss
Nik Mortimer
Michael Morwood
David Moss
Greig Muir
Alexandra Austin Muirhead
Robert Naylor
Angela Neale
Andrew Neve
Vivienne Neve
Paula Newens
Christopher J Newman
Alex Newsome
Simon Newson
John Nichol
Jess Nicholls
Al Nicholson
Chris Nicolson
David Nield
Andrej Ninkovic
Martin Nooteboom
Tom Northcott
Stuart O'Connor
Sean O'Rourke
Antony O'Sullivan

Anna-Maria Oléhn
Isabell Olevall
Kaylene O'Neill
Erwin Oosterhoorn
Matthew Orrison
Jim Osborn
Alan Outten
Stuart Owen
Brendan Owens
Lawrence Owens
Louise Paddock
S.J. Page
Sal Page
Keith Paine
Matthew Palmer
Michael Palmer
Ernest Panychevskyy
Kevin Parker
Mark Parkinson
David Parry
Kevin Pascoe
Andrew Paul
Shaun Payne
Neil Pearce
Dave Pearson
Bella Pender
Dan Pendleton
Michael Pennick
Mark Phelan
Amanda Phelps
Lorin Phenis
Chris (furrie) Phillips
David Phillips
Eric Phillipson
Guy Phipps
Jennifer Pickup
Steve Pike
Brian Pitkethley
Justin Pollard
Edward Pollitt
David Poloni

Malcolm Porter
Craig Portsmouth
Rachel Poulton
Nick Powell
Jon Prendergast
Edward Price
Christopher Pridham
Jim Prince
Morgan Prior
Simon Prior
Johnny Pritchard
Adam J Purcell
Jenny Puttock
Huan Quayle
Ethan Race
Mark Randall
Hans Rasmussen
Colette Reap
Julia Rees
Ian Reeves
Georgina Helen Reid
James Reid
Craig Reilly
Paul Renold
Lauren Rhodes
Andy Rice
Mark Richards
Christopher Richardson
Andrew Riddell
Laura Riggall
Heather Ringstead
Craig Risk
Robert Ristroph
Andy Roberts
Ian Roberts
Andy Robinson
Katy Robinson
Anne Rock
Petre Rodan
Mike Roest
Charles Ross

Craig Ross
Lorna Ross
Ian Roughley
Lynn Rowlands
Chloe Rowley-Morris
Allan P. Russell
Emma Ryal
Paul Sadler
Jon Salt
Evan Salway
Christoph Sander
Steven Saunderson
Neil Sayer
Hugh Scantlebury
Claire Scott
Ryan Scott
Chris Scutcher
Adrian Seale
Pat Samhain Seery
Lee Sei-Macfhearchair
Annie Self
Daniel Sendall-King
Katherine Setchell
Jennifer Seymour
Lee Shannon
Robert Sharp
Jonathan Sharpe
Joanna Sharples
Darran Shepherd
Karl Sherratt
Jennifer Shipp
Jon Shute
Sam Sibbert
Richard Sickinger
Darren Sillett
James Sinclair
Vicki Sivess
Angela Skinner
Claire Slade
Alasdair Smith
Alison Smith

Eric Smith
Laura Smith
Neil G. Smith
Nic Smith
Paul Smith
Russell Smith
Adam Smithson
Nat Snell
Peter Snell
Jason Soroko
Chris Spath
Tom Speller
Peter Spicer-Wensley
Mat Stace
Lee Stamper
Graham Starkey @grezzaa
Craig Stewart
Bent Stigsen
Glenn Stokes
Jack T. Stonell
Andrew Storm
Karen Stott
Alison Strange
Charlie Styr
Stéphanie Suchecki
Patrick Sugrue
Mark Sundaram
Mark Suret
Ian Sutherland
Lindsay Swann
Trina Talma
Jack Tams
Alan Taylor
Gregory Fenby Taylor
Lee Taylor
Mark Taylor
Nick Telford-Reed
Edward Thomas
Jo Thomas
Mark Thomas
Paul Thomas

Alexander Thompson
Andrew Thompson
Alex Thomson
Mark Thorpe
Barry Tipper
James Tombs
Samuel Toogood
James & Helen Townsend
David Tubby
Nicholas Tufnell
Daniel Tumilty
Ben Tumney
James Tunnicliffe
Richard Turner
Paul Tyler
Pete Tyler
John Underhill
Rav Vadgama
Mark Vent
Steve Wadsworth
Yasuhiro Waki
Steve Walker
Stewart Walker
Antony Wallace
Bobby Wallace
Nick Walpole
Stuart Walsh
Hui-chang Wang
Ashley Ward
Rachel Ward
Adam Warn
Marc Warner
Paul Warren
Emma Watkins
David Watt
James Watts
Paul Wayper
David Wegmuller
Glenn Wehmeyer
Carl Weller
Philip Weller

Karen Wells
Tom West
Johan Westlin
Amy Wheaton
Devlin Hugh Francis
　　Whitfield-Martin
Matthew Whittaker
Carol Whitton
Jason Wickham
Rob Widdowson
Andrew Wilcox
Dave Wild
Tom Wilkinson
Christopher Williams
Craig Williams
Graham Williams
Gwylim Williams
Trevor Williams
Joan Wilson
Martin Wink
Tim Winstanley
Graham Wise
Stuart Witts
Ian Wolf
Cindy Womack
Charlotte Wood
Rupert Wood
Steven Wooding
Katie Woodman
Barney Worfolk-Smith
Bryan Worth
David Wright
John Wright
Rachel Wright
Simon Wright
Ian Yates
Yin-chien Yeap
Stewart Young
Goldie Yule
Lynn Zarb

A note about the type

HE BODY TEXT OF THIS BOOK IS SET IN LTC Cloister, designed by Morris Fuller Benton (1872–1948). Benton was chief designer at the American Type Foundry from 1900–1937 and was America's most prolific modern type designer, responsible for Century Schoolbook, Franklin Gothic and the revivals of Bodoni and Garamond. Cloister is a roman face based on the work of the 15th century French engraver and type designer Nicholas Jenson (1420–1480), who was based in Venice and had been a pupil of Gutenberg. Jenson is credited as the inventor of roman type. Previously, books had been set in the gothic 'blackletter' style. Jenson's elegant type was much admired by William Morris (1834–1896), the founder of the arts and crafts movement. Chapter headings are set in Morris Troy, an adaptation of William Morris's semi-Gothic Troy type designed for use in his Kelmscott Press books. The Kelmscott Press's great project was the production of a hand printed edition of Chaucer's *Canterbury Tales*, which contained eighty-seven illustrations by Edward Burne-Jones. A masterpiece of book design, it is the embodiment of Morris's theory that work should be collaborative and the results both beautiful and useful. Burne-Jones called it 'a pocket cathedral'. The ornamented initial letters are also adapted from Morris's designs for his Kelmscott Press editions.